Something sharp jabbed hard into Gerald's ribs.

"Mr. Wilkins," the thin man breathed, "are you familiar with the stiletto blade?"

Gerald froze. His back arched as the thin man pushed harder on a long pencil-thin dagger.

"The stiletto is a marvelous thing," the thin man whispered, his top lip curling in a tight snarl. "Much favored by assassins. The blade is very thin indeed but extremely strong. It can pierce clothing, flesh, muscle . . . heart. But it leaves almost no sign on the skin. The victim falls to the ground, as if in a faint. By the time a doctor arrives, the lungs have filled with blood and the target has drowned in his own vital fluids. Most effective."

Gerald stared straight ahead. Constable Lethbridge was less than ten yards away. And there was nothing he could do to reach him.

The thin man leaned even closer, pressing the dagger right through the fabric of Gerald's shirt until the point nicked his skin.

"We are going to walk out this door, past this policeman, and away. Who knows, Mr. Wilkins? You may live to enjoy that fabulous fortune of yours."

Books by Richard Newsome

The Archer Legacy
Book One: The Billionaire's Curse
Book Two: The Emerald Casket

THE ARCHER LEGACY ◆ BOOK ONE

THE BILLIONAIRE'S CURSE

RICHARD NEWSOME

ILLUSTRATED BY JONNY DUDDLE

WALDEN POND PRESS

An Imprint of HarperCollinsPublishers

Library of Congress Cataloging-in-Publication Data
Newsome, Richard.
The billionaire's curse / Richard Newsome ; illustrated by Jonny
Duddle
    p. cm.
Summary: When thirteen-year-old Gerald finds himself the heir to
twenty billion pounds from an aunt he never met, he inherits with
it a mystery surrounding his aunt's death and various artifacts in the
British Museum.
ISBN 978-0-06-194491-8
    [1. Mystery and detective stories. 2. Inheritance and succession—
Fiction. 3. London (England)—Fiction. 4. England—Fiction.] I. Duddle,
Jonny, ill. II. Title.
PZ7.N486644Bi 2010   2009042518
[Fic]—dc22   CIP
                                                                 AC

Typography by Amy Ryan
11 12 13 14 15   CG/CW   10 9 8 7 6 5 4 3 2
❖
First paperback edition, 2011
First U.S. Edition, 2010
Originally published in Australia in 2009 by
The Text Publishing Company

For Ella, Kath, and the other two,
and Mum and Dad as well.

Acknowledgments

Thanks first, and most importantly, to my family—Kathryn, Sam, Ruby, and Ella (and Pippin the cat)—for giving up holidays and agreeing to up stumps and move city so this book could finally be completed.

To three people who deployed the right words at the right time: Ali Lavau (who was there at the very beginning), Colleen Lewis von Eckartsberg, and Frank Leggett.

To my parents, Phil and Dorothy, and my sister, Nicola, who all taught me the value of perseverance.

And, finally, to everyone at the Text Publishing Company—in particular Michael Heyward, Jane Pearson, Penny Hueston, Anne Beilby, Bridie Riordan, and Kirsty Wilson.

THE BILLION

GERALD'S JOURNEY AND

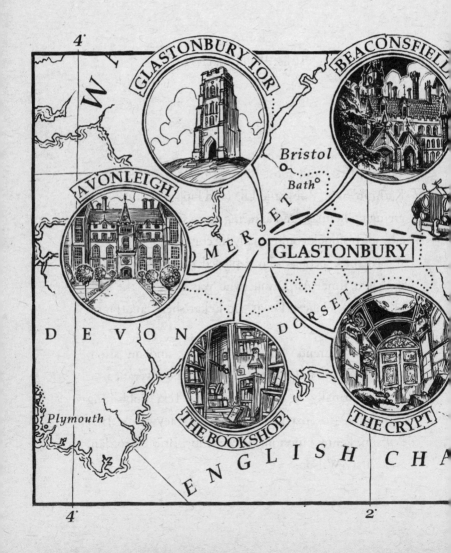

AIRE'S CURSE

VARIOUS POINTS OF INTERESTS

The clock on the wall chimed twice. Two o'clock in the morning. Constable Lethbridge of the London Metropolitan Police was bored.

He had finished the last of his take-out dinner—a rather disappointing chicken curry. He didn't have the luxury of a table, so a fair amount of it was dribbled down the front of his shirt and spattered on the marble floor around his boots.

Lethbridge eased back in his folding chair and loosened his belt a notch. The last of the curry completed the trek down his gullet, his head lurched back, and a tremendous belch burst through his lips. It shot up the walls like a gas-fired Ping-Pong ball.

"Whoops," Lethbridge burbled to himself. "Pardon I."

He removed a crumpled newspaper from the jacket that

was slung over the back of the chair. Sighing, he settled in for a long night.

A half-moon shone through the glass dome that formed the roof high above, illuminating the cavernous circular room in a dull glow. Apart from the occasional scraping of Constable Lethbridge's chair on the floor and the rustle of his paper as he turned the pages, there was nothing to be heard. As you might expect at two o'clock in the morning in the Reading Room of the British Museum, not a great deal was afoot.

The British Museum is one of the world's finest museums. And the Reading Room is one of the museum's finest rooms. Its walls are lined with bookcases that stretch up over three stories, and its elaborate glass-paneled dome is trimmed in gold and duck-egg blue. The room houses an extraordinary collection of leather-bound volumes of rare antiquity: a majestic warehouse of the learning of all Western civilization.

In the middle of all this sat Constable Lethbridge, scratching his bottom with the plastic fork from his dinner. There was nothing at all extraordinary about him. His sandy hair was thinning, his face was pale, he was on the tubby side of plump, and he was in desperate need of a holiday.

Lethbridge shifted uncomfortably in his chair. He lowered the newspaper to his lap and muttered, "Gawd, this is dull."

His voice disappeared into the gloom. With a low grunt, he hauled himself to his feet, hitched up his sagging trousers, and shambled across the floor.

In the center of the room, bathed in moonlight and free from the museum clutter and dinnertime debris, stood a circle of identical statues. A dozen ancient archers carved from gray stone, each one aimed a crossbow at a black marble pedestal in the very middle of the room.

On top of the pedestal rested a glass case. And inside the case there shimmered a soft light.

Lethbridge stepped into the circle of stone sentries and crossed to the case. He bent down and peered through the glass.

Inside the case, on a stand like a red velvet egg-cup, nestled a single gem—a diamond—about the size and shape of a duck's egg. Shards of moonlight hit the stone. Tiny rainbows reflected in Lethbridge's watery eyes. The diamond looked as if it burned with a flame of gossamer in its heart.

"Not that impressive," snorted Lethbridge, wiping a patch in the glass that his breath had fogged up. "Who'd pay a hundred million quid for that?"

He straightened up and plodded across the room, still clutching his waistband and grumbling to himself. He hated working nights. But with security guards on strike across London and police having to step in, his duty sergeant had assigned him the task of watching the diamond until dawn.

Lethbridge lumbered across to a large white sculpture of an elephant in the shadows at the edge of the room. The elephant was taller than a good-sized man and it sat plump-bellied and cross-legged on a cushion of pink rose petals. Garlands of blossoms were draped around its neck. Four arms poked out from its rounded sides; one hand held a coil of rope, another a bamboo flute, while a third clutched a bunch of roses. The fourth arm stretched out, like a cop stopping traffic.

Lethbridge peered into the statue's face. The statue stared back. Their gazes locked.

Lethbridge went cross-eyed. He lost focus and half stumbled forward. He shuddered. Being locked in a huge circular room where the slightest noise seemed to come from every direction at once was giving him the creeps.

He turned and trudged back, his graying underpants peeking out above a drooping trouser line. At that moment the elephant statue blinked. A crusty white eyelid flickered. Hairline cracks spread across the statue's surface, like a giant boiled egg being cracked with a teaspoon. Flakes of white plaster sprinkled onto the bed of rose petals as the elephant slowly began to move. It plucked a flower from one hand and guided it bud-first into the bamboo flute it held in another. Then it waited.

In the center of the room, Lethbridge passed between

two of the stone archers and stopped in front of the glass case. He unhitched his belt again and bent over to take another look at the diamond. The back of his trousers sagged low.

A sharp burst of air splintered the silence. Lethbridge lifted his head. But before he could turn, something sharp buried itself deep in his left buttock.

He yelped, his eyes popping in their sockets in a rush of pain and surprise. He clamped his hands behind him to clutch at his underpants, out of which now sprouted a six-inch-long dart with a rosebud fixed to its end.

Lethbridge reeled. Grasping for support, he lunged at the glass case. His knees buckled. Numbness drained into his legs, his face flushed from red to purple. His jaw clamped shut and white froth spurted from his lips. His belt fell undone and his trousers collapsed around his ankles. Lethbridge lurched to the floor, crashing onto his elbows and knees, still hugging the glass case in his arms.

Across the room in the shadows, the elephant statue slid another flower into its flute.

Raising the instrument to its mouth like a blowgun, it let loose another bolt that shot across the room, this time skewering Lethbridge's right buttock.

"Bleedin' heck," Lethbridge whimpered through clenched teeth. He laid the side of his stunned face on the cold marble floor. "That really hurts."

His vision blurred. The world tipped on its edge and spun crazily inside his eyeballs. The numbness in his legs washed through him. The stone archers swam in and out of focus—almost laughing at him. Lethbridge could have sworn the elephant statue stood up from its nest of rose petals and took a step toward him. Then he blacked out.

And that is how Constable Lethbridge of the London Metropolitan Police was found by his colleagues the next morning: slumped facedown on the marble floor, asleep on his elbows and knees, his trousers around his ankles, his underpants exposed to the dome high above, and what appeared to be two red roses growing out of his backside.

Of the world's most valuable diamond, however, there was no sign at all.

CHAPTER ONE

"Nothing . . . is . . . certain!"

Gerald raised his head at the blood-freezing roar that boomed through the dank dungeon tunnels. Even under his heavy fur cape, he shivered. The beast was close. He cradled the unconscious Madeleine in the crook of his right arm, her auburn hair cascading over alabaster shoulders, her bottle-green robes spilling across the stone floor like a lily pad on a pond. Gerald muttered an oath. He cursed the foul fortune that had landed him in this benighted place. He cursed the cold and the stench. But, most of all, he cursed the realization that he would have to fight this beast with his left hand. He slid his long blade one more time from the worn leather sheath on his belt, and waited.

And what a beast it was. Barely recognizable as human,

the creature stood a good seven feet tall. Its skin rippled with muscles, like baseballs stuffed into socks. Its bristle-covered shoulders burst through the bare rags that clothed it. A shaggy head lolled to the side—a thick tangle of dark matted hair across one eye, the other glaring out with a bloodshot resonance that glowed in the dark mire of the castle's rank underbelly.

"Nothing is certain!" the beast bayed again, steam spewing from its nostrils and spittle showering from its coal-pit mouth. Its jaws opened wide, exposing rows of yellowed teeth, rotted through from the flesh of other adventurers. The beast lay ready. Waiting. Hungry.

Gerald cared not for this beast. He shot a fleeting look at Madeleine, lying in his arm as if in peaceful slumber, and steeled himself. He would not let her down. They might be mere teenagers, but neither man nor beast would stand in their way. His blade sliced slow silent circles through the fetid air, ready.

Without warning, the beast sprang from a corner about twenty yards from Gerald and the maiden. The creature raised a mighty paw and flung a fireball straight at Gerald's head. The boy hero ducked; the flaming missile grazed his temple, singeing his hair.

"Nothing is certain!"

The yell was deafening. The beast strode right at them, pelting fireballs at every step, its enormous feet pounding the flagstones like a pile driver. Gerald spun on his heel, clutching Madeleine tight to his side, weaving and dancing through the erupting firestorm. Molten death exploded all around them. His sword flashed through the air, deflecting lethal missiles left and right in a Catherine wheel of sparks and brimstone.

Gerald swung around to fight the fast-advancing foe. He scuttled up a corridor as quickly as he could, his sword a scythe of blazing metal. But then he felt the cold press of a stone wall at his back—and he knew with equal coldness that there was nowhere left to run. He stole a last glance at the vision of beauty at his side, his one true love. He looked back—in time to see the beast unleash one final, fatal fireball. . . .

A stub of white chalk bounced off the middle of Gerald's forehead and clattered onto the desk in front of him. Gerald blinked.

He blinked again. The face of Mr. Atkinson, his year eight history teacher, was glaring down at him. The vein in the teacher's temple was throbbing like some claustrophobic earthworm trying to wriggle free. Gerald watched the chalk as it circled to a stop on his desk.

"Not talking too loudly for you, I hope, Wilkins," the teacher said. "Hate to disturb the sleep of the simple."

The dank castle dungeon, which moments before seemed certain to be Gerald's final resting place, melted away. Instead Gerald found himself in the back row of Mr. Atkinson's history class. He rubbed the spot on his forehead where the chalk had hit. Everybody in the room was staring at him.

"Wilkins," the teacher breathed, his teeth clenched as if glued at the molars. "I was advancing the theory that nothing is certain—that we are all the masters of our destinies; with some effort we can conquer the obstacles that come before us." He paused for breath. "Now, apart from an inevitable jail career, what was it that you were advancing toward in your slumber?"

Gerald shifted in his seat.

"Um . . . you know, I was sorta thinking that same thing . . . about destiny . . . and stuff."

Atkinson was not Gerald's favorite teacher. Atkinson was tall and angular, with a box-shaped head, no hips to speak of, and a fashion sense that extended to a dozen shades of beige. His rimless glasses magnified his eyeballs and resembled a pair of rifle sights strapped to the front of his head. On this day, Atkinson had Gerald in the crosshairs.

The teacher leaped forward. He plucked a dog-eared notebook from under the boy's elbow, whipping it away before Gerald could grab it.

"And what do we have here?" Atkinson said in triumph, ignoring Gerald's protests. He flicked through the ink-smudged pages. "Oh, this is most interesting."

Gerald let out a low moan and slumped into his chair. This was not turning out to be his best day.

"Well, well. This is very entertaining, Wilkins," Atkinson said airily as he wandered between the rows of desks. "I suppose all these drawings of castles and little men on horses do have something to do with history." He held the book up to show Gerald's classmates a particularly detailed drawing of a dragon spewing fire at a knight who was cowering behind a shield. The room erupted in laughter.

"Please don't," Gerald groaned, his head now in his hands.

"Oh, but I must, Mr. Wilkins! I must!"

He flicked through the pages. "Yes, just the collection of juvenile scribblings and smudged adolescent angst that we could expect from you, Wilkins. Oh look—here's one with a little story under it."

Gerald sat up.

"No!" he blurted out loud. Then, in a softer voice, "Not that one." And then even softer, "Please."

Atkinson glared through his gun sights at Gerald. "But, Wilkins, this one wants to be shared."

Gerald closed his eyes.

"Let's see," Atkinson began in a cheery voice. "The story is under a drawing of a young man holding a young lady in his arms. The young lady has lovely flowing hair and it looks like the young man has been going to the gym rather a lot."

More laughter spewed from the class as Gerald's head sank toward the top of his desk. "Oh, crud," he muttered.

"And the young lady is gazing at the young man with such gratitude in her eyes, such adoration. And this is where Wilkins has written: 'Brave Sir Gerald saves the love of his life yet again!'"

The laughter showered over Gerald like acid rain.

"Wait, wait! There's more!" Atkinson said above the noise, waving his hand to quiet the class. "The terrific thing is, Sir Gerald has even named his fair maiden." The teacher wandered toward the front of the classroom and consulted the notebook again. "Let's see. It appears her name is . . . Lady Madeleine."

With that, Atkinson dropped the notebook onto a desk in the front row. The room fell silent. The girl who was sitting at the desk picked up the notebook and studied the drawing. She flicked a lock of auburn hair from her eyes and swiveled around to look at Gerald. Revulsion was etched across her face.

"Anything you'd like to add to the story, Madeleine?" Atkinson asked, drumming his chalky fingertips together with glee.

The girl in the front row looked very much like the girl in the drawing in Gerald's notebook—the same strong jaw, the upturned nose and intense eyes, even down to the lock of hair that fell across her face. But there was no adoring look, just a glare that would curdle milk.

The bell rang for the end of the period and the class dissolved into a clatter of voices and scraping chairs. Atkinson, obviously annoyed that his fun was being cut short, called over the rabble, "Enjoy your break, people! At least those of you who have earned it."

Gerald remained slumped in his seat at the back of the room, staring at the floorboards.

"Well, that could have gone worse," a voice said. "Not much worse, I grant you, but potentially worse."

Gerald raised his head to see a round face beaming at him. He grunted. "I notice you were laughing along with everyone else."

"Well, you gotta admit, it was pretty funny. But top marks for the artwork, anyway." Ox Perkins slapped his friend on the back and laughed.

"Yeah. Terrific," Gerald replied.

He went to get out of his chair but paused midway. Madeleine was in front of him. The look of revulsion had been replaced with one of loathing. Her eyes were narrowed to slits and her face was flushed redder than her hair. She held Gerald's notebook between a thumb and forefinger as if it were a dead fish and dropped it on his desk. The book landed open at the offending page. The face was completely scrawled out. Madeleine leaned down until her nose was an inch from Gerald's.

"You're possessed!" she spat. She turned on her toes and stamped toward the exit.

"Oi! Blood nut!" It was Ox, a huge grin on his face.

Madeleine stopped short and spun around.

"What?" she demanded.

"I guess a kiss is out of the question?"

Madeleine scowled death at him and extended a finger before storming from the room.

Ox chuckled.

Gerald dragged himself upright and stuffed his notebook into a worn backpack. He and Ox headed toward the door.

"Wilkins!"

Atkinson's voice rang out like fingernails down a chalkboard. Gerald cringed at the sound. He looked up to be confronted by his teacher's face, a smile on it like a split watermelon.

"I've seen the student lists for next semester's history classes. Guess who you've got as teacher . . . again!"

Gerald's shoulders slumped.

Atkinson's smile broadened even further. "Now you have a tremendous holiday, won't you?"

"So what's with the drawings?" Ox thumbed through Gerald's notebook as they waited in the school gym for the final lesson of the day to get under way—PE with Mr. Phillpotts. Ink and pencil sketches filled the book. Many were no more than airy doodles, but some were as intricate as the drawing that had inflamed Madeleine and delighted Mr. Atkinson.

"Dunno," Gerald mumbled. "Stuff I dream about."

Gerald was fastening a harness around his waist. He pulled a rope from a rock-climbing wall and looped it through a ring at the front.

"You must dream about a lot of dungeons and caves then," Ox said, lying on a mat at Gerald's feet. He stopped at one sketch and held the page up so Gerald could see. "Shame Atkinson didn't find this one."

It was a pencil sketch of a cloven-hoofed monster clutching a trident in one hand and a writhing, screaming child in the other. The monster's face bore a striking resemblance to Mr. Atkinson.

"Yep." Gerald grinned, pulling a knot tight. "That's one of my favorites. Here, belay for me, will you?" He held out a rope for Ox to take.

"What's with Madeleine?" Ox asked as he pulled in the slack on the line. "Is she one of your dreams as well?"

"Doesn't really matter, does it?" Gerald grumbled. He lifted his right foot onto a ridge. "You saw how she reacted."

"Women, eh?" Ox said. "I wonder if one'll ever talk to me?"

For the next twenty minutes, the class took turns scaling the various faces on the climbing wall. Gerald was trying to traverse a difficult overhang when he stopped for a breather.

"So we're leaving for the snow tomorrow at ten, right?" he called down to Ox.

"You suffering from short-term memory loss?" Ox called back. "How many times do we have to go over this?"

"Humor me, okay?" Gerald said. "It's two weeks at the snow with your family and two weeks away from my folks. I'm treating this as a four-week holiday. Okay, hold tight now."

Gerald eyed the gap to the next face. Then he coiled his muscles and sprang into the void. He soared across like a spider monkey and hit the wall hard. His hands scrambled to find a hold but slipped free, leaving him swinging back across the space on the end of his rope, arms and legs dangling.

"That's enough mucking around, Wilkins." Mr. Phillpotts strode across the gym floor. "You're dismissed early."

Gerald gazed down from his position hanging above everyone's heads. He was surprised to see Madeleine standing next to Mr. Phillpotts.

"You need to go with Madeleine to the vice principal's office," the teacher said.

Ox lowered Gerald to the floor and helped him out of his harness. "Now what?" he whispered as he scooped up his backpack.

Ox shrugged. "See you first thing tomorrow."

Madeleine ignored Gerald as they walked down the deserted corridors toward the school office.

"Um, Madeleine," Gerald said. "Does this have anything to do with that drawing, because I'm really sorry about that and . . ."

His voice trailed off. There was no response. For once, Gerald decided that shutting up might be the best option. When they got to the office, Madeleine marched off in the direction of the library, her hair whipping the air like an enraged rattlesnake.

Gerald watched her go, baffled by why he could never get a girl to like him—and why he should be summoned to the office twenty minutes before school ended for the mid-year break. Apart from infuriating Madeleine, he hadn't done much wrong that day. He faced the frosted glass on the door, took a breath, and gave three sharp knocks.

An unexpected voice called, "Enter."

A shiver shot up Gerald's spine as he turned the handle. He opened the door to reveal a familiar figure standing behind the desk.

"Mr. Atkinson!" Gerald yelped.

The history teacher sneered down the length of his nose at Gerald, as if inspecting the contents of a handkerchief.

"Don't worry, Wilkins," Atkinson said. "I haven't been promoted yet. I'm standing in for the vice principal, who apparently couldn't wait for his holiday."

They regarded each other awkwardly.

"Um . . . you sent for me, sir," Gerald said. "If it's about that drawing—"

"No," Atkinson said, cutting him short with a flick of his hand. He fixed Gerald with a curious eye. "Your parents are here to see you."

"My parents?" Gerald echoed in a stunned voice. He followed the direction of Atkinson's outstretched hand and saw that his mother and father were indeed sitting on a couch in a corner of the office. His mother's face was buried in a lace handkerchief and his father's arm lay tentatively around her shoulders. Gerald's mother was a short woman, stoutly conditioned, with a helmet of rigid blond hair. Violet Wilkins had a manner some described as brassy—which Gerald had never really understood. He thought she was just loud. Vi wore a bright floral dress that Gerald recognized as the one she kept for special occasions.

A sort of soft squeak emerged from behind her handkerchief. Vi's shoulders heaved in spasms.

"Um . . . Dad?" Gerald said.

Gerald's father was a large man with sparse red hair. His watery eyes sat like underpoached eggs on the front of his head, which, combined with a long blotchy nose that looked like someone had squeezed a raw sausage, gave him a face that resembled an uncooked breakfast.

"What is it, Dad?"

"Gerald," Eddie Wilkins said at last, "I'm afraid I've got some news." He stood up and took a step toward his son. "It's about your great-aunt Geraldine, back in London."

"Yeah, what about her?" Gerald asked, jiggling his head to get his thoughts straight. This is a bit random, isn't it? The last day of school; I'm going to the snow with Ox tomorrow. Why are we here talking about Mum's ancient aunt?

"Well," his father said. "There's been a phone call, and she's . . . um . . . passed away."

Gerald's expression didn't change. "And this affects me how?" he asked, not liking the direction things were going.

"I'm afraid your trip with Oswald will have to wait, son. We've got a funeral to go to."

Gerald's heart sank.

"Dead!"

The word shot from his mother's mouth like a bullet.

Both Eddie and Gerald jumped at the noise. So did Mr. Atkinson, who had been listening with interest from across the room. The three of them stared at Violet as she lifted her face from her handkerchief. Tears streamed down her cheeks, streaking mascara in their path.

"I can't believe she's dead!"

Vi's mouth tightened at the corners, then she sobbed: "Isn't it just . . . wonderful!"

In all his life, Gerald had never seen his mother look quite so happy.

Chapter Two

Gerald nestled into the airplane seat and munched on some peanuts. He gazed out the window at the city of Sydney disappearing beneath him as the jet climbed into the sky. He knew that somewhere down there Ox and his family were stuffing last-minute things into bags as they prepared for the long drive to Charlotte Pass in the Australian Alps. A journey they would now make without him. He dragged out his beaten backpack, pulled out his notebook, and began doodling.

Seated across from him, his parents were deep in discussion. His mother seemed particularly agitated.

"Mum?" Gerald said.

". . . which is why I don't trust any of them, Eddie. That's why I've asked for all the locks to be changed."

"Mum?"

"I will not leave anything to chance. The Lord only knows I've waited years for this, and it's not going to fall over now for the want of a bit of planning."

"Mum!"

Vi exhaled as she turned to face her son.

"For pity's sake, Gerald. It's going to be a long enough day without you whining all the time. Keep quiet. Your father and I have important things to discuss."

With that, Vi turned back to resume her one-sided conversation.

Gerald flopped back into his seat. This holiday wasn't turning out the way he'd imagined at all. He was supposed to be trying out his new snowboard with Ox—they'd been planning it all year. But now he was on his way to England for the funeral of some great-aunt that he'd never even met. And then there was the little matter of the plane they were flying in. Long-haul flights are cramped and noisy and smelly and plain awful. So why, Gerald wondered, was he cradled deep in a soft leather armchair aboard a private jet? An enormous, luxurious Airbus A380 Flying Palace, on which, from what Gerald could see, he and his parents were the only passengers.

"Another drink, sir?"

Gerald was shaken from his thoughts by the flight attendant, who was carrying a tray of bottles and various multicolored snacks in packets. He was a robust, barrel-chested Englishman with a bushy moustache and a manner as starchy as his shirt. His short dark hair was parted in the middle and held in place with a slick of oil.

"I do beg sir's pardon," the attendant said, "but would sir care for some refreshment prior to luncheon?" The offer was delivered with the warmth of day-old porridge.

Gerald blinked up at the man, then shook his head. The plane had been in the air for barely an hour and already Gerald could tell that the flight attendant hated him. The Englishman affected a glazed response, then turned to Gerald's mother.

"Some more champagne, madam?" he asked in an ingratiating tone.

Vi smiled at him. "Why thank you, Mr. Fry. That would be simply marvelous."

Gerald hadn't been able to break into his parents' conversation to find out why a private Airbus was taking them to his great-aunt's funeral. He had no idea how they could possibly afford the flight. His father was always complaining about the meager state of their savings. The sudden interest in family matters was another mystery. Gerald and his parents had emigrated from England when he was six months old. In all the years since, not one of his relatives had come out to visit them. He'd never even seen his great-aunt and now he had to miss out on snowboarding to go to her funeral.

Gerald tossed aside a gridlike pattern of squares and rectangles he had been doodling in his notebook and turned his attention to a copy of *Oi!* magazine that his mother had discarded. A line on the cover read: "The lowdown on London's high life." It contained page after page of photographs and gossip about the social lives of people he had never heard of.

He was about to dump it when a photo caught his eye. Under the heading "About Town" was a picture of an old man and a woman at some official function. The man wore a black dinner suit with white gloves and held what looked like a large glass egg. Gerald didn't recognize him, but the woman was a different matter. She bore a striking resemblance to . . . his mother! He read the caption:

This diamond would certainly be any girl's best friend. British Museum Trust Chairman Sir Mason Green shows off the priceless Noor Jehan diamond to philanthropist Miss Geraldine Archer at the much-awaited opening of the new India exhibit this week. The rock weighs in at a lazy 500 karats and is rumored to be insured for £100 million. Sir Mason thanked Miss Archer for her continued support of the museum and for the generous donation that has brought Noor Jehan to Britain for the first time. The diamond is on display until September—a must-see!

Gerald was astonished. Her hair was white and her chin sagged, but there was no mistaking it—the woman in the photo looked like an older version of his mother. He flipped to the cover. It was dated a week ago. He got out of his seat, waving the magazine at his father.

"Hey, Dad! Is this Great-Aunt Geraldine?"

Vi intercepted the magazine before Eddie could take it. She looked at the page.

"Yes, that's her," she sighed. "More of her charities."

Gerald caught the magazine on his chest as it was flung back. He looked again at the photograph of his great-aunt and then back at his parents, who had returned to their squabbling. He tore out the page and stuffed it into his jeans pocket.

"I'm going to the toilet," he mumbled, and wandered toward the rear of the jet. Despite being irritated by his parents' weird behavior and the grim start to his holidays, Gerald couldn't help being impressed by his lavish surroundings. This certainly wasn't like any plane he'd ever seen.

He walked by a cluster of leather armchairs positioned around a fully stocked bar, then past a lounge area complete with cinema seating in front of a huge flat-screen TV on the wall. Further on was a dining table big enough to seat a dozen people, already laid out with white linen and crystal stemware for lunch. Everything was smooth edges and sweeping designs—like something from those "house of the future" shows on TV. Beyond the dining area and to one side was a galley kitchen hidden behind heavy blue curtains, from which came the rattle of dishes. A rich aroma of something delicious wafted from within.

The thrum of the jet engines grew a little louder as Gerald neared the tail. At the rear of the plane, his path was blocked by an enormous set of black lacquered doors that stretched the width of the jet. They were inlaid with cherry-stained wood in a pattern depicting a man with a bow and arrow set against a radiant sun. Gerald ran his fingers across the smooth wood and marveled at the perfect fit of the inlay into the dark paneling. It made his woodwork projects at school look pretty lame. He glanced back over his shoulder, but there was no one around. He turned a golden door handle and slipped inside.

Gerald stood still as his eyes adjusted to the dim light. After a moment he let out a low whistle. He was standing in a fully kitted-out bedroom suite, complete with a king-size bed bearing an enormous midnight-blue quilt, sewn in gold cloth with the same elaborate archer design that was on the doors. The dark ceiling was speckled with pinholes of light that gave the impression that the bed was in the middle of the outback under a star-filled night sky. Gerald recognized his mother's overnight bag on the floor by the bed and what looked very much like her pajamas laid out on a blue velvet couch at the far end of the suite.

"I guess I'm sleeping in a chair then," he grumped. He gave the bag a sulky kick and it toppled onto its side. A few of his mother's things spilled out. With a groan, Gerald knelt down and scooped up some toiletries and makeup. As he tipped them back into the bag he noticed something in a side pocket. He pulled out a bulky buff-colored envelope about the size of a large notebook. On the front was his mother's name—Violet Wilkins—in ornate handwriting. Flipping it over, he saw that the flap on the back was sealed with a large splodge of red wax. There was a design pressed into the seal but it was too dark to make it out. Gerald was about to crack open the wax when there was a faint sound behind him. The sound of doors being opened.

Gerald moved quickly. In an instant he had stuffed the envelope back into the side pocket and pushed the bag half under the bed. He jumped up—the moment he regained his feet a stripe of bright light crossed his face as the doors from the main cabin were thrust open. In the doorway was the imposing shape of the flight attendant, Mr. Fry.

"So this is where young sir has been hiding." The voice dripped with accusation. Fry's eyes darted around the suite. They came to rest on the overnight bag, lying on its side by Gerald's feet, half shoved under the bed.

"Tsk, tsk. How did this get under here?" Fry said. He hauled the bag out and settled its contents back into place.

He zipped it shut and bent down so he could look Gerald square in the eye.

"Now, will sir be joining his parents for luncheon or does sir have some more snooping to do?"

"I wasn't snooping!" Gerald protested. "I was looking for the, um, toilet."

Mr. Fry regarded Gerald as he might a hair floating in his soup.

"Yes, of course sir was."

Gerald screwed up his face and pushed his way back into the main cabin. He found his parents at the dining table, Vi holding a fresh glass of champagne. Gerald was surprised to see a small balding man sitting opposite his mother. A row of documents was set out in neat piles on the table between them. The man's head, his shoulders, even his manner, all seemed shrunken. He was dressed in a pale gray suit at least two sizes too large, and he had a pair of wire-rimmed spectacles perched on the end of what could best be described as a beak. In another life, the man could well have been an owl.

Gerald sat next to his father and studied the small man with interest, wondering where he had been until now.

"This must be Gerald," the man said pleasantly, half standing and extending a tiny hand, which Gerald shook softly for fear of crushing it like a dried leaf.

"Yes, this is him," Vi said, as if identifying a bag snatcher in a police lineup. "Gerald, this is Mr. Prisk. He'll be helping us with your great-aunt."

"What help do we need?" Gerald asked.

Mr. Prisk smiled at him from across the table.

"Gerald, I have been your great-aunt's solicitor for many years. She left specific instructions in the event of her death—quite specific instructions."

"Uh . . . instructions?"

"From what I am told"—the lawyer gave Vi and Eddie some sharp glances—"you are unaware of the extent of the situation."

Gerald saw an opportunity at last to get some answers. He cleared his throat, and said in his politest voice, "By 'situation' do you mean my parents coming to school yesterday to tell me that the high point of my holiday will be going to a funeral? Do you mean being driven home at twice the speed limit, told to pack a bag and get to bed early because we have a flight to catch first thing in the morning? Then today getting picked up in a stretch limo longer than our house and being taken to the airport where no less than a private jet is waiting? Being told to shut up and sit quietly in my seat, where I'm treated like an infestation of head lice by that guy?" Gerald jerked his thumb at Mr. Fry, who was laying out plates of poached salmon on the table, impervious to Gerald's tirade. "And all the while my mother's acting like she's been named the next queen of England.

Would that be the 'situation' you're referring to?"

Gerald looked at Mr. Prisk, who had removed his glasses and was cleaning them with a corner of his napkin.

"Gerald!" Vi was livid. Her eyes blazed from beneath her lacquered helmet of hair. "How dare you speak in that tone!"

Gerald crossed his arms and sank back into the chair, glaring at the salmon on his plate, and what looked suspiciously like a thumbprint in the potato mash.

There was an awkward silence, then Mr. Prisk cleared his throat.

"Yes . . . well, perhaps there are a few questions that need to be answered." Turning to Vi, he ventured, "Would you like me to provide some family history?"

Gerald's mother sniffed sharply and drained her champagne glass, which was refilled almost immediately by Mr. Fry, who had been hovering in the background.

"Thank you, Fry. You are a dear," Vi said.

The attendant bowed low and, with an almost inaudible "Madam is too kind," withdrew to a serving cart at the rear of the dining area, still within earshot of the conversation around the table.

"Gerald," Mr. Prisk began, picking up one of the piles of documents on the table and consulting the top sheet through his glasses, "your great-aunt was a most interesting woman."

"Well, I wouldn't know. I never even met her," Gerald said. "But I get to go to her funeral. Oh joy."

"Gerald!" His mother spluttered through a mouthful of salmon.

Mr. Prisk raised an eyebrow. "Gerald, your great-aunt was a woman of many dimensions," he continued. "Tomorrow she will be buried in a small cemetery in London. There will be a great number of people there to say their farewells. She was a unique woman."

"Unique? In what way?"

"Well, Gerald," Mr. Prisk said, clearing his throat. "There is probably no tactful way of saying this, so I guess I'll have to say it straight out. Your great-aunt was—"

"Just about the richest woman in the whole world!" burst out Vi with a gleeful shriek. She banged her champagne glass on the table, sending a fountain of bubbles over Mr. Prisk's papers.

For the second time in twenty-four hours, Gerald marveled at how happy his mother looked.

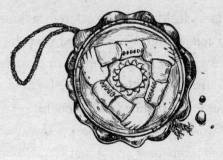

CHAPTER THREE

"Yes, Gerald," Mr. Prisk continued, dabbing his sodden paperwork with a napkin. "It is true that your great-aunt was a woman of means. She was heir to the Archer estate and managed her affairs with tremendous skill. She built a small fortune into a great one."

Mr. Fry fussed around Vi with a cloth, sopping up her spilled drink, before pressing another glass of champagne into her hand.

"Mr. and Mrs. Wilkins, your entrée is getting cold," Mr. Prisk said. "Why not eat your lunch and I'll bring Gerald up-to-date?"

"Very well, Mr. Prisk," Vi said, stabbing a forkful of salmon. "But don't take too long. You and I have much to discuss."

Excusing himself, Mr. Prisk stood and indicated that Gerald should follow him. They walked past the lounge area to the front of the plane and climbed to the upper deck to a spacious office suite. This must have been where Mr. Prisk was earlier in the flight, Gerald thought.

"This is a working plane," the lawyer explained as he sat down behind a tidy desk and waved Gerald into a seat opposite. "Your great-aunt insisted that she be able to operate the family business from anywhere in the world."

Gerald sat bewildered.

"Mr. Prisk," he started, "I have no idea who my great-aunt was. I just want to go to the snow with my friend and enjoy my holiday."

Mr. Prisk regarded Gerald carefully.

"How old are you, son?"

"I'm almost fourteen," Gerald said.

"Yes," Mr. Prisk murmured. "You ought to learn a bit more about your great-aunt. You know you're named after her, don't you?"

Gerald took a breath. He loathed his name. Gerald. Ger-ald. He could never understand why his parents had lumbered him with such a boat anchor to drag around for life.

"I was named after her?" he said in disbelief. "Oddly enough, I don't consider that a bonus."

Mr. Prisk ignored the remark and went on, "The funeral

is tomorrow. Your family has made an unusual request. Immediately after the ceremony there will be a reading of the will. Now, this is much sooner than is customary but, because of the sheer scale of Miss Archer's fortune, you can imagine there are a lot of people keen to hear what she might have left them."

Realization dawned on Gerald's face.

"My mother included," he said. "Yes, things are getting a bit clearer now."

That was why his mother had been acting so strangely. The glasses of champagne, the hysterical tears, that grasping smile. Because her wealthy aunt had died and might have left her some money. All Gerald's relations in England were probably behaving the same way, he thought. Relatives and money—what a toxic mix.

"But what about this jet? Why couldn't we just fly out on a normal plane? Why are you even here?" The questions tumbled out of Gerald.

Mr. Prisk said nothing. He reached into his breast pocket and pulled out a length of pink ribbon. Tied on the end was a silver key. He pushed the key into a cabinet by his desk, opened the top drawer and removed a buff-colored envelope, about the size of a notebook.

"Here," Mr. Prisk said, handing the package to Gerald. "I have been instructed to give this to you. It may provide some answers."

Gerald took the envelope.

On the front was his name, in the same neat but old-fashioned handwriting he'd seen on the envelope in his mother's bag. Under his name, in the same hand, was written: NOT TO BE OPENED UNTIL AFTER MY FUNERAL. Beneath that was: AND GERALD, I MEAN IT! He turned the package over and saw that the envelope was sealed with red wax. Pressed into the wax was the image of a triangle consisting of three forearms, hands clutching elbows, with a small sun at the center.

"That's the Archer family seal," Mr. Prisk said. "It dates back almost seventeen hundred years. You should understand that any attempt to open this envelope prior to the funeral will result in the forfeiture of any inheritance that may or may not be coming your way."

Gerald looked at the envelope with renewed curiosity.

"Who instructed you to give this to me?" he asked.

Mr. Prisk looked surprised.

"Your great-aunt, of course. That's her handwriting on the front."

Fry gave Gerald a look of intense suspicion when he emerged from the upper deck with a large envelope under his arm. Gerald stuffed the package into his backpack and out of sight.

The jet refueled in Dubai and Gerald managed to catch

a few hours' sleep. He watched a couple of movies on the big-screen TV, but mostly he stayed in his seat, occasionally scribbling in his notebook. He couldn't settle. The questions kept piling up onto the backs of one another. What was in the envelope? And what about the envelope in his mother's overnight bag? What was in that one? And why on earth would his parents name him after his mother's aunt and then have no contact with her for thirteen years? And why would a woman who hadn't seen him since he was a baby leave him anything in her will?

Gerald had finally fallen into a light doze when he was woken by the pilot's announcement that they would be landing in twenty minutes.

"Righto then, Gerald—seat belt on." Eddie emerged from the bedroom suite and was settling in a chair. "We'll be there soon enough now."

Gerald looked down the cabin and saw his mother speaking with Fry, who appeared to be offering her yet more champagne. He turned to his father. "Dad, about Geraldine—how did she die?"

Eddie peered at his son through his poached-egg eyes and considered the question for a moment. "Everyone's gotta go sometime. I guess this was her time. I know you were looking forward to the snow, but you'll still have a good holiday."

Gerald stared out the window. It was about ten in the

evening London time, and the long summer twilight was almost at an end. The jet touched down with a light bump and cruised to a halt outside a modest terminal building. Gerald peered out but could only see that they had landed at a small airfield surrounded by trees—they certainly weren't in the middle of a big city. At the front of the plane, Fry opened the main access door and a large set of steps was rolled into position. A young official in a navy blue uniform stepped inside.

"Evening, everyone," he said. "Passports, please."

He sat at the dining table going over the paperwork, stamping the documents.

"Welcome to the United Kingdom," the man said as he returned Gerald's passport. "You must be very popular."

"Why's that?" Gerald asked.

"A few of your friends have turned up," the man said with a flicker of a grin. Then he packed up his stamp and inkpad and disappeared out the door.

"A few of my friends?" Gerald said. "Who do I know in England?"

He hoisted his backpack onto his shoulder and followed his parents to the doorway. The moment they walked out onto the steps the night erupted. Lights exploded all around them. Shouts and sharp cries came from the bottom of the steps.

"Over here. Over here!"

"This way! This way! Over this way, Vi! One more."

"C'mon! Over this way, love. Keep coming."

The shouts grew in volume and intensity and the lights kept flashing in Gerald's face. He covered his eyes from the glare, stumbling on one of the steps and colliding with Eddie in front. Gerald blinked hard to clear his vision and after a second he made out the cause of the firestorm.

At the bottom of the steps a swarm of television crews and photographers was bursting flashes, raking spotlights, and yelling for Vi and Eddie. For a moment, Vi stood frozen halfway down the steps, unsure what to do. And then, as if some long-dormant instinct deep within sparked back into life, she took charge.

She strode down the steps onto the tarmac and stood directly in front of the cameras. She squared her shoulders to the crowd, tilted her head back, and threw her arms wide, barking, "It's great to be back in England!"

There was a renewed barrage of flashes as Vi waved to the cameras. From his position back on the steps, Gerald could see that she even waved to corners of the airfield where there weren't any people. He was surprised to admit his mother was pretty good at this.

"Vi! Vi," a young male reporter in the front called out. "How does it feel to know you could inherit one of England's greatest fortunes? How are you going to spend it?"

Vi smiled (another blast of flashes), closed her eyes,

lifted her chin, and affected a coy laugh (more flashes) and then cocked one hand on her waist and waved a reproving finger at the reporter (yet more flashes).

"Not so fast, sweetie," she cooed. "The will won't be read until tomorrow. But there's one thing for sure: I won't be spending any of it on you, you naughty boy. I'm a married woman!"

Vi bathed in the reporters' laughter and opened her mouth to speak again. Before she could say anything, Mr. Prisk materialized at her elbow and whispered into her ear. Vi's eyes widened and her expression changed.

"Of course this is a time of tremendous sadness for our family," she said in a hushed tone. "An occasion of great personal loss and we all deeply mourn the tragic passing of Geraldine Archer. We all miss her terribly . . . terribly." She cast her eyes to the tarmac for a moment. Then the smile burst back onto her lips. "Now then . . . who's next? Yes, you in the white pants—I love your shoes, by the way."

For the next fifteen minutes Vi and Eddie answered questions. Flashes still burst sporadically into the night as Vi struck a variety of poses. Gerald found a spot by one of the jet's tires to watch the show.

He was sitting with his chin resting on his fist when a sudden coldness clamped onto his shoulder. A hand encased in a black glove gripped him. Gerald wrenched around and leaped to his feet, knocking the hand away.

"Mr. Wilkins," a lean male voice rasped in Gerald's ear. "Did I startle you?"

Gerald stumbled back and looked up into the thinnest face that he had ever seen. The man was dressed entirely in black: elegant black boots disappeared up black stovepipe trousers, met at the hips by a tight-fitting black suit coat over a black shirt that was buttoned to the neck and fastened at the wrists with black cuff links. A black homburg covered the top of his head; wisps of snow-white hair peeked out at the sides. While the man's clothing was the color of coal dust, his face was like chalk—he had a deathly white complexion that may never have seen a sunny day. A narrow gray scar ran the length of one gaunt cheek. His lips were thin, barely darker than the surrounding skin, and drawn tight across yellowed teeth. And, in spite of the evening now being quite dark, the man wore sunglasses. Against the night sky, it was as if a skull were floating in front of him. But for Gerald, the overwhelming impact was not the man's gothic appearance or even his intense thinness, but his smell: a choking aroma of bleach made Gerald cover his nose. He took a gulp of air and another step backward.

"Who are you? What do you want?"

The thin man stretched two hands toward Gerald like a giant puppet controlled by invisible strings.

"Mr. Wilkins," he said in his rasping voice, his head jerking to one side, "there is nothing to fear. I merely wanted to . . . to welcome you . . . back to your home."

"Th-thanks . . . I guess," Gerald said, not taking his eyes off the outstretched hands that hovered near his face.

"I knew your great-aunt," the thin man continued. "I got to know her quite well, you know, toward the end."

"Really?"

"Yes. Well enough." The thin man paused and looked Gerald up and down. But because of the dark glasses it was impossible for Gerald to tell exactly where he was looking. The thin man tilted his head and sniffed the night air, as a dog might if another animal ventured nearby.

"Sadly," he said, as if talking to himself, "she wasn't able to help me the way I had hoped she would."

Gerald took another step back. The smell of bleach was overpowering. Then, in a blur of rapid movement, the thin man shot out a hand and grabbed Gerald hard around the wrist.

"Hey!" Gerald protested. The man may have been thin, but he was very strong.

"Perhaps you might be able to help me," the man said, a mirthless smile spreading across his narrow lips.

"Let . . . go . . . of . . . me . . ." Gerald grunted as he struggled to free his hand. But the grip tightened until Gerald was sure his wrist would break.

"Yesss," the thin man hissed through gritted teeth, drawing his face so close that all Gerald could see was his own stunned reflection in the dark glasses. "I think you may be of enormous help to me."

A flash exploded behind Gerald's ear, slicing through the darkness. The thin man recoiled, loosening his grip for a second. It was all Gerald needed—he whipped his hand away and fell backward onto the tarmac.

"Look! Here's the kid," a voice rang out.

Three photographers appeared out of the night and surrounded Gerald, firing a series of shots. "Just a coupla frames," said one burly snapper, the pockets of his red vest stuffed with camera lenses. Gerald snatched his backpack from the ground and, pushing past the cameras, hurried toward his parents.

"There you are," Eddie called as Gerald ran over. "What have you been up to?"

Gerald looked back behind him. The thin man had disappeared. "A man . . . over there. He tried to grab me," he panted, holding his wrist.

"Yes, they can get a bit pushy," Vi said as she fare-welled the last of the photographers. "Never mind. I'll have Mr. Prisk appoint a PR company tomorrow to handle all requests for interviews."

"Mum, I don't think he was after an interview," Gerald said. "I think he was after me."

Vi let out a shrill laugh. "Don't be hysterical. Why on earth would anyone want you?"

Mr. Prisk emerged from the plane, a large briefcase in each hand.

"Come along," he said. "Time to get going."

He ushered them across the tarmac to a black Rolls-Royce parked near the terminal building. Their bags were already in the trunk, and Mr. Fry sat behind the wheel, a chauffeur's cap on his head.

Gerald stared out the rear window as the limousine drove through the gates. They passed the reporters filing their stories and the camera crews packing their equipment away. There was no sign of the thin man.

CHAPTER FOUR

Gerald had been impressed by the luxury of the private jet, but his reaction didn't compare to the trills of ecstasy that his mother emitted when they stepped inside Geraldine's five-story house in Chelsea later that night. Vi spent much of the evening wandering from opulent room to opulent room with an expression of rapture plastered on her face.

In the morning, Gerald was surprised to find Mr. Fry serving breakfast in the dining room. He did notice a slight thawing in the Englishman's attitude, even offering Gerald seconds of bacon.

They left for the funeral service soon after breakfast. Mr. Fry was dressed in an immaculate chauffeur's uniform and doffed his hat as Gerald climbed into the back of the Rolls.

In the backseat, Gerald leaned across to whisper to his father, "Dad, what's the story with Mr. Fry? Is he going to go everywhere with us?"

Eddie pondered the back of the chauffeur's head and, in a hoarse whisper, replied, "Not sure, son. He was Aunt Geraldine's butler for years—he's part of the furniture. I don't think we can get rid of him."

Vi shifted in her seat and looked up from a newspaper report of their arrival at the airfield.

"And why would we want to get rid of him?" She sniffed. "He's a dream, and he knows how a lady ought be treated in her own home."

Gerald and his father looked at each other.

"Uh, Mum," Gerald said. "It's not your home."

"Oh really?" Vi said to Gerald, her eyes affecting a half glaze as she returned to her newspaper. "Let's see what the day brings, shall we?"

She let out an indignant grunt. "Listen to this. 'Vi Wilkins touched down in the Archer corporate jet last night to lay claim to one of Europe's greatest fortunes. She boldly predicted that she would inherit the lion's share of the grand estate, built by teabag baron Dorian Archer and later by his daughter, Geraldine.'" Vi snorted derisively. "I never said that."

Eddie flicked through a stack of newspapers in the back of the car, each one opened to the page with the news of their arrival.

"I think you'll find all the papers are saying the same thing. Here, look at this."

Eddie turned up the volume on the television in the back of the limousine. It had been flickering away silently, tuned to an early-morning news program. Behind the onscreen announcer's right shoulder was a photograph of Great-Aunt Geraldine.

". . . meanwhile, the funeral of businesswoman and philanthropist Geraldine Archer takes place in Chelsea today. Friends and relatives from around the world are converging to see how the vast estate will be split among them. Her niece, Vi Wilkins, jetted in from Australia overnight and had this to say . . ."

The story then cut to footage of Vi and Eddie at the airfield. Vi was standing with both fists on her hips, her feet set well apart and her chin jutting out. "I won't say that I was Geraldine's favorite, but compared to the rest of the family, let's just say I wouldn't be quitting my job yet if I was one of them!"

From the back of the Rolls, Vi frowned at the TV and muttered something about context, but Gerald wasn't listening. His eyes were fixed on the screen. As Vi talked to the cameras, a tall slightly hunched figure clad in black drifted behind her toward the jet. The figure turned to the cameras. But that was all Gerald needed to recognize the white face and the impenetrable sunglasses.

"Dad!" Gerald burst out, stabbing his finger at the

screen. "That's him. That's the man from the airport last night, the one who grabbed me."

Eddie glanced at the TV, but the thin man had melted into the night. The only thing Eddie saw behind Vi was his own face, staring out embarrassed.

"Oh Gerald," Vi said. "Will you get over it. One autograph hunter and you go to pieces. I don't want to hear another word about it. Look, we're coming to the church now."

The Rolls glided to the side of the road. Vi fixed a determined eye on both Gerald and Eddie. "Right, you two—I've waited half a lifetime for this. Don't make a hash of it!"

The scene at the church was almost a replay of their arrival at the airfield the previous evening. Banks of cameras exploded in a whir of shutters and flashes as the Wilkins family emerged from the car.

"Right, let's go!" Vi ordered, and grabbing the others' hands, she pulled them scuttling up the path, past a line of mourners waiting to get inside—"Excuse me, we're family!"—and into the church, the photographers' cries still ringing in their ears.

Vi dropped Gerald and Eddie's hands and rearranged her large black hat. She inspected Gerald for the fourth time since breakfast. Clicking her tongue, she batted off his protesting hands to adjust his tie, licked her fingers, and pressed down a patch of unresponsive hair. Satisfied that everything was in place, Vi led the way to the front of the church. She flicked a RESERVED sign off the seat closest to the altar and settled into her place. Gerald and Eddie followed close behind.

The church was full. The pews, which faced each other across the central aisle, were lined with silver-haired men and tight-faced women, all dressed in somber suits and speaking in hushed whispers. The men wore an assortment of club ties and lapel pins indicating some honor or other, and the women wore black hats of all dimensions. In front of the altar sat a coffin on a wheeled stand, draped with the white-and-red flag of St. George. A green laurel branch lay on the coffin lid. Organ music played softly in the background, and despite it being a sunny summer day, it was distinctly cool in the low light of the church.

Gerald found himself staring across at a boy and a girl of roughly his own age. The boy sat hunched forward, his bulky shoulders supporting a pumpkinlike head. The girl had long dull hair, parted sharply down the middle and tied back in two stringy pigtails. Her face was a picture of determined boredom.

"That'd be yer cousin Octavia," a gravelly voice whispered into Gerald's right ear.

Gerald swiveled around to come face-to-face with a man in the pew behind him. The man's round head sat atop an even rounder body.

"She's yer cousin on yer mother's side," the man said, chewing on something. After a moment's reflection, he added with a grunt, "Nasty piece of work she is, too."

Gerald blinked. He had a cousin?

He stared agog at the stranger. The man was about the same age as Gerald's father, but his skin was the color and consistency of old floorboards, like he'd spent half his life in the tropics.

Gerald went to speak but before he could utter a word the man raised his hand and flicked a small white ball into the back of Gerald's mouth.

"Here," the man said. "Have a peppermint."

Gerald gagged as the sweet bounced off the back of his throat.

"Not too strong for you, I hope. I likes the strong ones."

Gerald couldn't respond. Tears started to well in his eyes.

"She's the daughter of yer mother's brother—yer uncle Sidney," the man continued, indicating the girl across the aisle with a nod. "He's the large brick outhouse over there."

Gerald turned back and saw that the girl was sitting next to a hulk of a man, bald headed and looking uncomfortable in an ill-fitting suit and a shirt that couldn't quite fasten around his tree stump of a neck. This man was clearly also the father of the pumpkin-headed boy.

The stranger leaned forward and whispered into Gerald's left ear, "And yer know why they call that there hairstyle of young Octavia's a pigtail?"

Gerald sucked his peppermint and looked across at the freckled nose of his newfound cousin. He felt the man's lips brush close to his ear. "Well, have ya ever, at any time in yer life, seen a face that looks more like a pig's arse?"

Gerald coughed to dislodge the peppermint from his windpipe.

From the head of the pew, Vi glared at him with a look that would stop a clock. Gerald tried to mime that he had been talking with the man behind him, but when he turned to look over his shoulder the seat was occupied by an elderly woman busy adjusting her hearing aid. Gerald cast about to his left and right but could find no sign of the round-headed man. He gave his mother an apologetic shrug and slouched back into his seat, chewing the peppermint and trying to spy the strange man among the other mourners.

The funeral service seemed to go on forever. The reverend said a few words, and people from a number of charities got up to praise Geraldine for the large sums of money that she had donated over the years. After the fourth person spoke about a particularly generous gift, Gerald noticed that his mother's hands were gripping the front of the pew so tightly that her knuckles were white. A couple of hymns were sung, a few more words said, and then the coffin was wheeled down the aisle.

Gerald had sat impassively throughout the service. He had never met this woman. He didn't feel anything toward her. The only thing that seemed to link them was a shared name—a name that Gerald detested. As the casket passed him, though, Gerald said a quiet word of good-bye under his breath, and he wondered whether he would have liked his great-aunt Geraldine.

The church began to empty through the front entrance, but Vi took Gerald by the elbow and guided him across to a side door.

"Come along, Gerald," she said. "The main event's in here."

They walked into a church hall that had been set with rows of white plastic chairs. Along one wall was a table laid out with sandwiches and pots of tea. At the front was a fold-up table behind which sat Mr. Prisk. Vi pushed Gerald into a chair at the back of the hall.

"You stay there, Gerald. Out of harm's way," she said, a hand heavy on his shoulder. "This bit won't concern you, but your father and I need to talk with some people."

Eddie had already made a beeline for the refreshment table and Vi edged her way into a group at the front of the hall near Mr. Prisk. "Ah, you must be Sir Mason Green. So good of you to come."

The hall filled quickly and people gradually took their

seats. Gerald noticed that Fry, whom he hadn't seen during the funeral service, sat in a chair in the second row, directly behind Vi and Eddie. At the other end of the front row sat Gerald's cousin Octavia with her brother and their father, Sidney. It seemed that Vi and Sidney were taking great care not to acknowledge each other's existence. The other rows filled with people of all ages, none of whom Gerald recognized. He was staring at a white-haired man who looked sort of familiar when a voice grated in his ear, "What a bunch of hyenas!"

Once again Gerald startled. The round-faced man had appeared from nowhere and pulled up a plastic chair to sit next to Gerald. Gerald declined the offer of another peppermint.

"And aren't they all eager to see what's comin' to them." The man popped a mint into his mouth and began chewing loudly. "Greed's an ugly thing to see red raw in the flesh."

Gerald saw the chance to get a word in.

"Who are you? How do you know so much about my family?"

"Who am I? Now there's a question!" The man rasped out what Gerald assumed was a laugh, but there was no smile on the face. "I, my boy, am an old friend of yer great-aunt's family. We go back a few years now." The man stood up, wiped his right hand on his jacket, and offered it to Gerald.

"My name is Hoskins. You can call me Mr. Hoskins, or you can call me Sir—the choice is yours."

He gave Gerald's hand a crushing shake.

"Your great-aunt told me a fair bit about you. You even look a bit like her—did yer know that?"

Gerald shook his head in confusion.

"But I never even met her," he said. "How could she know anything about—"

Before Gerald could finish, Hoskins raised a finger.

"You may never have met the lady, but she knew all there was to know about you," he said. "Family was very important to her."

"Not so important that she'd jump on that giant jet and visit us," Gerald said.

Hoskins bristled.

"Listen carefully, young fellow," he said, jabbing a finger in Gerald's chest. "That lady had good reason to keep her distance. She needed to protect the—" He stopped abruptly and turned away, concentrating on his mint.

"To protect what, Mr. Hoskins?" Gerald asked.

"Never you worry. But family was the first thing in Geraldine's mind in everything she did."

Gerald looked around the room. Vi and Eddie never spoke about family. Eddie was an only child and his parents were long dead. Vi's parents had died before Gerald was born. He grew up with no grandparents, no aunts and uncles, no cousins. So who are all these people? Gerald wondered. Who's that old woman half asleep leaning against the wall over there? And those two white-haired men chatting by the urn; who are they? What about the rest of the collection of eyeglasses, silk ties, long gloves, false teeth, and ear hair in the room? Who are you all?

Gerald's eyes came to rest on his cousin Octavia, fidgeting in the front row.

"Ah, yes," Hoskins murmured. He had been following Gerald's gaze with interest. "The next of kin."

"How do you mean?" Gerald asked.

"Yer mother and her brother are the only two of Geraldine's line: niece and nephew to as fine a woman you could ever hope to meet. Then comes you, of course, and yer cousins—the disgraceful Octavia over there and her equally rotten brother, Zebedee."

"Uh, Zebedee?" Gerald said, wrinkling his nose.

"Yes, I know. What are some parents thinking, eh?"

Gerald stifled a laugh.

"Geraldine never married. She had no children of her own. And when her brother died—your grandfather—that left her the sole beneficiary of the Archer fortune," Hoskins said.

"And now Mum and Sidney are the next in line?" Gerald asked.

Hoskins nodded.

"Who are the rest of these people?" Gerald asked.

"A mixed bunch. A lot of very distant cousins many times removed, a few old employees from the family firm, some servants from the country house. Anyone who reckons they could be due a few bob from the old girl," Hoskins said.

Just then, at the front of the room, Mr. Prisk stood up and a hush settled over the gathering.

Gerald opened his mouth to ask Hoskins something, but the man raised his finger to his lips. "I suggest you listen very carefully," he rasped. "You'll find it concerns you."

Gerald sat mesmerized as Mr. Prisk started proceedings.

"Good morning, everybody," he began. "This is the reading of the last will and testament of Geraldine Archer, daughter of Dorian and Cassandra Archer. In drawing up her final wishes, Miss Archer was very clear about how the estate was to be divided."

A murmur swept across the hall, and plastic chairs scraped the floor as bottoms adjusted in anticipation.

Mr. Prisk reached down and took a buff-colored envelope from the desk. He held it up.

"You see this document has been secured with the Archer family seal, which is intact," he said.

With a flamboyant wave of his hand, Mr. Prisk broke the red wax seal and opened the envelope. He pulled out a single sheet of white paper.

"Miss Archer asked that I read this statement: 'Over the last few days all of you have been given envelopes by Mr. Prisk or his agents. Inside each of these envelopes is a brief personal message from me, as well as details of what has been left to you from the Archer estate.'"

Mr. Prisk continued, "The Archer estate was valued as late as May at approximately twenty billion pounds. You should now read the contents of your envelopes."

Buff-colored envelopes appeared from suit pockets and handbags. The sound of tearing paper ripped through the hall.

The buzz grew louder as people scanned their letters. But then the voices started to break out.

"What? A toast rack!"

"Her old magazines?"

"Teaspoons!"

But it was hoarse cries of "Nothing!" that were heard the most.

In the front row, Vi tore her envelope open, the wax seal shattering across Eddie's lap. She hauled out a thick wad of paper and gave Eddie an excited look. "This is it," she said, cradling the paper in her arms. She burrowed into the pile, reading as quickly as she could.

At the other end of the row, her brother, Sid, was half-way through a similar-size bundle, a knot of concentration growing on his forehead. Even Mr. Fry had discreetly pulled an envelope from his suit pocket and was busy reading its contents.

At the back of the room, Gerald sat on his hands and kicked his feet back and forth, watching the tension build. He had left his envelope at Geraldine's house, in his backpack.

"I guess I'll read mine later," he said, turning to Hoskins, only to find the man was no longer by his side. Gerald could see no sign of him. "How does he do that?" he asked himself.

There was a loud cry at the front of the hall. Sidney was on his feet. He was not happy.

"What's the meaning of this, Prisk?" Sidney railed, the veins in his neck bulging. "Says here we get a million quid in cash. Where's the rest of it?"

Mr. Prisk cleared his throat. "That is a considerable sum of money."

"Considerable sum be stuffed," Sid growled back. "The old cow was worth billions!"

Sid's outburst encouraged others to stand and voice their disappointment at receiving collections of old crockery rather than the sacks of cash they thought were coming their way. In the second row, Mr. Fry folded his letter back into his pocket and sat stony faced.

More and more people stood to raise objections. Gerald

tried to see what his mother was doing, but the forest of protesting relatives made it an impossible task. He jumped out of his seat and began forcing his way toward the front of the hall.

He got to a point where he could glimpse his mother and found that she was still reading intently through the ream of papers. Finally, she tucked the sheaf back into its envelope and sat with a thoughtful look on her face.

Gerald struggled on.

Mr. Prisk held up his hands.

"Please. Please. Let's calm down," he implored. "Remember where you are."

The room quieted at this and most people took their seats, though Gerald still had to squeeze between bodies as he continued toward his parents.

"Thank you. I have one last document to read from Miss Archer," Mr. Prisk said. "Miss Archer's final wishes were these." He cast a quick glance at the thirteen-year-old boy who was making for the front row. "She said: 'My estate is worth approximately twenty billion pounds. This consists of my home in Chelsea, the manor near Glastonbury, my shares in Archer Enterprises, my island in the Caribbean, the Archer yacht, the Archer air wing, various investments, artworks, properties, and holdings, as well as about two hundred million pounds in cash. Apart from the few trinkets and minor cash sums I have distributed to people in this room, I leave all of my estate to one person . . . '"

The intake of breath around the hall could be heard from across the street, followed by a unanimous demand of: "Who?"

At just that moment Gerald popped out from between two large women and stumbled across the floor, right in front of Mr. Prisk.

"To my great-nephew, Master Gerald Archer Wilkins," Mr. Prisk announced.

Gerald looked up at the sound of his name.

"What?" he said.

The uproar that followed frightened dogs four blocks away.

CHAPTER FIVE

Gerald was sucked into a clash the likes of which the church hall hadn't seen since the German air force bombed it to its foundations in World War II.

The room was in uproar. Gerald was the primary heir to a fortune worth twenty billion pounds. A mob formed around Mr. Prisk, hungry for answers.

The most vocal was Sidney, who brayed that he would be "seeing his lawyers about this outrage!"

Everything happened at such a pace and with such intensity that it was hard for Gerald to keep up. Sidney was yelling at Mr. Prisk, and Mr. Prisk was doing his best to be heard back.

Gerald stood mute—ignored by the mob but, at the same time, the center of its fury.

He felt a jab on his arm. He turned to be confronted by the unsmiling Octavia and Zebedee.

"Oh, hello," Gerald said, a nervous smile forming on his lips. "I guess we're cousins. I'm Ger—"

"We know who you are," Octavia snapped.

Zebedee glowered at Gerald.

"Do you have any idea how much time we had to spend with that woman?" Zebedee demanded.

"Uh, what?"

"Afternoon teas, trips to the park, walks in the country, visits to that boring museum." Octavia counted off on her fingers.

"I'm sorry, what?" said Gerald.

Octavia shook her fists with frustration. "With Aunt Geraldine, you idiot!"

"Dad made us grovel to her for years and what do we get? A lousy million quid," Zebedee said.

"A million pounds is pretty good," Gerald said. "I mean, I wouldn't mind getting—"

Octavia looked like she was about to smack Gerald in the head.

"Weren't you listening, you clot?" she shouted. "You just inherited twenty thousand million quid!"

It still hadn't sunk in. Gerald counted himself lucky if Eddie remembered his pocket money each week. But now . . . twenty billion pounds.

The world was pressing in on him: the inheritance, the mob, his newfound cousins. The only thing missing from the sideshow was his mother. Where was Vi?

His question was answered almost immediately.

Vi shouldered her way to the center of the crowd.

"Right, you lot," she snapped. "Time to listen to me!"

Her tone made it clear she wasn't going to ask a second time. People took a few steps back.

"There's nothing to argue about," she said. "I'm assured by Mr. Prisk that this will is as watertight as a fish's bum. The estate goes to Gerald."

The crowd howled.

Vi wasn't deterred. "Naturally, as Gerald is not yet of age, the estate will be held in trust for him over the next five years. And it is up to us, as responsible parents, to manage that estate as we see best for our dear son. Now, in case any of you get wild ideas about making some sort of claim"— she gave Sidney a piercing glance—"I have instructed Mr. Prisk to change the locks on all of Geraldine's . . . I mean Gerald's properties. Which means, Sidney, you will no longer have access to the country house. Don't worry. Any personal effects will be forwarded to your little bungalow."

The vein on Sid's forehead bulged even further.

"That does it, woman," Sid bawled. "You've gone too far!" He shoved people aside to confront his sister. "Naming your little brat after the old cow was bad enough, but this is too much."

Vi clamped her hands on Gerald's shoulders and started to pilot him out of the throng.

"Come on, Gerald. We've spent far too much time with these unpleasant people." She threw a parting gibe at her frothing brother: "If you have any complaints, Sidney, I suggest you take them up with my new lawyer, Mr. Prisk."

On hearing this news, Mr. Prisk emitted a high-pitched yelp. The mob descended on him like lions at feeding time.

Vi bustled Gerald and Eddie back into the church. Mr. Fry followed at a polite distance. She pushed Gerald into a pew and sat down next to him.

"Right, Gerald," she said. "There's been a change of plan."

"Uh, Mum?"

"We won't be staying in London after all."

"Mum?"

"Well, when I say 'we,' naturally I mean your father and I."

"Mum?"

"We'll be undertaking a thorough inspection of the entire Archer empire to make sure everything is in order."

"Mum!"

"I thought we might start with a few weeks on the Archer

yacht sailing around the Archer island in the Caribbean. It would be best for you to stay here for safety reasons, and Mr. Prisk has a few things he needs to go over with you. So I've arranged for Mr. Fry to look after you here in London. Now, doesn't that sound fun?"

"Mum!" Gerald yelled at last.

Vi looked at Gerald as if she had only just noticed him. "Yes, dear, what is it?"

"Is it true?" Gerald asked. "Is it true you named me Gerald so you could suck up to Great-Aunt Geraldine?"

Vi looked at her son with surprise.

"Why, Gerald," she said. "Of course it's true. Best investment I've ever made. I was only doing it with your long-term interests in mind, my lovely boy. Now, be a darling and calm down. Your father and I will call you once we get to the island."

Vi squeezed Gerald's cheeks and planted a wet kiss on his forehead. "Such a good boy," she purred. "Come on, Eddie. There's a car waiting to take us to the jet."

Gerald's father gave his son an apologetic shrug. Vi hugged Gerald, and with a sharp laugh of triumph, she and Eddie disappeared out of the church.

Gerald sat speechless for a full minute as the enormity of the morning's events sank in.

His thoughts were interrupted by a cough. He looked up to see the sour face of Mr. Fry looming above him.

"You ready to go, or what?" Fry said, his plummy accent mysteriously disappearing.

Gerald guessed that Fry's cheery demeanor was unlikely to be seen again any time soon.

The drive back to Geraldine's house—to Gerald's house—was as quiet as you might expect it to be, sitting alone in the backseat of a Rolls-Royce limousine.

Fry made a big show of raising the privacy screen behind the driver's seat, but not before Gerald caught his muttering "ungrateful" and "twenty years of service" and "this is the thanks I get."

For most of the trip, Gerald sat there thinking.

Now, let me get this straight, he pondered. I had a great-aunt named Geraldine. I never met her in my life, even though apparently I was named after her. She dies and it turns out she's worth a gazillion dollars. And she leaves pretty much the lot to me. My folks have jumped onto my new private jet and are heading to my luxury yacht to sail to my island in the Caribbean. And I'm stuck in London being babysat by my new English butler who totally hates my guts.

Gerald stewed on all this.

And it's only day two of my holidays.

The Rolls entered the Chelsea street of smartly presented houses, festooned with window boxes alight with summer color. Up ahead Gerald could see a crowd had gathered on the footpath outside Geraldine's place. It was the now-familiar scrum of press cameras and television crews, waiting for Gerald to arrive. Fry pressed the accelerator and the car responded, gliding past the front door and along the street. The media pack was slow to react and only a few photographers bothered to chase the car, cameras held outstretched. Looking out the rear window, Gerald recognized some of them from the airport the previous night. The last one to give up the chase was the burly photographer with the red vest who had allowed Gerald to escape the grip of the thin man. He was sweating and swearing as he stumbled to a halt in the middle of the flagstoned street, trying to catch his breath.

Fry brought the car around a corner and into a narrow lane that ran behind the line of houses. About halfway down the alley a pair of iron gates opened to reveal a driveway. The Rolls pulled in off the street and the gates moved back into place. Fry got out to open the car door for Gerald, who climbed out and faced his butler.

"You don't like me, do you?" Gerald said.

Fry closed the car door with a metallic clunk.

"I'm not paid to like you," he said. He turned and marched across the white pebble drive to open the back door for his new master, his boots crunching on the stones.

* * *

65

About an hour later Mr. Prisk arrived at the house, a tiny ball of anxiety. He struggled past the cameras and through the front door. "I told you I have no comment," he said over his shoulder, heaving the door closed. "Vultures," he muttered, straightening his tie.

Mr. Prisk found Gerald sitting in a bay window in the downstairs drawing room, peeking through a gap in the curtains at the media pack on the footpath.

"Ah Gerald," Mr. Prisk said in a businesslike manner. "Good to see you're making yourself at home." He pulled up a chair and sat next to his youngest client. "Seeing as it is your home now."

"It doesn't exactly feel like home," Gerald said. The walls were hung with floral wallpaper and adorned with expensive artwork. Antique furniture stood on plush woolen carpets. An ancient clock ticked loudly on the mantel above the fireplace and an enormous crystal chandelier hung from the ceiling. It was an old woman's house—from the porcelain figurines in display cases to the clusters of framed photographs on the side tables. Gerald had been surprised to find that one of the frames included a photograph of himself.

"Perhaps not to everyone's taste," Mr. Prisk said, fidgeting with his briefcase.

Gerald looked at the tiny man.

"Is everything all right?" Gerald asked.

"Um, not really, no," Mr. Prisk began. "I mean, there's

no need to be alarmed, but I've been on the phone to the police."

"The police! What for?"

Mr. Prisk pulled a white handkerchief from his coat pocket and dabbed his top lip.

"It seems that news of your inheritance has spread rather quickly."

Gerald pulled the curtains back to reveal twelve television cameras perched on the doorstep. "I can't imagine how," he said.

"There have been a few threatening phone calls—just nutters—but the police don't want to take any chances," Mr. Prisk said.

"Any chance of what?"

"Um . . . well, not wanting to worry you . . . you know . . . any chance of . . . unpleasantness. So they've asked that I keep you in the house for a little while."

"What? In here!" Gerald said. "For how long?"

Mr. Prisk cleared his throat.

"Just till you go home."

Gerald was horrified. "But that's weeks away!" he cried. "You want me to sit in here for the next three weeks?"

"Yes, actually. Possibly even longer. That is exactly what I want you to do," Mr. Prisk said firmly.

Gerald flopped back into his seat with an exasperated sigh.

"Some holiday this has turned out to be," he grumbled.

Mr. Prisk frowned at Gerald.

"Look, Gerald. I'm not sure you appreciate what happened today. You have inherited one of the largest fortunes in Europe. You are now probably the richest thirteen-year-old on the planet."

Gerald considered this. "Fat lot of good it does me if I'm stuck in here," he said.

"Gerald, from today everything is changed. This amount of money brings new challenges, new responsibilities. And, frankly, it brings new dangers. When you're talking this kind of money . . . Gerald, there are people who are willing to do almost anything to get even a small fraction of it. I promised your parents that I'd keep you safe. I promised your great-aunt that I would keep you safe. And I intend to keep my word."

Gerald thought it over. The memory of the sinister thin man clutching his arm was still fresh in his mind. He rubbed his wrist and looked at the lawyer.

"But why leave it to me?" Gerald asked, picking up his photograph from the side table. "Why would she leave it all to me?"

Mr. Prisk retrieved his briefcase from the floor.

"You asked before why I flew out to collect you and your family, Gerald, instead of leaving you to take a commercial flight. It was for your protection. Your great-aunt wanted you safe. Her last instruction to me, in fact the very last words she ever spoke to me, were: 'Look after Gerald.'"

Gerald stared into the photo—into his own eyes.

The lawyer stood up, preparing to leave. "It's strange," he said. "She seemed her normal self, then in the last few days she insisted that her will be brought up to date, that documents be prepared. It was as if she had some premonition of . . ." Mr. Prisk let his voice trail off for a second. "Gerald, I worked for Miss Archer for a very long time. She was never one for the grand gesture. Everything she did was well planned and done for a reason. Her decision to leave almost everything to you wasn't because she liked the color of your eyes. The purpose she had in mind for you is something that you will have to discover for yourself."

Mr. Prisk glanced at the boy sitting at the window, and said with an encouraging tone, "Cheer up, Gerald. The time will pass quickly enough; all this excitement will die down. And remember—you've got Mr. Fry for company."

Gerald spent the rest of the day exploring his home and his prison. He started in the basement, rummaging through some ancient crates and tea chests. But beyond a collection of old Turkish postage stamps and a faded tourist brochure of the pyramids in Egypt, he found nothing of interest. He worked his way up to the kitchen, the lounge room, several drawing rooms, the library, the dining room, the six bedrooms and bathrooms, the home cinema, Aunt Geraldine's office, the enormous games room, and finally the attic above the fifth floor. He didn't venture into the staff quarters; he had no desire to spend any extra time with Mr. Fry.

In the office, Gerald picked up the phone to call Ox but realized his friend would be at the family holiday house in the mountains, out of cell phone range. And anyway, what would he say? Hey, Ox. You'll never guess what happened to me today.

He tried to picture his parents. Were they on the yacht? Or still on the luxury jet? He guessed that no matter where they were, the smile on his mother's face hadn't faded.

Dinner was unremarkable. Mr. Fry prepared scrambled eggs and Gerald ate by himself in the formal dining room. Apart from the brief visit from Mr. Prisk and a few wordless encounters with Fry, Gerald had not seen anyone all afternoon. About eight o'clock, he began to feel incredibly tired and took the lift up the three stories to his bedroom.

He closed the heavy oak door, reassured by the click of the brass latch behind him. The shower was warm and relaxing, the bed welcoming and comfortable. Gerald couldn't believe how exhausted he was. He leaned across to flick off the bedside lamp and let the darkness wash over him. It had been a bit of a day. He listened as the sound of his breathing filled the room, and his eyelids closed.

* * *

The bedside light suddenly sparked back to life. Gerald flung himself from under the covers and onto the carpet. He scurried across the floor and threw open the door to the closet. He tossed his shoes aside and hauled out his beaten old backpack, tore at the zipper, and grabbed what he was looking for: a buff-colored envelope, about the size of a large notebook. He carried it back to the bed, his great-aunt's writing clearly legible in the lamplight: NOT TO BE OPENED UNTIL AFTER MY FUNERAL. AND GERALD, I MEAN IT!

Gerald flipped the envelope over and cracked the wax seal. He lifted up the flap and tipped the envelope upside down.

Out fell a jumble of loose sheets of paper and newspaper clippings, as well as a bundle of small envelopes, tied together with brown string. Gerald spread everything across the bed and tried to make sense of what looked like a scrapbook that had been torn apart at the spine.

He picked up a sheet of notepaper. It was decorated with a floral design and covered in an old lady's handwriting— the same writing as on the front of the envelope. He lay on his stomach and read the note:

Hello, Gerald. I hope this isn't too weird for you—a letter from beyond the grave! By now you are my heir and worth a good deal of money. I hope you don't mind.

Bit late to be asking me that now! Gerald thought. He read on.

I have a favour to ask. I am told you are a bright chap. I know we never met, but your mother kept me up-to-date on your achievements and whatnot in her letters. So I expect you've figured out that I was murdered. I want you to find out who did it.

CHAPTER SIX

Gerald's eyes locked on the word *murdered*. As if the day hadn't been bizarre enough. He continued to read:

> It's a long story, and I've tried to explain it here as best I can. I'm afraid it has all been a bit of a rush. But the harsh fact is that if you are reading this, then I am dead. Murdered dead.

Gerald was so tired he wasn't sure what to think. Was this for real? A joke? The ramblings of a madwoman?

> You will meet a lot of people in the next few days, many of whom will claim to have been my friend. I advise you to trust no

one, not even the police. Because, Gerald,
I have been murdered for a reason—the
same reason people will now want to get hold
of you. Maybe even murder you.

Had Gerald's eyes bulged any farther they might have bounced onto the blankets like soggy Ping-Pong balls. Someone wanted to kill him? He turned the note over to read on, but the back was blank. On the edge of panic, he rifled through the papers on the bed hunting for the rest of the note. But among the mess of clippings and official-looking documents he could find nothing that matched. He shoved his hand back into the envelope. It was empty. He cast wild-eyed about the room, not sure what to do. Then he leaped off the bed and flew across to the door, pushing hard against the brass bolt to lock it. He gathered all the bits of paper, stuffed them back into the envelope and shoved it under his pillow. He lay back down on the bed and pulled the covers under his chin, his eyes still threatening to pop out of his skull. When he finally fell asleep, the bedside lamp was still on.

Gerald woke with a start. He was in a strange bed in an unfamiliar bedroom. Sunlight seeped through a gap in the heavy curtains and the faint sound of birdsong rose from the street below. Gerald checked his watch: seven o'clock,

Monday morning. He sifted through the random thoughts rattling around inside his skull. He remembered where he was: London. His great-aunt's house. His murdered great-aunt's house. He shoved his hand under the pillow. The envelope was still there. Gerald's heart sank. He hoped it had been one of his ridiculous dreams.

Sitting cross-legged against a pile of cushions, Gerald turned the envelope over and over, desperate to look inside but also petrified about reading any more about murder. About his great-aunt's murder. About his murder. He swallowed hard and pulled out the sheaf of papers. This time he sorted them, building a number of small piles on the bedspread: a stack of newspaper and magazine clippings, some typed pages, the bundle of envelopes tied with string, and the handwritten note from Great-Aunt Geraldine that had shaken him the night before. He was relieved to turn up another page of the same floral notepaper, also in Geraldine's handwriting:

It's all to do with this blasted diamond of course. You need to find Professor McElderry at the museum. He'll point you in the right direction. Gerald, I have left you in charge of the Archer estate because in time you will learn to use its resources wisely. In time, you will know what to do—or not to do—as

*the case may be. Now, do an old woman
a favour and find my killer. And do it
quickly. Because rest assured, they are
looking for you.*

*Take care,
Geraldine*

Gerald shook his head. School holidays weren't meant to be like this. Who was this professor? What was this diamond? And how was he supposed to know what to do? Gerald read the note three times but it was still no clearer. Then, as if a door in his brain swung open, he jumped from the bed and grabbed his jeans from the floor. He fished into the pocket and pulled out the page from *Oi!* magazine that he'd found on the jet. He flattened the crumpled paper and looked again at the photograph of his great-aunt Geraldine: the photograph of her, an old man in a dinner suit, and an enormous . . .

"Diamond," Gerald breathed out loud.

He stared at the egg-shaped gem in the picture.

This diamond would certainly be any girl's best friend . . . priceless Noor Jehan diamond . . . much-awaited opening of the new India exhibit this week . . . rumored to be insured for £100 million . . . on display until September . . .

Gerald's eyes were drawn to the pile of newspaper clippings. He fanned through the stash of stories. Every one was about the Noor Jehan diamond: about how Geraldine had donated a large sum of money to bring it out from India; about how it was the first time the diamond had left that country since its discovery, expertly cut and polished, nearly eighteen hundred years ago; and about its daring theft from the Reading Room at the British Museum a few days before. For the next twenty minutes Gerald read about the break-in. How the room was locked from the inside and there was no sign of how the thief escaped. Rumors that the policeman on duty was found asleep on the floor with two roses sticking out of his buttocks. Another clipping outlined a theory that the thief had hidden inside a statue of an elephant. The last article featured a photograph of a fierce-looking man with bushy eyebrows and an unruly red beard, his sharp eyes boring holes out of the page. According to the caption, the man was Professor Knox McElderry, curator of the India exhibition. The story said that Professor McElderry had hurled the newspaper reporter out of his office and threatened violence if he ever returned.

Gerald tried to soak it all in. His mind was awash with questions about murder, stolen diamonds, elephants, and fierce professors, but one thing was clear: He had to get to the British Museum as soon as possible. He had to escape his newfound prison.

Gerald got dressed and grabbed his battered backpack. It was now almost eight and he needed to get moving. He put the newspaper cuttings and the other documents back into the large envelope. He picked up the bundle of smaller envelopes tied with string and was about to do the same with them when he realized he still hadn't opened them. He undid the brown twine and spread them on the floor. Geraldine had scrawled a few short words on the front of each of them, but they made no sense to Gerald. One was labeled "Fraternity," another was "Family Tree," and a third was a string of random shapes: the number 10, a circle with a line through it, a Y, an arrow, a triangle. One envelope caught Gerald's eye. In Geraldine's handwriting on the front was: "Young Billionaire's Survival Kit." He tore the flap and pulled out a small leather wallet. He flipped it open, let out a low whistle, and counted out two thousand pounds in crisp new notes. He also pulled out a black American Express card, with a neat Gerald A. Wilkins embossed on the front. He searched the other pockets and flaps of the wallet and found a passport photograph of his great-aunt and a small pocket mirror. Taped to the back was a square of paper. Gerald peeled it off and unfolded another note in Geraldine's handwriting:

> Every young billionaire needs some walking-around money. The credit card is for emergencies. The mirror is so you can take a good look at yourself before you use it!

Gerald turned the mirror over and gazed at his reflection, smiling to himself. He was starting to like his great-aunt Geraldine. But his smile disappeared at the sound of a sharp knock on the bedroom door.

"Breakfast is served in the dining room." It was Fry. His humor had not improved overnight.

"Yeah," Gerald called out. "I'll be right down."

He shoved the unopened envelopes in with the other documents and looked for a hiding place. Geraldine had said trust no one, and Fry was a good enough place to start. He finally settled on a spot in the back of the closet, under a loose corner of carpet. He stuck an old suitcase on top, closed the closet door, and locked it. He stuffed the key and wallet in his pockets and hurried down to breakfast, his backpack slung over his shoulder.

A long solid-oak dining table was set out with a selection of juices as well as a steaming platter of eggs, bacon, cooked mushrooms, tomatoes, hash browns, and a couple of things Gerald didn't recognize.

"What's this?" Gerald asked Fry, picking up a lid from a silver tray and poking a fork at the shriveled contents.

"Kidneys and black pudding," Fry replied from his position by the sideboard.

"Kidneys!" Gerald gagged, dropping the lid with a clatter, splashing water onto the polished table. "For breakfast? No thanks. And what's a black pudding?"

Fry flinched at the sight of water on the table. He

rushed across to wipe up the drops. Then he replaced the lid squarely on the tray, taking care to make sure the table setting remained immaculate.

"The main ingredient of black pudding," Fry said, his face just inches from Gerald's, "is blood. Lots and lots of blood."

Gerald looked into the blank mask that was Fry's face and swallowed.

"Uh, I think I'll have some toast," he said.

Fry marched back to the kitchen, muttering to himself. Gerald noticed some newspapers on the sideboard and wandered over to leaf through them. Every one led with the amazing story of the instant boy billionaire. There were photographs of Gerald rushing into the church with his parents for the funeral and shots of him climbing into the back of the Rolls for the journey home. Gerald had forgotten about the media pack. He went to a window that looked down on the street, and sure enough, at least thirty photographers and reporters were still parked on the pavement. A couple of the photographers had lenses trained on the front windows, and the moment Gerald's face appeared a shout went up from below. Egg-and-bacon rolls and cups of coffee hit the footpath as breakfasts were tossed aside and cameras were hoisted toward Gerald. He waved a couple of times, which had as much calming effect as prodding a stick into the middle of an ants' nest. Then he poked out his tongue and closed the curtains.

Gerald sat at the table and thought. If he was to get out of the house, the front door was not going to provide an easy exit. And after the Rolls snuck in via the rear lane the previous day, it was likely that the media would be covering the back door as well. Then there was the small issue of getting past Mr. Fry.

Just then, the butler appeared with a plate of warm toast, which he placed in front of Gerald, then fussed around, deftly wiping some crumbs from the table into his palm. As Gerald watched Mr. Fry rearranging the newspapers into a tidy pile on the sideboard, an idea popped into his head. He took the wallet from his back pocket and pulled out his shiny new credit card. Between mouthfuls of toast and honey, he spun it between his fingers.

About an hour later Gerald positioned himself in a quiet corner of the ground-floor drawing room and waited. From this spot, he could keep an eye on the front door, as well as see through to the kitchen and the only door that led to the back drive. He flicked through the pages of one of the morning papers. In the kitchen Mr. Fry cleaned up after breakfast, a crisp white apron over his dark suit. Then from outside, there was a sudden clamor of voices. Gerald went to the window and looked between the curtains. There were three delivery vans at the front door and the drivers were busy handing out boxes of pizza to the photographers and reporters, together with trays of coffee.

"From the young man inside," one of the drivers announced. "He says he's sorry if you dropped your breakfast earlier." The free food and drink was too much for the media pack to resist. Hands grabbed at whatever they could take, upending pizza boxes across the footpath. Gerald grinned as the shouts outside grew louder. He let the curtains fall and wandered across to the kitchen.

"Mr. Fry," Gerald said, idling over to the butler. "The people outside seem to be dumping pizza boxes in the flower beds."

"They're doing what?" Fry was incensed. He dashed out of the kitchen and straight through the front door, almost slipping on a slice of ham-and-pineapple pizza on the doorstep before hurling himself headlong into the feasting mob.

"What do you disgusting people think you're doing?" he demanded.

Gerald leaped into action. As soon as Fry disappeared out the front, he scooped up his backpack and dashed through the back door, vaulting the porch railings onto the white-pebbled driveway below. He dropped to his stomach behind the Rolls Royce and inched forward to peer around the front wheel. His suspicion that there would be photographers in the back lane had been correct. He spied at least three between the bars of the tall iron gates, looking uneasy about the commotion coming from the front of the house. Gerald's entire escape plan depended on these photographers doing one thing and doing it quickly. He didn't have much time. He breathed heavily and waited. The tallest of the snappers was pacing about and looking increasingly anxious—the noise from the pizza riot was getting louder. Gerald could hear snatches of conversation in the lane: ". . . something's up . . . missing it . . . boss'll kill me . . ."

The tall photographer grabbed his camera gear and sprinted up the alley. The other two looked at each other, then set off in pursuit, cameras and lenses dangling and bouncing over their shoulders. Gerald got up from his hiding spot and skittered across the drive to the back gate. The first two photographers had already rounded the corner. But the last one, the burly photographer with the red vest, was making heavy work of it.

"Come on!" Gerald hissed to himself. "Hurry up."

The fat photographer was still twenty yards short of the corner when one of the pizza vans appeared around the bend. The man had to throw himself up onto the curb to avoid being hit as the van raced past. He turned with a volley of abuse at the driver. But as the van slowed and then stopped at the back of Gerald's house, the photographer came to a stuttering halt. From inside the back gate, Gerald could see that he was going to have to move now, even though the lane was not deserted. He slammed his hand onto the release button and slipped through the sliding gate, straight into the open passenger-side door of the delivery van.

"Where to?" the young driver asked. "This is a bit of fun, innit?"

Gerald glanced in the van's side mirror and saw that the red-vested photographer was now running toward them, camera gear flapping wildly.

"The British Museum," Gerald said, one eye still on the reflection of the advancing cameraman.

"Do I look like a tour guide?" The driver laughed. "Yeah, no problem."

The van lurched forward and accelerated down the alley, spraying gravel into the face of the puffing photographer and drowning out his shouts for them to stop.

They rounded the bend at speed. As they reached the corner, Gerald grinned at the scene he had created at the front of the house. The combination of extreme boredom and the prospect of a free feed had worked a treat; the assembled media had gone berserk at the endless supply of pizza and coffee. Cardboard boxes and paper cups were strewn across the road. Entire pizzas lay upside down trodden into the footpath. Spilled coffee flowed into the gutters. Some of the greedier photographers were still hoeing through the pizza boxes that had been dumped outside Gerald's door.

In the middle of the melee stood Mr. Fry, railing at one reporter about the tomato paste that was smeared across the doormat. The van sat idling at the end of the street with

Gerald beaming at the window. The reporter with Mr. Fry spotted him. He sprayed pizza crumbs all over the butler with a yell of: "The kid's gettin' away!"

Gerald nodded at the driver and the van lurched off. Reporters and cameramen dumped their food and drink where they stood and scrambled to their cars, pulling out into the street in pursuit. Several slammed sideways into other vehicles as they surged down the road and ended up mounting the curb or ploughing into railings. Others weaved around the wrecks only to find that each end of the narrow road was blocked; the remaining two pizza delivery vans were parked across both lanes, sealing off any hope of a quick exit from the street.

Gerald smiled as the van trundled away from his prison, satisfied that his plan had worked. He was about to ask the driver how far to the museum when a flash of red caught the corner of his eye. He looked into the side mirror and gasped. Sweeping out of the lane after them was the red-vested photographer astride a motor scooter.

Gerald turned to the driver. "There's an extra fifty pounds if you lose the guy on the scooter."

The driver glanced into the mirror, and grinned.

"Not a problem."

Gerald was only six months old when he'd last been in London, so it's fair to say that he didn't remember anything about the place. It's equally fair to say that the next twenty minutes of tearing down back lanes, taking tire-bursting turns across the flow of traffic, dashing through red lights, and speeding the wrong way up narrow one-way streets gave him a view of the city he hoped never to have again. The pizza van driver rose to the challenge of losing the red-vested photographer. But while the driver fancied himself as a rally champion, the van was not rally material. Gerald was tossed in his seat like a tennis ball in a clothes dryer. He clung onto his seat belt with white-knuckle intensity as the van hurtled over potholes and speed bumps, tailed by the fat photographer on his scooter.

At last the van tore out of a side street near Hyde Park Corner and, in a purple cloud of screeching brakes and dis-integrating tire rubber, joined the flow of traffic toward Bloomsbury and the museum.

"I think we've lost him," the driver panted.

Gerald straightened himself up and looked out the back window. There were cars and vans of all shapes but no sign of a red vest on a scooter.

"Fantastic. Is it far from here?" Gerald asked.

"Shouldn't take more than fifteen minutes."

Gerald caught a glimpse of Buckingham Palace and the long green stretch of St. James's Park. For the first time since arriving in England, he felt like he was in a foreign country.

The young driver glanced at Gerald.

"You're not from 'round here, are you?" he asked, buzzing from the morning's excitement. "What brings you to town?"

Gerald hesitated.

"Well, I'm on my own in London because my parents are sailing around the Caribbean on my new super-yacht. I'm going to the British Museum to ask a professor I've only seen in a newspaper photograph about the murder of my great-aunt. I never actually met her but I inherited twenty billion pounds from her yesterday."

The driver blinked.

"All right, if you don't want to say you don't have to," he said, raising his eyebrows. "Just tryin' to be polite."

They continued in silence until the van pulled into Great Russell Street and came to a halt outside the main gates to the British Museum. Gerald counted out some cash and the driver pocketed the notes and drove off.

Gerald gazed across the front lawns to the building's imposing Greek façade, took a breath, and joined the flow of tourists heading toward the main entrance for the ten o'clock opening.

CHAPTER SEVEN

Gerald made his way up the steps and between the towering columns at the museum entrance. He paused beneath the front portico and gazed at a row of statues high above: a lineup of ancient Greeks that stared, marble cold, at the people below. He let the flow of tourists take him inside.

The museum had just opened and already there was a crowd in the foyer. It was a mixed bunch: parents with children (who would rather be almost anywhere else on their school holidays), a clutch of older folk (filling in time before lunch), and tour groups from all corners of the globe (not really sure why they were there but it was on the itinerary for that morning). Gerald jostled his way through the throng, finally stumbling into an enormous open space—the Great

Court. The contrast with the confines of the dark foyer could not have been greater. The huge area was defined by sandstone buildings on all four sides and was filled with natural light that beamed through a vast glass roof high above. Gerald looked up in wonder. A pattern of triangular glass tiles spread out from the center as if a colossal crystal jelly bowl had been upended over the surrounding buildings. For a moment Gerald forgot why he was at the museum, entranced by the spectacle above him.

He spotted an information desk and wandered across. The man behind the counter was dealing with a dozen flustered tourists who were apparently searching for the *Mona Lisa*. It looked like he could be some time. Gerald was about to ask a security guard for directions when he spied the police tape.

The blue-and-white checkered tape was strung across a doorway at the base of a large circular building in the center of the Great Court. A police constable stood at the entrance and a number of people were hanging around, trying to peek inside. Gerald saw two words carved into the stone wall next to the doorway: READING ROOM. The policeman on duty was talking in an exasperated tone to an elderly man.

"I'm sorry, sir, this area's off limits to the public at the moment. You can't go in."

The old man screwed up his face.

"Is this something to do with that diamond robbery?"

the man asked, craning his neck across the tape to get a better look. The policeman shuffled sideways to block his view.

"I'm not at liberty to discuss anything about—"

The man squinted into the policeman's face: a pale, podgy face with fine sandy hair that poked out from under his bobby's helmet.

"You look familiar," the old man said. He turned to the even older-looking woman at his side. "Doesn't he look familiar, then?" he yelled into her ear.

The policeman recoiled as the woman shoved her prune-like face close to his.

She declared at the top of her voice, "He's the copper wot was in the paper."

"In the paper?" the old man shouted back.

"You remember," the old lady said. "The one with the flowers up his bum!" Clearly quite deaf, the woman could have been heard across the deck of an aircraft carrier.

The policeman was mortified. His eyes darted about as heads across the Great Court turned. A boy and girl about Gerald's age wandered up. The boy whispered something in the girl's ear and they both started giggling.

The policeman had had enough.

"Okay. That's it," he said, ushering the growing crowd away from the taped-off entrance. "Move along. Nothing to see here. Go on, clear off!"

The old woman shrugged and, casting a sideways glance in the direction of the policeman's bottom, placed her hand on the old man's arm. They tottered off toward the coffee shop.

"I guess I'd be upset too if I'd had some flowers, you know, up there," the woman shouted.

The girl who had been giggling caught Gerald's eye and smiled. Gerald grinned back. She was a touch shorter than he with short blond bangs and a ponytail.

A tall man appeared and put his hands on the girl's shoulders. "Come along, you pair. There's a lot to see."

"Okay, Dad," the boy and girl answered, resigned boredom in their voices. They headed toward the Egyptian sculptures at the other end of the Great Court.

Gerald was left standing with the policeman, who was still flustered after his run-in with the elderly couple. He noticed Gerald staring at him.

"What are you lookin' at?" the officer demanded.

"Um, nothing," Gerald said as innocently as he could. From the corner of his eye he could make out a good deal of activity inside. In the middle of the room at least five people in white overalls were crawling on their hands and knees around the base of a black pedestal. Occasionally, one would stop and pick up something in rubber-gloved fingers and drop it into a clear plastic bag. To one side a group of uniformed police and some men in blue suits chatted and sipped from paper cups. At the very far end of the room, beneath a huge gold clock on the wall, more men in overalls hefted chunks of what appeared to be broken plaster into a Dumpster.

The police officer at the door shunted in front of Gerald.

"I said clear off, all right?"

At that moment, two policemen emerged from the Reading Room and ducked under the blue-and-white tape.

"Interviewing a prime suspect, are we, Constable Lethbridge?" one asked, smirking.

Lethbridge swung around but before he could open his mouth the other officer said, "Haven't you got better things to do than harass innocent children, Crystal?"

Lethbridge flinched.

"What's this?" the first officer asked in mock confusion, winking at Gerald. "Why'd you call him Crystal?"

"You know . . . crystal vase."

The pair erupted in laughter and sauntered off, leaving Lethbridge seething.

Gerald decided it was time to find Professor McElderry.

He went back to the information desk, but it looked like the tourists were still arguing over the whereabouts of the *Mona Lisa*. He spotted a museum attendant.

"Excuse me," Gerald said. "Could you tell me where—" He stopped midbreath. Over the attendant's shoulder he saw the photographer with the red vest step into the Great Court.

The snapper had a camera slung over his shoulder and another clutched in his hand. He stood inside the entrance, his eyes sweeping the space like searchlights. His face shone bright with sweat and the thrill of the hunt. Gerald was too stunned to move. He had clean forgotten about his pursuer. And now he was standing barely thirty yards from him.

The crisscrossing tourist traffic provided Gerald with some cover but he felt painfully exposed.

"Can I help you?" the museum attendant asked.

"Um. No, it's all right," Gerald mumbled. He looked about, darted across to a large plinth, and slid down behind it. It held a statue of a Roman youth on a horse. Gerald sat with his back against the cold white marble, half wishing he had a horse to escape on. He took a deep breath and poked his head around the corner. The photographer hadn't moved—he stood feet apart like a big-game hunter waiting for his prey to break cover. Gerald knew there was no way he could get through the museum entrance without being seen. And to go either left or right from his hiding spot would put him out in the open. He thought about staying where he was, sitting behind the statue. If the photographer moved off to one of the galleries on the western side, he could make a dash for the exit. All he needed was a few minutes.

"Can I help you, young man?"

Gerald winced. He looked up to find the museum attendant glaring down at him.

"Um . . . no," Gerald said in a hoarse whisper. "I'm quite all right. Thanks."

"Well, you can be quite all right somewhere else," the attendant said. "No sitting on the floor and no leaning against the exhibits!"

Gerald looked back around the plinth and saw in alarm that the photographer was staring in his direction, watching a museum attendant talking to someone hiding behind a statue. The snapper took a step closer. Then another.

It was time to act. Gerald leaped to his feet and grabbed the attendant by the arm.

"Watch out for that guy with the camera," Gerald said to the bewildered guard, pointing a finger toward the photographer. "He doesn't look like a tourist to me."

Gerald bolted. He glanced over his shoulder just as the photographer spotted him, just as the photographer shouted a loud "Oi!" and broke into a run. And just as the museum attendant stepped forward, extending his hand with a firm, "Not so fast, sir," they collided in an awkward embrace of arms, legs, and tangled camera straps.

Gerald slid sideways through a doorway and almost tripped as his feet met a floor of uneven wooden boards.

At the end of a long narrow room he saw an exit sign and made for it. Galleries flashed past as Gerald bounced and weaved his way between exhibits and people. He rounded a corner and ran down a flight of stairs. He flung himself against a wall inside a small alcove on a landing, pressing his back into the bricks and gulping in air. He waited. A few tourists wandered by, as well as a cleaner pushing a trolley loaded with mops and brooms. But there was no sign of the photographer.

Gerald's breathing eased and he bent down to rest his hands on his knees. He wasn't even sure why he was bothering to run away. It was only some guy wanting to take a few photos for a newspaper. It wasn't like any real harm was being done. But it bugged him. No one cared who he was last week. He hadn't done anything special. So why should anyone care who he was this week? He couldn't put his finger on it. It just bugged him.

The cleaner rolled his trolley past again and Gerald caught a whiff of cleaning fluid. That smell, he thought. Where have I . . . ?

Four bony fingers and a thumb dug deep into the flesh of Gerald's left shoulder. A strong hand wrenched him upright, almost yanking him off his feet. A searing pain shot down Gerald's side. The acrid stench of bleach burned into his throat. Through the pain jolting into his shoulder, Gerald felt something brush against his cheek.

"Mr. Wilkins," a voice hissed into his ear. "We need to talk."

Chapter Eight

Gerald could barely open his eyes. His shoulder felt like it would dislocate. He balanced on the tips of his toes, desperate to stop the torture. But the agony was relentless, hot like a blowtorch.

"Would you like me to stop?" the voice rasped.

Gerald nodded through his pain.

"Very well. But do not make a sound or try to run. Or things will get very much worse."

The thin man twirled Gerald around with his gloved hand, like a spider spinning its prey in a web. Gerald danced on his toes, unable to fight back. The thin man's head was almost touching Gerald's face.

"Do you understand?" he whispered. With each syllable his thumb twisted deeper into Gerald's shoulder.

Gerald gasped and nodded. At last, the thin man released his grip. Gerald's knees buckled and he stumbled forward. He grabbed at his shoulder with his right hand. His left arm hung, useless.

Gerald looked up. The thin man's eyes were hidden behind the same sunglasses that he was wearing at the airfield a few days before.

"You are in very real danger, Mr. Wilkins," the man said softly. "No one knows where you are. No one has seen us here. And even if they had, to a casual observer we are just another pair of museum patrons. There have been no raised voices, no outlandish struggles. I have merely been talking with you whilst laying a caring hand on your shoulder." He paused, tipping his head. "How is your shoulder?"

Gerald peered into the sunglasses.

"Who *are* you?" he spat. "What do you want?"

The thin man stooped and looked Gerald in the eyes.

"The same thing I wanted from your great-aunt." His strange voice raised the hairs on the back of Gerald's neck. "Information. The information that she refused to give me."

The thin man stretched out a hand and ran his index finger over Gerald's throbbing shoulder. "And look what happened to her."

Gerald gagged. What was he saying? Was this the man who'd killed Great-Aunt Geraldine? He stepped back—thought of running. But before he could move, a bony hand shot out like a bolt from a crossbow and grabbed his shoulder again. It took only the slightest touch to squeeze a whimper from Gerald.

Lean lips drew tight across two uneven rows of yellowed teeth. "I want to know where the diamond casket is," the thin man whispered, clenching Gerald's shoulder hard. "And I want you to tell me now!"

A jolt of pain shot across Gerald's back.

"I . . . I don't know what you're talking about," he panted, his eyes awash. "I don't know anything about any diamonds. Or any casket."

The thin man's face was as expressionless as any statue in the museum.

"You wouldn't lie to me, Mr. Wilkins?" His thumb pressed deeper into Gerald's shoulder. Gerald took a sharp breath and shook his head in an urgent spasm. The first tear rolled down his cheek. The thin man regarded it without emotion.

"Tell me, Mr. Wilkins," he said. "Did your great-aunt leave you any messages? Any notes or letters?"

Gerald nodded. He couldn't help it.

A corner of the thin man's mouth curled upward, just the merest fraction.

"Most interesting," he said. "They are at your house? Let us go then, you and I, on a little journey."

The thin man turned Gerald around and guided him to the bottom of the staircase. Gerald, slumped and crestfallen, shuffled across the floor. He felt sick. It was like a black void had opened inside him, all his feelings draining into life's sewer. He was thousands of miles from home, alone in a strange city and held by a man who may well have murdered his great-aunt. *If he murdered Geraldine, what will he do to me?*

The thin man pressed his shoulder as they rounded a corner. The exit to Montague Place at the rear of the museum was in front of them. To Gerald's astonishment, so too was a policeman. His eyes widened when he recognized it was the same one he'd seen outside the Reading Room.

Constable Lethbridge stood in a courtyard outside the museum, on the other side of a set of glass doors. He was leaning against a large plant pot, holding his helmet in one hand and drawing on a cigarette. *He must be taking a break,* Gerald thought. *If I can just make a run for him.*

Something sharp jabbed hard into Gerald's ribs.

"Mr. Wilkins," the thin man breathed, "are you familiar with the stiletto blade?"

Gerald froze. His back arched as the thin man pushed harder on a long pencil-thin dagger.

"The stiletto is a marvelous thing," the thin man whispered, his top lip curling in a tight snarl. "Much favored by assassins. The blade is very thin indeed but extremely strong. It can pierce clothing, flesh, muscle . . . heart. But it leaves almost no sign on the skin. The victim falls to the ground, as if in a faint. By the time a doctor arrives, the lungs have filled with blood and the target has drowned in his own vital fluids. Most effective."

Gerald stared straight ahead. Constable Lethbridge was less than ten yards away. And there was nothing he could do to reach him.

The thin man leaned even closer, pressing the dagger right through the fabric of Gerald's shirt until the point nicked his skin.

"We are going to walk out this door, past this policeman, and away. Who knows, Mr. Wilkins? You may live to enjoy that fabulous fortune of yours."

Gerald pushed the heavy glass doors and he and the thin man stepped outside the museum. Lethbridge was only a dozen paces in front of them. The policeman cocked his head back and blew out a stream of smoke. His face was drawn and tired. He inspected the cigarette end, then flicked the butt onto the ground.

Gerald and the thin man were now just steps away. Lethbridge patted his pockets, in search of another cigarette. He paused and looked at Gerald's face. Gerald's eyes beseeched Lethbridge to do something. To stop them, to ask the thin man for a light, anything. But Lethbridge went on rifling his pockets. Gerald was pressed forward, the stiletto pricking his back.

"Tony! Tony Valentine!"

A girl's voice rang across the courtyard. Gerald came to a sudden halt, right beside Lethbridge. The thin man bustled into the back of him. The policeman raised his head from a veil of smoke, to see what the ruckus was.

"Tony! Where have you been? Dad's been worried sick."

Gerald looked in surprise as a girl with short blond bangs and ponytail ran up and grabbed him by the elbow. He recognized her at once—she and her brother had been giggling at Lethbridge outside the Reading Room.

"Come on," the girl said. "We've still got loads to see inside." She turned her back on Lethbridge and the thin man and flashed her eyes at Gerald. Gerald stood stunned.

"Uh . . . yes," he responded at last. "Lots to see."

The girl tugged Gerald's hand. The thin man still clutched Gerald's other arm. The girl yanked harder, and before Gerald was caught in a tug of war in front of the policeman, the thin man loosened his grip. Gerald pulled free. The thin man's lips tightened.

"My cousin," the girl explained to Lethbridge with a laugh. "He's always wandering off." She strengthened her hold on Gerald. "Come along, silly."

She wrapped both her hands around Gerald's wrist and skipped toward the museum doors. Gerald went gladly, leaving the thin man fuming next to a confused-looking Constable Lethbridge.

The pair burst back into the museum and bolted toward the safety of the Great Court, leaving the glass doors juddering on their hinges. The place still teemed with people.

They collapsed into some chairs near the coffee shop.

"Th-thanks," Gerald said, finally finding his voice.

"No problem," the girl replied. "You looked like you needed some help."

"You could say that. How did you know?"

"My brother and I were hanging around the back stairs. We saw that guy pull a knife on you."

A fair-haired boy about Gerald's age appeared and dropped into a chair.

"That all seemed to go to plan then," the boy said, clapping a hand on Gerald's shoulder.

Gerald winced.

"Oh, sorry. Sore, is it?"

The boy had a happy face, with a strong jaw and a scattering of freckles across the bridge of his nose. His blond hair was short and his skin looked ready for the first tan of summer. He was shorter than Gerald and looked pretty fit.

"We figured your bad guy wasn't going to cause a fuss if we grabbed you right in front of a policeman," the boy said. "Lucky he was there or we'd have needed Plan B."

"What was Plan B?" Gerald asked.

His rescuers looked at each other.

"Um, we were still working on that," the girl said. "But Plan A seemed to go okay."

Gerald let out a small laugh. "Yeah, I guess so."

"Do you think that guy'll come back? Y'know, looking for you?" the girl asked.

Gerald shook his head.

"Not with all these people about. And not after that policeman got such a good look at him. Who is Tony Valentine, then?"

"Our cousin. It was the first name that popped into my head," the girl said. "I mean, you had to be someone."

Gerald grinned. "My name's Gerald," he said. Then, as an afterthought, "Stupid name, eh?"

"Only if your last name is Grasshopper," the girl said. "I'm Ruby. Ruby Valentine. This is my brother, Sam."

"What's your story, then?" Sam asked, resting his elbows on the table. "Who wants to kidnap you?"

Gerald looked at the two sets of inquisitive eyes. He reached around, pulled out his wallet, and opened it. Sam gaped at the wedge of fifty-pound notes poking out.

"Who feels like hot chocolate?" Gerald asked.

Twenty minutes and two rounds of hot chocolates later, Gerald finished the tale of his holiday so far: a funeral, a fat inheritance, abandoned by his parents, chased by photographers, a stolen diamond, a possible murder, and a knife-wielding kidnapper.

Sam scraped bits of chocolate from the bottom of his mug.

"You don't want to go to the police because your great-aunt said they can't be trusted?" he said.

"That's right. Why would they believe any of this anyway? I can't even believe it," Gerald said. He paused. "You believe me, right?"

"Why not?" Ruby said. "That guy had a knife at your back. You didn't make that up."

"Who's the professor we're trying to find? Mackelberry?" Sam said, pushing his chair back from the table and half standing up.

"It's McElderry, but you don't need to—"

"Oh, come off it, Gerald," Ruby said. "Our dad had to go back to work. He left us to look around here all day. There's only so many Greek relics you can stand in one go. Your quest sounds a lot more fun. Besides, you need some local knowledge."

"Yeah," Sam said, clapping Gerald hard on the shoulder again. "We're family, remember, cousin?"

The elevator to the administration wing opened onto a narrow corridor lined with dark red carpet. A board on the wall opposite listed a number of offices. Professor McElderry's was down the long hallway.

"You guys are twins?" Gerald said, leading the way.

"Yep," Sam said. "I'm older by two minutes."

"But not identical twins?"

Gerald stopped.

"I can't believe I said that."

"Don't worry," Ruby said. "We get it all the time."

"Really?"

"Nah. Just trying to make you feel better. Identical twins! Pfft!"

Sam shouldered past his sister. "Ignore her, she's a pain. What do you want to get from this professor?"

"He's the only lead I have to my great-aunt's death," Gerald said. "He was the one who brought the diamond out from India, which seems to be the thing that got everyone excited. The thin man wanted to know about a diamond casket. Maybe the professor knows something about it."

They stopped outside a dark wooden door with PROFESSOR K. MCELDERRY in gold letters across the central panel. As Gerald reached out to turn the handle, they heard a bellow from inside.

"I don't care if he's the queen's uncle! I don't have time to see him!"

The door opened to reveal a small reception area. A timid-looking woman sat behind a wooden desk in the corner. An enormous man leaned over her. His face was a spectacular red that outshone his thatch of auburn hair and unkempt beard. He looked like a strawberry jelly that had been dropped on a barber shop floor. The woman held a telephone to her ear, a tiny hand trying in vain to cover the mouthpiece.

"But what should I tell the prime minister's office?" she said. "He wants a meeting."

"Tell him I died in a mine explosion," the man fumed. "And I'll call him tomorrow." He stormed into an adjoining office, slamming the door behind him.

The woman looked at the telephone receiver and took a deep breath.

"I'm afraid Professor McElderry is unavailable today. Perhaps Tuesday?"

She finished the phone call and made a note in a diary on the desk. Then she turned to the three children in the doorway.

"Yes?" she said wearily.

"We'd like to see Professor McElderry, please," Gerald said.

The woman folded her arms across her chest and stared at him.

"The professor is busy."

She snapped the diary shut and returned to her work.

Gerald looked at the others and shrugged.

"I guess that's that," he muttered. "Come on, Valentines, let's go."

"Rubbish," said Ruby, who had been studying the room. "You haven't said the magic word yet."

"What?" Gerald said. "Please?"

"No," Ruby replied. "Money."

She pushed past Gerald and strode up to the desk.

"Excuse me," she said in a clear voice. "My friend would like to see Professor Mackelberry."

The woman lifted her head and glared at Ruby.

"As I have told your friend, Professor McElderry is busy."

"I'm sure he is, but—"

"And if the prime minister of Great Britain can't see him, I don't think your friend is going to skip to the front of the queue."

Ruby eyed the woman.

"I noticed the plaque on your desk," Ruby said. "The one that thanks the Archer Foundation for funding this section of the museum."

"What about it?" the woman said.

"After the sad death of Geraldine Archer, I believe the sole director of the Archer Foundation is standing in the doorway." Ruby pointed to Gerald, who was watching with a look of wonder. "And while the prime minister can't get in, I'm sure the person who pays the professor's salary might be able to buy five minutes of his valuable time." Ruby leaned closer and whispered to the woman, "I guess he probably pays your wages, too."

The woman looked at Gerald, then back at Ruby. She glanced at a copy of the morning paper on her desk, which had a large photograph of Gerald on the front page. She cleared her throat.

"I'll see what I can do."

She edged out from behind the desk and scurried to the door through which the professor had disappeared. She closed her eyes, summoning strength, then tapped on the wooden doorframe.

A thunderous roar blasted back.

"What in the blinking blue blazes do you want? I am not to be disturbed!"

The woman swallowed tightly and opened the door just wide enough to poke her head through.

Gerald couldn't make out what the woman was saying but within seconds Professor McElderry's enormous frame filled the doorway.

"Gerald Wilkins?" he asked.

Gerald held his hand up timidly.

"Why didn't you say so? Come in!"

Gerald, Sam, and Ruby squeezed past Professor McElderry and found themselves in what could have passed for a war zone. There was stuff everywhere. Great towers of paper were stacked on every surface. If the place was a bomb site, then the desk was ground zero. Old teacups nestled atop leather-bound volumes. Great sheaves of notes and pencil sketches spilled across the surface like water overflowing from a bath. A bookcase behind the desk was stuffed with statuettes and carvings, shoved in at all angles on the shelves, but, curiously, not a single book. The books were piled on the floor next to the stuffed head of some sort of antelope.

They found some chairs and sat down among the carnage.

The professor pushed his way through the debris and went to settle behind his desk. McElderry had barely sat down when he leaped up, cursing to himself, and removed a tortoise from his chair.

"Found this little chap on the slopes of Parnassos," he said, moving it out of the way.

"Is it alive?" Gerald asked.

"Alive? Course it's alive," the professor said. "Smell something awful if it was dead." He looked around for a place to put the tortoise and eventually decided on the pile of books closest to the antelope. The tortoise stuck out its head and peered around, then withdrew inside its shell.

"Can't say the same for this fellow," the professor said, pointing at the stuffed head. "Bagged that one in India twenty years ago. Bit moth-eaten now but still has its uses.

Here, watch." He picked up a battered hat from behind a rubbish bin and flung it across the room. The hat sailed well clear of the antlers and careened into a tower of folders and old shoe boxes, sending the lot tumbling onto Sam.

"You get the idea," the professor muttered. "Now, you're Geraldine's nephew, are you?" He studied Gerald from beneath a canopy of shaggy red eyebrows.

"Uh, great-nephew."

"Not come here to cut off my funding, have you?"

"No," Gerald said quickly.

"Well, that's a relief," the professor said. "Couldn't do what we do without the Archer Foundation's cash. In that case, what do you want?"

Gerald mustered some courage and wriggled upright in the chair. "Um . . . Geraldine left me a note saying that you might be able to help me."

The professor appeared surprised.

"Help you? From what I read it doesn't look like you need much help from anyone. A tick over twenty billion quid, wasn't it?"

Gerald flushed. He was still getting used to the idea of being a billionaire.

"Look, Professor Mackelberry," Sam piped in, shoving the last of the shoe boxes from his lap onto the floor, "Gerald's great-aunt reckons she was murdered because of the diamond that was on display here at the museum. And she said you might know something about it."

The professor swung away from Gerald and locked his gaze onto Sam like a gun turret turning on a battleship.

"Geraldine reckons she was murdered, does she?" McElderry said.

"That's right," Sam said.

"And how does a dead woman—God rest her soul—tell you she's been murdered? Pop by for a chat, did she?"

"Um, no. She wrote a letter, actually."

"A letter! And how was it delivered, may I ask? Through the ghost post?"

"Well, I—"

"I expect she has a bit of spare time to be writing nice little notes now, her being dead and all."

Sam shifted in is chair. "No, no. You misunderstood. She wrote it before she was killed."

"Yes, that would be more traditional. And predicting her own demise, was she?"

"Well, yes."

"At the hands of the same person who nicked my diamond?"

"Um . . . I guess."

"From my recollection the diamond was stolen the day before Geraldine Archer passed away. Are you suggesting that a master criminal who has just flogged the world's most valuable gem from under the nose of a policeman, rather than fleeing the country, wakes up the next day and pops down the road to snuff out an old lady for no personal gain and every risk of capture by the police? Is that what you're saying?"

Sam paused. "Um, yes. That is what I'm saying."

Professor McElderry motioned for Sam to lean in closer.

"You know something, son?" he asked.

"What?" Sam said.

"I think you might possibly be the stupidest boy in the world."

The tortoise sitting on top of the stack of books poked its head out.

McElderry stood up and pushed his way around to Gerald.

"Listen, Gerald, I admired your great-aunt. She was a very generous supporter of our work and she had a genuine love for science and discovery. About a year ago the opportunity came up to bring the Noor Jehan diamond out here to be the centerpiece of an India exhibition. It was a coup for the museum to get it. But the insurance cost was ruinous. Your great-aunt offered to pay for the lot. A remarkable woman."

"What's so great about this diamond?" Gerald said.

McElderry let out a ripe snort.

"Noor Jehan—it means 'the light of the world.' It's the

largest flawless diamond ever discovered. It's the big sister to the Koh-i-Noor diamond in the British crown jewels. That one-hundred-million–pound value everyone's talking about? It's meaningless—there are collectors out there who would write a check for that without blinking. It hadn't left India for seventeen hundred years and now it's been stolen. I've got the insurance company breathing down my neck, the prime minister's worried about relations with India, and the gem's owner is due to arrive any moment. He's not going to be blowing me kisses."

McElderry placed an arm around Gerald and led him toward the reception area.

"It is a great tragedy that Geraldine passed away. But she was old. And I hate to say it, the last few times I spoke with her she didn't seem altogether there. You know, a bit batty. Maybe she was imagining things. It can happen. But linking her death to the theft of the diamond? Nonsense."

Gerald stopped as they reached the door.

"One more thing, professor," he said. "This diamond, is there some sort of casket that goes with it?"

McElderry looked at Gerald.

"There have been tales over the centuries that Noor Jehan was once stored in a fancy box, but I've never seen any evidence of it. Why do you ask?"

"Just curious," Gerald said, rubbing his still-tender shoulder. "Thanks anyway."

Gerald was out in the corridor before he realized that Sam and Ruby weren't with him. He was about to go back when two things happened. First, a roar from behind the door confirmed that the twins were still inside. And secondly, three people emerged from the elevator at the end of the corridor. A tall and elegantly dressed man led the way, limping slightly on a wooden walking stick. His short silver hair was combed neatly with a gun-barrel part on the side, suggesting an early life in the military or, at the very least, boarding school. His back was ramrod straight, though he did tilt a bit to the right on account of the limp. He was followed by a plump, middle-aged Indian man in a bottle-green suit, his neck swelling at the collar and his face a deep shade of purple. Gerald guessed from his expression of bottomless anger that this was the owner of the missing diamond. With them was a girl, perhaps two years older than Gerald. She wore a sari, the same bottle green as the plump man's suit. Her dark hair was pulled into a single thick braid that reached well down her back. The girl glanced at Gerald, revealing dark almond eyes and a beautiful face, but she looked away, tilting her slightly upturned nose even higher, as if she'd just passed a dodgy fish shop.

The door behind Gerald opened and Sam and Ruby bundled out into the corridor, followed by a blustering Professor McElderry.

"Blasted cheek. Going through my papers!"

Sam stood defiantly and held up his index finger, which bore a livid red mark.

"I was not," he said. "Your stupid turtle bit me. Look!"

"It's a tortoise, you twit," McElderry said, looming over Sam. "Better than a guard dog, he is. He knows when someone's up to no good."

"Pity he wasn't guarding your precious diamond then, isn't it!"

McElderry's awninglike eyebrows shot up and he opened his mouth to speak when the silver-haired man stepped forward.

"Knox, I hope we haven't arrived at an awkward time?" It was a voice of quiet authority.

McElderry looked up and was startled to find three new faces in the corridor, each one staring at him.

"Sir Mason," he said, withdrawing his raised fist. "What a pleasant surprise."

"Hardly a surprise, Knox, I'm sure," the tall man said. "You remember Mr. Gupta?"

The plump man elbowed past Sam and barreled up to the professor. His head came up to McElderry's hairy chin but he didn't appear at all intimidated.

"Remember me? He'll rue the day he met me if I don't get my diamond back!"

McElderry's whiskers bristled.

"That diamond was under the protection of the

Metropolitan Police, and I'll be blowed if I'm going to take blame for any—"

The silver-haired man coughed into his hand.

"Perhaps, Knox, this conversation would be best held inside your office?"

The professor and Mr. Gupta eyed each other. McElderry mumbled something and opened the door.

Mr. Gupta motioned to the girl, who had been standing sullenly to one side.

"Come along, Alisha," he said. "This concerns you as much as anyone." The girl glided past Gerald without sparing him a glance, jasmine-laced fragrance wafting after her. The silver-haired man went to follow his companions when his eyes came to rest on Gerald.

"I think I know you," the man said.

Gerald looked up, surprised, and shook his head. "Um, I don't think so."

"You're Gerald Wilkins. I was at your great-aunt's funeral. Mason Green, chairman of the Museum Trust."

He shook Gerald's hand in a firm grip. Gerald thought maybe he did recognize the man from the church hall.

"I'm sorry about this unpleasantness," Green said, nodding toward McElderry's office. "Touchy business, this diamond thing. Mr. Gupta and his daughter have been on a plane all night to get here from Delhi and he's not in the best of humor."

"So I see," Gerald said.

"Once all this is sorted, I'd like to have a chat with you. I knew Geraldine very well and I think it most appropriate that we become acquainted." He reached into his suit pocket and took out a business card. "Give me a call and let's have lunch, shall we?"

Gerald looked at the card in his hand. It said simply: Sir Mason Green GCMG, with a London telephone number.

"Um, sure," Gerald said. "Thanks very much."

"Not at all, Gerald. The pleasure is all mine. Now, I best get inside and make sure those two remain gentlemen."

He swung the door closed behind him.

"Watch out for the turtle!" Sam called out as the door pulled to.

Chapter Nine

"Well, you're mixing with the muckety-mucks, aren't you?"

Gerald, Sam, and Ruby made their way down the broad marble staircase to the museum ground floor, leaving Professor McElderry and Mr. Gupta to argue in peace.

"You know who just invited you to lunch?" Ruby said.

"Nope," Gerald replied. "Some bloke from the Museum Trust?"

Ruby laughed. "That's Sir Mason Green, dopey. He's one of the richest men in Britain. He's in the papers all the time, doing charity stuff. He's worth squillions."

"Yeah," Sam said. "He's almost as rich as you."

Gerald blushed and tried to change the subject. "So, were you looking through the professor's stuff?" he asked Sam.

"Course I was," Sam said. "Couldn't help it, could I? Half of his office landed in my lap."

"While you and Mackleberry were outside we managed to find one thing of interest," Ruby said. "Look."

She pulled a crumpled piece of paper from her pocket and handed it to Gerald. He flattened it out to reveal a rough pencil sketch of a rectangular box, decorated on the sides with a pattern of suns and moons. In a barely legible scrawl under the drawing was written: *Sketch of Noor Jehan casket copied from papyrus believed originally from Library of Alexandria (c200 AD).*

Gerald studied the drawing, trying to divine some meaning from the pencil lines on the paper.

"It was on top of his desk," Ruby said. "Seems it might be top of mind for the professor, as well as for your skinny mate."

Gerald ran a hand across his forehead. "Why would the professor say he didn't know anything about a diamond casket when this was sitting on his desk?"

"Dunno," Sam said. "But I don't fancy going back and asking him."

They reached the Great Court and stepped into the vast space under the glass roof.

"Now what?" Ruby asked.

"Beats me," Gerald said. "We're no closer to finding out anything about Geraldine or the diamond. Professor

McElderry was no use at all."

"Look," Sam piped up. "They're taking down the police tape."

Across the Great Court they saw Constable Lethbridge rolling up the tape outside the Reading Room.

"Wanna take a look inside?" Ruby asked. She didn't have to wait for a response. In no time, they were across the floor and through the open doorway. Just inside, Gerald pulled up short and the others bustled into the back of him.

"Far out," Gerald exhaled.

The sheer expanse of the Reading Room took their breath away. It opened up in an enormous circle around them, three stories lined with volume upon volume of books of all sizes—hundreds of thousands of them. Two sets of narrow balconies ringed the insides like ribs, providing access to the upper levels. Above them, light streamed through a bank of arched windows that lined the base of a huge pale blue and gold dome.

Fifty yards away, on the opposite side of the hall, was the Dumpster that Gerald had seen earlier.

"Come on," Gerald said. "Let's have a look."

They crossed the room and found that the Dumpster was filled with broken bits of plaster, including a long section that looked like an elephant's trunk.

"I guess this was where the thief was hiding, then," Gerald said.

". . . and I still can't find my elephant."

Sam raised his eyebrows and looked at Gerald.

"Did you say something about an elephant?" he asked.

Gerald shook his head. "No. I thought you did."

". . . a fifteenth-century statue of Ganesha gone without a trace. Must have weighed a ton and a half."

The disembodied voice seemed to come out of the air around them. Sam wriggled a finger in his ear. "There it is again," he said. "Something about a statue—"

"Shhh!" Ruby hissed. "Look!"

She pointed across the room. There, standing in a group, was Professor McElderry, Mr. Gupta, his daughter, Constable Lethbridge, and another policeman, who looked like he might be Lethbridge's boss. He was a fair bit older than the constable, and the gray of his short-cropped hair matched his moustache.

"It's the professor," she whispered to Gerald and Sam. "It's him we can hear."

"How can we?" Sam said. "He's miles away."

"The sound must be bouncing off the domed ceiling and coming down here," Gerald said. "You know, like a satellite dish. How cool is that?"

"Shushhh!" Ruby hissed again. "If we can hear them, they can probably hear us. Listen."

The three huddled their heads in tight and listened hard.

". . . you think the thief was hiding inside the replica statue for at least a day before the robbery, Inspector Parrott?"

"That's Mr. Gupta's voice," Sam said. Ruby's sharp elbow into his rib cage produced a muffled grunt and persuaded Sam to keep his thoughts to himself.

"Yes, that's right, Mr. Gupta," the inspector said. "We're dealing with a professional gang. To smuggle a fake statue into the Reading Room and remove the original was a feat in itself. To have overpowered one of our finest men here in Constable Lethbridge, well, that must have taken immense strength and planning."

Gerald popped his head up. Even from across the other side of the room he could tell that Mr. Gupta was less than convinced by the inspector's description of Constable Lethbridge.

"Is it not true that this policeman was found with his trousers around his ankles and a bunch of flowers up his—"

"Mr. Gupta!" Inspector Parrott interrupted, "I can assure you the Metropolitan Police Service is doing all it can to retrieve your diamond. We have a number of very promising leads and we'll keep Sir Mason posted on any breakthrough."

"That's all very well," Gupta said. "But the fact is this man was the last person to be with my diamond. So far the only evidence we have about a supposed thief is the constable's word for it. How do we know he didn't break the statue and take the diamond himself?"

"We have every faith in Constable Lethbridge and his story," Inspector Parrott said. "Not to put too fine a point on it, the state in which we found the constable required the involvement of at least one other person. It's just not possible to do that type of injury to yourself. We tried to replicate it in the forensics lab and the results were"—the inspector let out an involuntary shudder—"not pretty. Don't worry. We'll find your diamond. No reputable collector will go near it."

Gupta scoffed.

"It's not the reputable collectors I'm worried about," he said.

The professor grumbled a thank-you to the inspector and led Mr. Gupta and his daughter out of the Reading Room. Constable Lethbridge sighed with relief.

"That wasn't too bad," he said.

"Lethbridge!" the inspector barked. The friendly tone he had used with Mr. Gupta had evaporated. "Thanks to you, the Metropolitan Police Service is a global laughingstock. Someone manages to smuggle themselves into this room hidden inside a statue—a statue of an elephant no less—then proceeds to use your arse for target practice before disappearing with the most valuable diamond in the world, and you think it's 'not too bad'!"

"Well, I thought—"

"You're not paid to think, Lethbridge. Your diamond thief escaped, leaving the room locked from the inside. So there must be another way out. I suggest you round up any of your colleagues who'll still talk to you and find it."

"But we've already looked—"

"Well, look again!"

Inspector Parrott stormed out of the Reading Room, leaving Constable Lethbridge speechless.

Ruby motioned for the others to follow her to a nearby desk.

Before he moved, Sam said in a deep voice, "And hurry up about it, Lethbridge." Across the room, the constable spun around as if he'd heard a ghost. He shook his head, then hurried off.

"Very funny," Ruby muttered as her brother and Gerald laughed. "But if we're going to solve this mystery, we need to find how the diamond got out of this room."

Gerald turned a full circle, scanning the walls of books. It seemed impossible. How could anyone get out of a room and leave it locked from the inside? Then, high up on the second balcony, to Gerald's astonishment, one of the bookcases swung open. A woman stepped out from behind it and walked around the balcony, replacing books on shelves. Gerald noticed that every so often one of the bookcases had a doorknob on one end.

"Look," he said to the others. "Some of the bookcases open like doors. Maybe that's how the thief got out."

Sam and Ruby followed Gerald's gaze. A number of bookcases on both balconies popped open and police officers stepped out, searching for clues.

"Not much chance of getting up there to have a look with that lot stomping around," Ruby said. "Let's have a look down here."

Like the higher levels, the ground floor was ringed by bookcases. But they couldn't find any sign of doorknobs. They moved around the room until they came to a small alcove under a section of the lower balcony. Inside the alcove, they were hidden from the rest of the library. There was a closet on one side that was full of jackets on hangers, and a glass-paneled door on the other. Gerald tried the handle.

"Locked," he muttered. Next to the door was a set of pigeonholes, some of which had mail and other bits of paper stuffed into them. Like the rest of the alcove—the ceiling, walls, and floor—they were made of dark polished wood.

"Well, there's nothing much in here," Sam said. "Want to look somewhere else, Gerald? Gerald?"

Gerald's eyes had glazed over. A dull ache throbbed across his brow. The pattern of pigeonholes seemed to lift off the wall and wash in front of his eyes. The grid of squares weaved and shimmered like a flag in the breeze. All the squares were dark, deep holes, openings to endless tunnels.

Except for one. One square shone with a harsh blue light.

"Gerald!"

The sensation of Ruby tugging hard on his elbow yanked Gerald out of his apparent stupor.

"Are you okay?"

Gerald rubbed his eyes.

"I'm fine," he said. "I sort of blanked out, I guess." Gerald was used to wandering off in his thoughts during school lessons—especially during history classes—but he'd never wandered off on his own time before.

"That's weird," he mumbled. "I thought one of these boxes—" He stuck his hand deep into one of the pigeon-holes and let out a surprised grunt.

"What is it?" Sam asked.

"It feels like a metal handle. You know, like on a cabinet."

"Give it a twist. See what happens."

Gerald turned the handle clockwise a quarter turn. There was a dull click. He pulled his hand out of the pigeonhole and looked at the others. "Maybe this bit of the wall opens up like those bookcases," he said.

He pushed on the far edge of the shelf but it wouldn't budge.

"That was a bit useless," Gerald said.

Then the wooden floor beneath their feet dropped dead away.

CHAPTER TEN

Gerald, Sam, and Ruby landed in a knot of arms and legs and bounced onto a thick mat with a chest-flattening "oof." A rectangle of light from the Reading Room alcove above disappeared as the trapdoor swung back into place. They were left in absolute darkness.

"You all right?" Gerald grunted, shoving what he guessed was Sam's knee off his face. He elbowed himself into a sitting position and blinked hard. No good. Couldn't see a thing.

Muffled grumbles on either side of him suggested Sam and Ruby were okay.

"I guess this is how the thief got out of the Reading Room, then," Ruby's voice came out of the darkness. "Where are we?"

"Dunno," Sam said. Gerald could hear him patting about with his hands. "I can't see a thing."

Sam's attempts at discovery continued for a while, then he called out, "Hold on! I think I've got something."

The blackness was broken by a spark and the smell of burning sulfur. A small flame appeared, illuminating Sam's face.

"Found some matches," he said. "And a half pack of Dunhills—looks like our thief is a smoker." The match burned out and they were thrown back into darkness.

Another match ignited. Gerald could make out the vague shape of Sam's head in the distance.

"Well, hel-loo," Sam murmured, "what do we have here? Ow!" The match extinguished, and the darkness engulfed them again.

"What is it?" Ruby asked.

Her face was suddenly lit up. She shielded her eyes. "Hey!"

"Ta-dah!" Sam cried. He emerged out of the murk with a flashlight strapped to his head. "Found this on the ground."

"What is it?" Gerald asked.

"It's a headlamp," Sam said.

He moved his head and the flashlight beam shone around the room, like a slow-turning lighthouse. They had landed on a large padded mat, the type used in school gyms.

They were in an open space that disappeared in all directions into the darkness. To one side, near the mat, a bank of scaffolding stretched up toward the trapdoor.

"Here," Sam said to Gerald. "Steady this and I'll climb up for a look."

Gerald and Ruby grabbed hold of the lower sections of scaffold as Sam clambered his way toward the top.

"What do you see?" Gerald called up. The light from the flashlight bounced around the dusty ceiling.

Sam's voice came back to them, "There's some rope and pulleys and an electric winch. But I can't see how to open the trapdoor. I don't think we're getting out this way."

He climbed back down and jumped the last section to rejoin Gerald and Ruby. In the light from the flashlight they could see the floor was littered with food wrappers, drink containers, and cigarette packets, as well as a few candle stubs. A pile of discarded teabags lay by a small camp stove.

"Here, give me the matches," Gerald said to Sam, and he lit a candle, standing it upright in a plastic cup. "I'd say they were down here for a while. Look at all this rubbish."

"I'll take a look over there," Sam said, and headed off into the darkness.

Ruby took the matchbook from Gerald and flipped it over. A single letter on each side—a large *R* in a deep russet red—was the only marking.

"You don't think the thin man might be lurking down here?" Ruby asked, keeping close behind Gerald as he poked about.

"I doubt it," Gerald said. "There's not much at all down—"

A shriek cut through the shadows. The light from Sam's head flashlight suddenly disappeared, leaving Gerald's candle emitting a pathetic glow.

"Sam!" Ruby called out. "Are you all right?" She grabbed the candle and moved in the direction of Sam's cry.

She stumbled a few steps, then a light flickered on and she found herself just inches from an enormous white face. Her mouth opened in a piercing scream.

Gerald caught up and grabbed Ruby by the arm. "What's the matter? What is it?"

Ruby opened her eyes to find Sam looking sheepish, his headlamp shining on the face of a large statue.

"I think I found the professor's elephant," he said.

The elephant rested on a wooden cargo pallet, its proud features looking out of place in the dank surrounds.

"You idiot!" Ruby said.

Gerald snorted. "You two like screaming, don't you?"

Ruby snatched the flashlight from Sam's head. "I'll be in charge of lighting from now on," she said. She shone the lamp onto the statue and bent down to pick up a small brass plaque. "'Ganesha—one of the most revered of Hindu gods,'" Ruby read. "'Few major tasks are undertaken in India without first making an offering to Ganesha.'"

"Hey, look at this," Gerald said. A forklift was parked behind the statue.

"That must be how they did the switch," Ruby said. "Winch, ropes, forklift: They came prepared."

"What makes you think it was more than one person, genius?" Sam said, still smarting after being called an idiot.

"You heard the professor," Ruby said. "This statue weighs over a ton. It would take at least two people to maneuver it, even with a forklift. And how about getting the fake elephant up into the museum? How do you think a guy hiding inside a statue is going to operate a forklift or a winch, genius?"

Sam bristled. "Cretin!"

"Imbecile!"

"Hey, I'm two minutes older than you, moron!"

Gerald intervened. "Hold on, you two. Let's concentrate on how we get out of here first. Then you can argue about how many people it takes to corral a marble elephant."

Sam said something about stupid sisters and Ruby spat back a "What did you say?" But then they settled down and listened to Gerald.

"Okay. If they got into the museum from down here,

there must be a way out from here as well. Light another candle and we'll have a proper look around. There must be some stairs up to the street."

Ruby picked up the longest candle stub she could find and lit it from Gerald's flame.

"Here," she said to Sam, handing him the candle, "do you think you can look after this without hurting yourself?" Then, under her breath, "Poltroon."

They made their way deeper into the darkness.

"So what is this place?" Sam said.

"Some sort of cellar, maybe?" Gerald said.

"Must be the world's biggest cellar—seems to go on for miles."

"And what's that smell?"

The air around them was heavy with a metallic tang.

"Dunno," Ruby said. "But it reminds me of something."

They padded along in the darkness. On one side they could just make out a gray-tiled wall. The sound of dripping water came from somewhere in the distance. They walked for what seemed an age, following bends and twists in the never-ending blackness.

"Wait up!" Sam said suddenly. "Check this out."

"What is it?" Gerald asked.

"My candle. Look."

The flame was flickering.

"See! It's moving, like something's blowing it," he said. "There must be some air getting in. That means a door or window or something."

"And a way out!" Ruby said. "Maybe you're not such a numbnut after all."

Sam ignored her. "Come on, follow me."

He disappeared around a bend, leaving Ruby and Gerald struggling to keep up.

"Sam!" Ruby called out. "Slow down. We can't see you."

Sam's voice came back: "Come on, you two. The breeze is stronger here. We must be near a—blast!"

Ruby looked at Gerald.

"Sam? What is it?" she called.

"My candle's blown out. Hurry up. I can't see any—ouch!"

"Now what?"

"I've fallen into a ditch or something," Sam's voice echoed back. "And onto some sharp rocks."

"Just stay where you are, you moron."

Ruby grabbed Gerald's hand. "Come on, before the idiot does himself any more damage."

Then, in the distance, came a screech of metal grinding metal.

Ruby came to a halt. "What was that?"

"Dunno. But it came from over there." Gerald pointed toward where Sam had disappeared. The metallic shriek tore through the darkness again, this time much closer.

"Come on!" Gerald shouted, hauling Ruby along. The screeching seemed to grow out of the blackness. They rounded a corner and by the light of Ruby's lamp caught sight of the top of Sam's head. He was sitting in a trench about three feet deep, dazed and with his hands on his knees. The metallic howl now surrounded them, tearing at their ears. The beam from Ruby's flashlight was just enough to light Sam's face—a thin trickle of blood ran down his forehead. He tried to stand, but wobbled and flopped onto his backside.

A spotlight suddenly filled the void, blinding them. Sam was silhouetted, like a rabbit in a searchlight. Gerald looked in disbelief. A train had appeared from around a corner in the darkness and was bearing down on Sam.

The candle tumbled from Gerald's hand as he dived headlong across the concrete floor, his chest skidding out over the edge of the platform. He lunged down and grabbed Sam by the collar, his fingers gripping whatever cloth they could find. Hauling with all his strength, Gerald screamed at the searing pain in his shoulder. He rolled Sam up and over the edge, wrapping him in his arms a split second before the train hurtled past, inches from their heads. They could make out the faces of commuters in the train's carriages as they flickered past.

The train shot by them. A pale red light on the last carriage disappeared around a bend, returning them to darkness and quiet.

Sam and Gerald lay on the cold floor.

"You all right?" Gerald asked.

"Yeah," Sam panted. "Th-that was a bit close. Thanks."

Ruby appeared out of the darkness and dropped to her knees to hug her brother. She held him for a full minute, not saying a word.

Sam broke the silence. "Why is there a train in a cellar under the British Museum?"

Ruby swung the torch around. The beam picked out a row of bench seats along a wall, and some yellowed posters peeling at the corners.

"It isn't a cellar," she said. "It's a Tube station—it must have once operated under the museum."

"A ghost station," Sam said.

"Tube?" Gerald asked.

"London's underground trains," Ruby said. "That's what that smell is—the whole underground reeks of it. Like a mix of grease and metal shavings. There's a few abandoned Tube stations; I think some of them were used as air-raid shelters during the Blitz and then never opened up again."

She inspected the cut on Sam's head.

"You'll live. Come on. If this is the station platform, there must be an exit somewhere."

At the end of the platform Ruby saw a dusty exit sign pointing up a set of stairs. A long corridor sloped up to a pair of old wooden doors.

They tumbled into the daylight and fresh air, and found themselves in a narrow cobbled alley lined with tall buildings. Gerald shut the doors. They were covered in years of grime and disuse. There was no sign that they led to a station below.

"It doesn't look like these get opened every day," he said.

Ruby peered at the buildings around them. Only a few small windows faced onto the lane where they stood.

"Easy enough to smuggle a statue in here in the middle of the night," she said. "Even an elephant. There wouldn't be anyone around."

Sam dusted the last bits of gravel and muck off his jeans and touched the lump that was forming on his forehead.

"Okay, we've found out how they did it," he said. "Now what? We're not any closer to figuring out who it was or how it ties in with Gerald's great-aunt or that thin guy."

"Well, if the thieves came out here, maybe they didn't travel very far," Ruby said.

"Are you kidding?" Sam said. "There would've been a car ready to take them straight to the airport. They could be anywhere in the world by now."

"Yeah, I know," Ruby said, deflated.

"Come on," Gerald said. "Let's find out where we are."

They wandered up the alley until it opened out onto a smart residential street.

"We can't be too far from the museum," Ruby said. "But some of these roads wind around a bit. It's easy to get lost."

Sam groaned. "I'm exhausted," he said. "My feet are killing me and I'm starving. I vote we find something to eat."

"Okay, let's get some lunch," Gerald said. He pointed to the end of a row of terrace houses. "Seems to be a lot of people up that way. Maybe there's some shops."

They'd only gone half a block when Sam spoke up. "Gerald, why did you stick your hand into that pigeonhole back in the museum?"

Gerald thought for a moment. "I don't know. I had this . . . vision, I guess you'd call it. One of the boxes was glowing like there was a candle in it or something. Turned out to be the right one, I guess."

They turned into a street, busy with lunchtime crowds and traffic. Just ahead, a cab pulled over and a man in a dark suit got out and brushed by them as he hurried up the footpath. Gerald stopped and grabbed Ruby by the arm. "Do you still have the matches? The ones from under the museum?"

Ruby dug into her pocket and Gerald snatched the matches from her hand. A satisfied grin spread across his face. Just as the cab was pulling back into traffic, Gerald jumped onto the road, slapping his hands on the hood. The driver slammed on the brakes. The squeal of tires echoed a half dozen times as a line of cars behind screeched to a halt. The cab driver stuck his head out the window.

"Oi!" he yelled at Gerald. "What d'you think you're playing at?"

Gerald rushed around to talk with the driver, who, after a peek at the contents of Gerald's wallet, calmed down and nodded his head. Gerald called to Sam and Ruby to get into the cab.

"What's going on?" Sam asked as they bundled into the back. The cab took off up the street. Horns blared from the cars behind them.

"He's taking us to where he picked up that guy—the one who just got out," Gerald said, looking pleased with himself.

The twins stared back with matching puzzled looks. "Why?" they asked.

"Because of the tie he was wearing."

"What's his tie got to do with anything?" Sam said.

"His tie had this on it." Gerald held up the matchbook. "The same red *R*. It was covered in them. The cabbie said he picked him up from some club."

"Club?" Ruby said. "What club?"

The driver leaned over from the front seat.

"The Rattigan Club," he said. "Exclusive place, that one."

A few minutes later they pulled up outside a four-story

sandstone building. The front was marked by a row of tall columns, each decorated at the top with a globe of the world. To one side of the front doors was a brass plaque embossed with a single *R*.

Gerald, Ruby, and Sam climbed out of the cab at the bottom of a flight of marble stairs.

"What do you think?" Ruby asked.

"I'd say our diamond thieves have been here," Gerald said. He walked up the stairs and pushed against one of the large oak doors.

Chapter Eleven

The heavy portal opened and Gerald led the way inside. As the door closed behind them, all noise from the outside world was silenced. Not a bird, not a car could be heard. The only sound was the dull ticking of a clock somewhere inside the building.

They stood in a grand foyer. The floor was an intricate parquetry in a pattern of roses and ivy. In the center was an enormous green carpet with the letter *R* woven in red in the middle. Long green-and-gold–striped drapes lined the tall Georgian windows, blocking all outside light. The main illumination came as a restrained glow from a crystal chandelier that hung from the ceiling high above. In front of them was a huge Y-shaped staircase that split left and right at the landing, leading to the upper floors beyond. The place reeked of a mixture of wood polish, stale cigar smoke, and privilege.

Gerald, Sam, and Ruby took some cautious steps into the foyer until they were standing beneath the chandelier and on top of the red *R* in the carpet. Before they could decide what to do next, a sharp voice broke the silence.

"What are you doing?" A short pigeon-chested man in a black suit with a gold fob chain suspended across his middle emerged from a vestibule tucked away on one side of the entrance. His heavy black shoes shone with parade-ground precision, and they squeaked as he walked. He carried a bright yellow cloth in one hand and a tin of polish in the other. The man reminded Gerald of a bonsai version of Mr. Fry.

"You can't just wander in!" the porter said as he advanced across the parquetry. "This is a private club."

Sam winked at Gerald and walked up to the man.

"You mean this isn't the . . . um . . . Ruby . . . the Rubicon Hotel?" Sam asked.

"Never heard of it!" the man said. "This is the Rattigan Club. Members only. So shove off."

"Oh," said Sam in a disappointed voice. "See, we're supposed to meet our father at the Rubicon Hotel, and my sister over there—"

"Not interested," the man said, waving a hand as if shooing a fly.

"My sister has an unfortunate medical condition, you

see. When she has to go—"

The man looked at Ruby. She was doubled at the waist. Her face contorted as if she was about to burst.

"It comes on suddenly, you see, and once she starts going, well, there's no stopping her."

The man's eyes shot out. Ruby was standing right on the *R* of the Rattigan Club's foyer carpet. "I can't hold on much longer," she said through gritted teeth.

"Not there!" the man squeaked. "It's just been shampooed." He rushed across and grabbed Ruby by the shoulders, pushing her in front of him like a shopping trolley. "Hurry. This way." He bustled Ruby toward a side door, shouting back over his shoulder, "You pair stay right there."

"Of course," Sam called back. "Wouldn't dream of going anywhere else."

The moment the man and Ruby disappeared through the door, Sam grabbed Gerald by the elbow and dragged him toward the staircase.

"What's that all about?" Gerald asked.

Sam smirked. "There's nothing a grown-up fears more than somebody else's kid with a full bladder. Come on!"

"You've pulled that trick before, then?"

They took the stairs two at a time.

"That medical condition has got us out of so many history lessons."

They reached the second floor and paused. "You go that way and we'll meet downstairs in ten minutes, okay?" Gerald said.

Sam nodded and turned to go, then stopped in his tracks. "What are we looking for?"

"I have no idea," Gerald said. "But let me know when you find it."

Sam grinned and headed off.

Gerald walked down a long corridor, his feet scrunching into thick maroon carpet. The walls were hung with rows of oil portraits of former club members, each with a brass lamp attached above it, spreading a yellow glow over the unsmiling faces. Closed doors ran the length of the passage. Above a number of the doors were small hand-painted signs. Gerald passed the Green Room and the Blue Room, and when he came to the Pink Room he decided to try the door handle. It pushed down easily and Gerald opened the door and stepped inside.

He found himself in a room decorated in a dozen shades of pink. Pink roses woven into the carpet, pink striped wallpaper, pink curtains, a pink upholstered sofa, and pink armchairs. In the middle of the room was a square dining table set for two (pink tablecloth to the floor, pink napkins), and along one wall was a buffet, covered with a selection of cold meats, salads, and desserts. Gerald glanced at his watch—it was almost two o'clock and he realized that he was incredibly hungry. He hadn't eaten since breakfast and his stomach was crying out for something. He picked up a plate and piled on some chicken legs and dinner rolls. He sank his teeth deep into a drumstick.

Behind him, the handle on the door started to turn. Gerald let out a high squeak through a mouth stuffed with chicken meat. His eyes darted about the room. There was another entry on the wall opposite the buffet but it was too far away. The door opened an inch. The curtains only came halfway down the wall so there was no chance of hiding there. A dusty brown shoe appeared through the gap. The only place to hide was under the dining table. Half a leg clad in tweed trousers emerged through the doorway. Grabbing his plate, Gerald dived under the tablecloth just as the door to the pink room swung wide. He sat hugging his knees, his plate balanced on his shoes. Two voices floated over from the direction of the buffet.

"Get yourself some lunch, Arthur," said a gravelly voice, sounding like the product of a lifetime of whiskey and cigarettes. "There's a lot to go over."

Plates clattered and serving forks scraped before two sets of shoes appeared on the carpet on either side of Gerald—a pair of old brown shoes belonging to the tweed trousers and a pair of pointed black boots that came connected to legs in a black pinstripe suit. It was Tweed Trousers who sounded like he'd swallowed a distiller's ashtray.

"Glass of claret, Arthur?"

"No, thank you. Never before five."

"Don't mind if I help myself, do you? I can barely hold off till noon most days."

The man didn't wait for a reply. There was a sound of bottle clinking crystal and a generous glush of liquid, followed by an equally generous slurp and a deep "Aaaah."

"That's more like it. Sure you won't have one? No? Well, eat up anyway."

Under the table, Gerald shifted from side to side. His buttocks were going numb. He looked at the chicken legs on the plate balanced on his feet but didn't dare touch them. Above him, food was being stuffed into hungry mouths.

"So, Major," Pinstripe Trousers said eventually, "the . . . uh . . . thing, you know . . . it's all secure? Got it safely locked away?"

Tweed Trousers let out a moist belch then took another long slurp. "You mean the diamond?" he asked.

The black boots under the table shot up and almost collected Gerald's ribs. Gerald's eyes bulged. Did Tweed Trousers just say *diamond*?

Pinstripe Trousers gagged. "Don't say that! We agreed to only talk about . . . you know . . . it . . . remember? Who knows who could be listening?"

The sound of bottle on crystal rang out again.

"Don't be such a big girl's blouse," the major gargled

through his drink. "You're worse than your father. Yes, it is locked away at Beaconsfield. I'm heading down tomorrow to make sure everything is in order."

"Excellent," Pinstripe Trousers said in a calmer voice. Then even softer, "We need to keep this between you and me."

Tweed Major grunted. "I only got you in to help because I'm getting too old for this," he blustered. "And I owe your father a favor."

Pinstripe Trousers bristled. "And a large sum of money, too."

The major lowered his voice to a doglike growl. "I haven't forgotten. You and your father will get your cash."

There was an uneasy pause in the conversation as a knife scraped across china. Pinstripe Trousers was first to speak again. "Well, what about the . . . you know . . . other item? What's the latest on that?"

"Other item?" the major rumbled. "You mean the diamond casket?"

A black boot threatened to take out Gerald's front teeth. A bread roll bounced off his plate onto the carpet and Gerald scooped it up just in front of Pinstripe Trousers' flailing feet.

"For pity's sake, will you stop doing that," the younger man demanded.

The major let out a low wheeze. There was another long

slurp, then the sound of paper being unfolded and smoothed out. "This page is all we've got to go by," Gerald heard the major say. "From that book I found in the town."

There was a long silence before Pinstripe Trousers spoke. "'*Pic de la lumière éternelle,*'" he read slowly. "The peak of eternal light—'*indiquera le chemin*'—will show the way. What on earth does that mean?"

"Pardon my French, but it means what it says," the major said. "We need to find the peak of eternal light and then we'll find the casket."

"Well, where's this peak then? On your estate?"

The major groaned. "I've got four thousand acres down there and hills all over the blasted place; it's got to be one of them."

Under the table, Gerald couldn't believe what he was hearing. These two had stolen the diamond—they'd all but admitted it. Did that mean they'd killed Geraldine? And why did everyone want to find the diamond casket?

"The buyer was very specific," the major said. "We have to locate the position of the casket by Midsummer's Eve—that's next Friday—or the deal's off. Mother is hosting her tiresome party as usual. There has been one held on the estate every midsummer since the Middle Ages, so she's insisting it goes ahead. Keeping up appearances and all that."

Gerald frowned. What did Midsummer's Eve have to do with anything?

"Won't that get in the way of what we're doing?" Pinstripe Trousers asked. "People all over the place?"

"If past years are anything to go by, they'll all be legless by midnight and pocketing the silverware. You know what these London types are like."

Pinstripe Trousers sat up stiffly. "I am a London type," he said.

"Yes," the major said midslurp. "I know."

Just then the door to the room burst open and someone rushed in. From his hiding place, Gerald couldn't see a thing, but he recognized the newcomer.

"Beggin' your pardon, Major Pilkington . . . your Lordship," a rough voice said. "Have you seen three kids running around the club? They've managed to get away from me."

The major's brown shoes disappeared from under the table. "No we have not," he growled. "What's the point of having a private dining room if I'm going to be disturbed? Out!"

The porter mumbled an apology and the door closed again. "Right, Arthur. Grab some pudding and then we can get stuck into this rather excellent port."

The black boots also disappeared from under the table and the sounds of serving spoons on crockery soon came from the buffet. Gerald lifted a corner of the tablecloth and peeked out. The diamond thieves had their backs to him.

For the first time, Gerald got to see them from the ankles up: a young man in a dark pinstripe suit cutting a slice of cake and an older gent—the major—helping himself to the port.

Now's my chance, Gerald thought, and he rolled out the other side of the table and scurried on hands and knees across to the door on the far wall. He opened it and disappeared through the gap just as the major turned back to the table.

Gerald was appalled to find himself buried in a forest of old coats.

Curse it, he thought. A closet. With his head surrounded by cloth, Gerald could only pick up a few snatches of the conversation in the pink room. It sounded like the major and Pinstripe Trousers were finishing up.

"See you in a week at Beaconsfield," he heard the young man say. "Let me know if you have any luck with . . . you know . . ."

The major made some rumbling noises and Gerald glanced down to see the door handle to the closet start to turn. His eyes wide, Gerald pushed hard with his feet, shuffling as far back as he could, pulling jackets across in front of him. The door flung open. The major rummaged about inside, looking for his coat. Gerald pressed against the back of the closet. He could smell the major's breath now—a toxic mix of alcohol and burned sausages. Then, just four inches from Gerald's nose, the major's gnarled hand appeared. It wrapped itself around the only coat left hanging between them and reefed it to one side.

Gerald stared, horrified, right into the major's bulging left eye.

Chapter Twelve

Gerald's mouth hung open. The major continued to rummage in the closet, his face half obscured by coats, his left eye still staring smack at the middle of Gerald's forehead. Gerald held his breath and waited for the major to let rip. Instead, he felt a sudden tug on his collar and, before he could react, he was jerked out of the back of the closet. He landed hard on the floor, his knees up around his ears, and looked up to find Sam smiling at him.

"What on earth?" Gerald spluttered.

Sam raised his finger to his lips. He put his ear to the door and listened.

"Two-way closet," he whispered. "A door on both sides." He grinned at Gerald's confusion. "Who were you expecting? Mr. Tumnus?"

Gerald sat up and found himself in a room identical to the one he'd just been in, though in this room everything was blue. Through the closed closet door he could make out the muffled sound of the major's voice on the other side: "Aah! Here it is. Come along, Arthur . . . the bar opens in twenty . . ."

Gerald stood up and massaged his numb buttocks.

"How did you know I was in there?" he asked.

"I had no idea. I was having a look around and heard scuffling through that door. Had a peek, which was lucky for you."

Gerald shook his head, trying to get his thoughts in order. "Why didn't he see me?" he muttered. "He was right in front of me."

Sam interrupted, keen to tell Gerald something. "While you've been hiding in the back of a closet, I've been finding out stuff," he said.

"Hiding!" Gerald protested.

"Don't sweat it. You'll muscle up in time. Anyhow, I headed up that corridor and almost straightaway I was fronted by a man asking me what I was doing there."

"What'd you say?"

"Well, I lied, naturally. I said my father was a member and I was meeting him for lunch."

"Didn't he ask who your father was?"

"Of course. I said the Duke of Doncaster."

"Who's the Duke of Doncaster?"

"Wouldn't have a clue. I made it up. But you know what these people are like—they love rubbing shoulders with aristocracy. Makes them feel special. After that it was all 'Your Grace' this and 'Your Lordship' that."

Gerald laughed. "How did you know he wasn't a duke himself? They must all know each other."

Sam rolled his eyes. "Because if he was a duke he wouldn't have spoken to me in the first place, dopey. He'd have sent a man across to do it for him. Honestly, Gerald, you really do need to learn how things work in this country."

"It's not easy," Gerald admitted.

"Anyway, this man was really helpful. Turns out there are only about three hundred members of this club and the memberships are handed down from father to son. It's almost impossible for anyone else to get in. Whoever had that matchbook under the museum was almost certainly a member. That narrows it down a bit. How's that for detective work?"

Gerald nodded. "Yeah. Pretty good. But I think I can narrow it down even more."

Sam's jaw dropped lower and lower as Gerald laid out every detail of the lunchtime conversation that had taken place across the table above his head.

At the end of the tale, Sam shook his head.

"Do you mean there's uneaten chicken legs in there?"

"Very funny," Gerald said. "Let's find Ruby. I think it's time to go to the police."

Gerald opened the Blue Room door and ducked his head into the passageway. It was deserted. They crept down the corridor to the top of the grand staircase and looked down to the foyer below. As they took the first step down the stairs a shrill whistle made them spin and look up. Standing on the landing above was Ruby, her cheeks bright and a huge grin cutting across her face.

"Come on, you pair, up this way!"

Gerald and Sam bolted up the stairs. Ruby was bursting with excitement.

"This is brilliant." She beamed. "I gave that porter the slip and I've been roaming all around this place ever since. It's amazing!"

"Not as amazing as what Gerald found out," Sam said.

Before Ruby could ask, Gerald cut in, "No time. We'll tell you outside."

They turned back down the stairs. But there on the lower landing, glaring up at them, was the porter, his face almost as red as the carpet.

"Stand where you are!" he bellowed.

"Not likely," Sam muttered, and the three of them spun around.

"Follow me," Ruby said. She led the boys up the next flight of stairs to the top landing. They darted along a dim passageway lined with doors. Behind them the squeaks of the porter's shoes gained intensity.

"This way," Ruby urged, and they tore around a corner only to find they'd run into a dead end, a wood-paneled wall boxing them in. They turned to go back but the porter appeared in the passageway, blocking their escape. He was a small man but he seemed to fill the space between them and freedom. Gerald, Sam, and Ruby retreated until their backs pressed against the wall. There was nowhere to go.

"This feels familiar," Gerald mumbled to himself, visions of castle dungeons and hideous beasts swimming in front of him.

"Right, you lot," the porter whispered. "You're coming with me."

Ruby smiled at the porter and crinkled her nose. The porter gave her a curious look. Then she grabbed Sam and Gerald by the hands and, digging her heels into the carpet, heaved back as hard as she could, hauling the other two with her into the wood paneling behind them. Gerald braced himself for the crunch. But instead, a panel in the wall gave way and he was flipped backward, feet in the air. And then they were hurtling down. The panel high above swung open and closed, like a window in a storm, and for a split second Gerald saw the enraged face of the porter glaring down at them.

"Wha—" Gerald yelled.

"Laundry chuuuuuuuuuute!" came Ruby's high-pitched squeal. Gerald, Sam, and Ruby were buffeted, bumped, and bounced as the chute fell and twisted away like a waterslide. They were finally dumped through swinging flaps onto a cushion of sheets in a huge wicker basket deep in the club's cellar.

No one moved. Then Gerald lifted himself above the lip of the basket. A pillowcase embroidered with a red *R* covered his ruffled head. He reached down and peeled back a striped bedspread to reveal Ruby and Sam in a sprawled heap. They all started giggling.

"How did you know?" Gerald said through his laughter, pulling Ruby upright.

"I told you I had a good look around," Ruby said. "Now let's—"

Before she could finish, there was a rumbling from above. They looked up in time to see the flaps to the laundry chute swing open again. A week's worth of sodden bath towels rained down on them. After a struggle, Gerald cleared a soggy towel from his face. He was met by the sight of the porter peering over the edge of the laundry basket, an evil grin on his beetroot-red face.

The main drawing room at the Rattigan Club was very much a British country gentleman's retreat. Richly uphol-stered chairs and couches were arranged in clusters in front of an enormous open fireplace, either side of which were glass-fronted bookcases, their shelves laden with every volume imaginable on the subjects of hunting, shooting, and fishing.

Gerald, Ruby, and Sam sat huddled on a sofa, a disconsolate group. Their clothes were still damp from the towel drenching they'd received in the cellar. Nearby, Inspector Parrott sipped tea from a cup bearing the club's red *R* insignia. He seemed to be enjoying the plush surroundings. He chatted with Sir Mason Green, chairman of the Museum Trust, who was leaning on his walking stick and listening politely. By the fireplace, Constable Lethbridge was jotting in his notebook as the porter recounted the afternoon's events. The major sat across the room in a wing-backed chair, flicking through a copy of *Horse and Hound*, and taking the occasional drag from a cigarette.

Sam turned to Gerald and said, "Well, you wanted to get the police in."

Gerald didn't bother responding.

The doors opened and a tall man strode into the room. He was dressed in a well-tailored navy-blue suit, a crisp white shirt, and a maroon tie decorated with a tasteful pattern of gold *R*s. His coiffed hair was flecked with gray but held enough chestnut to suggest the years were still on his side. He carried himself with the air of a man who was used to being in charge. He crossed straight to the inspector and thrust out his hand.

"Inspector? Lord Herring, chairman of the Rattigan. And at the outset, let me say the Rattigan Club has been a respected part of this city for more than two hundred years. In all its history never has an incident like this occurred. Frankly, it's disgraceful."

The inspector put down his cup of tea and shook the man's hand. "Your Lordship. A pleasure to meet you," he said. "I've long been an admirer of your work and—"

The man cut the inspector off with an impatient flick of his hand. "Can we get on with this? I'm due back at the Lords for an important vote this evening."

Parrott nodded. "Of course. Can't stand in the way of the nation's—"

Lord Herring brushed past the inspector and greeted Sir Mason.

"Mason! It's been ages. How are you mixed up in this?"

Sir Mason smiled. "Redmond, good to see you looking so well. Museum business. You've heard about our missing diamond no doubt?"

Herring nodded. "Most unfortunate."

"As chairman of the Museum Trust, I have a vested interest in finding out what happened to it. It seems the children here think one of the club's members might be involved."

Lord Herring's chest billowed out. "Nonsense! Children. Off the street. Running rampant around the club. Accusing honorable members of petty theft. It's unheard of."

Inspector Parrott cleared his throat. "The theft of a diamond valued at more than one hundred million pounds is somewhat more serious than petty theft."

Herring cut him short. "What exactly is being said here? Who is accusing whom of what?" He turned to Sir Mason Green. "Mason, I know this diamond thing could cost the museum a bit, but do you seriously think a member of this club would ever stoop to such a thing—to common burglary? I mean, who among the membership here would need the money?"

The inspector cleared his throat again. "Um . . . Your Lordship, in my experience money is rarely the prime motive for this kind of theft. You'd be surprised who nicks things sometimes."

Sir Mason put a hand on Herring's shoulder. "Redmond, I think the inspector is keen to follow any leads that may come his way, no matter how . . . ahem . . . unorthodox the source might be." At this, he threw Gerald a "what-have-you-been-up-to?" look. Gerald turned a light pink.

Herring let out a strangled moan. "All right, Inspector," he said. "What do you need from us?"

The inspector motioned toward Lethbridge, who was busy thumbing through his notebook. "Constable, can you please read back what young Wilkins has told you?"

"Yes sir," Lethbridge said. "The boy said that he over-head Major Pilkington and a gentleman by the name of Arthur discussing the stolen diamond and a box that they need to find before Midsummer's Eve. That's this coming Friday, I believe."

There was a pause as everyone stared first at the major, then at Gerald.

"And? What else?" the inspector asked.

Lethbridge flicked back through his scribblings before closing his notebook.

"That's it."

There was another pause.

Lord Herring turned to the inspector.

"Bit thin, wouldn't you say?"

Lethbridge blushed. "Erm . . . yes. It sounded better when he first said it."

Gerald couldn't contain himself.

"It's true!" he piped up. "They were talking about the diamond and whether it was in a safe place."

Every eye in the room turned to Gerald.

"Talking about the diamond and admitting to steal-ing it are two different things," the inspector said. "Half of London is talking about it. Did the major actually say, 'I stole the diamond'?"

"Well, no," Gerald said. "It wasn't like—"

"And what about you pair?" the inspector said to Sam and Ruby. "Did you hear this alleged conversation?"

They both mumbled, "No."

The inspector frowned at Gerald, then turned to Lord Herring. "I'm terribly sorry, Your Lordship. Had I realized the lead was this weak, I would never have bothered you."

Gerald couldn't believe it. "But I heard them! Why don't you ask him where he was when the diamond was stolen?"

Attention switched to the major. He put aside his magazine and stubbed out his cigarette.

Inspector Parrott glowered at Gerald and finally said, "Well, Major Pilkington? Where were you on the night of the robbery? Last Wednesday evening?"

Before he could answer, Lord Herring spoke.

"The major and I had dinner together that night, right here in the club. He was with me the entire evening."

The major nodded.

Lord Herring took Sir Mason Green by the elbow and walked him toward Major Pilkington. "Mason, you really ought to come to the dining room one night. The asparagus is still very good and the chef is doing some splendid things with mushrooms."

Gerald was appalled at the way things were going.

"But the papers said the robbery was at two in the morning," Gerald interrupted. "He could still have done it. And what about the other man the major was with upstairs?

Aren't you going to talk to him?"

"What cheek!" The porter, who had been standing by the fireplace, burst into life, his cheeks more crimson than ever. "How dare you talk to the major like that! The hero of the Second Battle of Bilghazi. He lost his eye in that campaign, he did, and all you can do is make up these ridiculous stories."

Gerald's ears pricked up.

"Lost an eye?" he said.

The major broke his silence.

"Thank you, Leggett," he said in his rumbling voice. "No need to gild the lily, eh?"

He trained his one good eye on Gerald.

"Took a piece of shrapnel while storming a machine-gun post." He tapped his left eyeball with a fingernail. It emitted a hollow click. "Got a good collection of glass ones now." The major turned to face the inspector. "What this young chap probably overheard was my plans for the diamond anniversary midsummer's bash that Mother's hosting down at Beaconsfield this weekend. Beaconsfield," he explained to the inspector, "is the family pile down near Glastonbury."

"I see," said the inspector. "Diamond anniversary of what exactly?"

"It's seventy-five years since . . . well, blowed if I can remember, but Mother's on top of the detail. You must come down for the party and stay the weekend, Inspector. You'll be there, won't you, Mason? Mother would be most pleased."

Green cocked an eyebrow. "Yes indeed. Sounds very interesting."

Gerald was stunned that the major seemed to be wheedling his way out of any investigation. Inviting the police to his party!

"But what about the diamond box?" Gerald blurted out. "You said you'd find it under the peak of eternal light or something."

The porter let out another outraged cry.

The major held up a hand. "No, it's all right, Leggett. Didn't lose my eye defending freedom to have youngsters told to shut up. You misunderstood, young man." He crossed to the inspector and urged him to take a seat. "I was lunching with young Arthur Chesterfield today—a good sound chap, you know, one of us. Mother has a party game planned for Midsummer's Eve and I mentioned I was still looking for the box where it's stored. I was complaining about the lack of infernal light under the stairs. That's all."

Gerald began, "But that's not what—"

The inspector lost his patience. "So we're all here because of some party plans?"

"Um . . ." Gerald fumbled.

Inspector Parrott turned to the major and Lord Herring.

"I am sorry to have wasted your time, gentlemen. A most regrettable—"

Gerald couldn't stand it any longer. The events of the past few days bubbled over.

"He did say he had the diamond. He did. And look." He crossed to the chair where the major had been sitting and scooped up a packet from an ashtray. "He smokes Dunhills. The same ones we found under the museum. He smokes the same brand as the diamond robbers. I guess a lot of people smoke them . . . filthy habit . . . possibly hundreds of thousands of people, but still . . . it's all there. And the thin man had a knife at my back and he threatened to stab me. . . ."

Gerald looked desperately at the faces that were now all staring at him. He pointed to Constable Lethbridge. "He was there. He saw the man with the knife. Only the knife was hidden so he couldn't see it. The man was going to kill me. Unless I told him about the diamond box. Just like he killed my great-aunt. Only Ruby saved me before he could do it. But he would have done it . . . because he said he was going to." Gerald's voice trailed off to a whisper. He realized he sounded demented.

He managed to mumble, "Well, it's true," before slumping defeated onto the sofa between Sam and Ruby.

Major Pilkington winked at the porter. "Australian," he muttered.

The inspector cleared his throat. "Yes, I don't think we need delay ourselves here any further."

He thanked the major for his kind invitation to the party and apologized once more to Lord Herring.

"But what about this lot?" Herring protested, pointing at Gerald, Ruby, and Sam. "We can't have people trespassing and running riot around the club. It's bad enough with women wanting to become members, but children! Can't they be prosecuted?"

Sir Mason stepped in. "I hardly think we need go that far, Redmond," he said. "It sounds like a misunderstanding, that's all. Young Gerald has had a difficult few days, what with the death of his great-aunt. You remember Geraldine Archer, don't you?"

Lord Herring and the major both gasped.

"You're that kid," Herring said. "You inherited the Archer fortune?"

The major sniffed. "All new money, of course," he said with evident distaste.

Herring frowned. "Well, I expect we can make an exception in this case," he said.

Green was delighted. "Excellent. If Gerald is anything like his great-aunt, he's a first-rate chap. Who knows, Redmond, perhaps one day he'll be offered membership here."

Herring looked at Gerald as he might at the sole of his shoe after stepping in dog poo. "I very much doubt that."

* * *

On the steps outside the Rattigan Club, Inspector Parrott held court over Gerald, Sam, and Ruby.

"Right, you three, your detective days are over. Do I make myself clear?"

They nodded.

A wry smile formed on Sir Mason's face. "Don't be too harsh, Inspector. After all, they discovered how the thief got in and out of the museum. And they recovered the statue of Ganesha, which must count for something."

The inspector was not convinced. "They're lucky they haven't been charged with disturbing a crime scene and removing vital evidence," he said. "I've got enough on my plate without having to deal with amateurs."

"I'm sure they'll promise to get on and enjoy their holiday now," Green said.

The inspector grunted something under his breath, then he and Constable Lethbridge marched off in the direction of the museum.

"Sir Mason?" Gerald said. "If that diamond is so famous and can never be sold on the open market, why would anyone want to steal it?"

Green pushed himself upright on his walking stick and pondered the question. "Greed can be a dangerous master, Gerald," he said. "If it takes hold, it can make people do shocking things—things they would never otherwise contemplate. And do you know what else?"

"What?" Gerald said.

Green nodded his head back toward the front doors of the Rattigan Club. "It's a curse that doesn't discriminate between the classes."

A deep-blue Bentley pulled up to the curb like a motor launch easing into its berth at a quay. A squat man dressed in a chauffeur's uniform leaped from the driver's seat and trotted around to open the passenger-side door.

"I'd offer you a ride but I'm afraid I have some business to attend to in the city," Green said, shaking each of the children by the hand. "I know the inspector said to leave the detecting to him, but if I recall my own childhood that sounds more like an invitation than a warning." Green grinned as if a distant memory had just returned to him. "If you get yourself into a bind, or you find out anything interesting, you have my number."

Gerald smiled. "Don't worry about us. We'll spend the next few weeks kicking a ball in the park."

Green's eyes shone mischievously. "Your great-aunt was a terrible liar too."

Chapter Thirteen

The black cab wound its way through the avenues of smart houses toward Geraldine's place in Chelsea. Gerald, Sam, and Ruby sat slumped in the backseat, too exhausted to talk.

Gerald broke the silence.

"That was all a bit of fun, wasn't it?"

The twins grunted.

There was silence again.

"You guys doing anything much over summer?" Gerald asked. "You know, going away or something?"

"Nothing much," Ruby replied. "Our parents both work, so we'll just hang around. How about you?"

"After today I reckon I'll be locked up in the very tallest tower of the castle."

Sam twisted around in his seat to look at Gerald. "Why

didn't you make the police believe you about the thin man?" he asked. "I mean, he stuck a knife in your ribs."

"What's the point?" Gerald said. "You saw how they looked at me. They thought I was nuts. And do you blame them?"

He sat sulking for a bit. "This is all a waste of time," he said at last. "Why go looking for this diamond anyway? It's not even mine. I've got a mountain of money, I'm in a new city in a new country with a couple of guides . . . why not just have some fun?"

"What about the thin man?" Ruby said. "Aren't you worried about him?"

"No," Gerald said, with more confidence than he felt. "He's a weirdo who read something in the papers and wanted to scare some cash out of me. You guys chased him off—we won't see him again. So what's to worry about?"

The cab rounded the corner onto Geraldine's street. The mess from the pizza vans was long gone, and the TV crews had moved on to other news events. Which was a shame for them, because in their place now stood three fire engines. From the front windows and door of Geraldine's house billowed a cloud of black smoke.

Mr. Prisk cast a sorry figure in the dark study. It was two hours since the fire had been extinguished and the electricity was still off. The only light came from the late afternoon sun that found its way through the tall windows. Mr. Fry had pulled the curtains back and propped open the casements in a mostly unsuccessful effort to clear the acrid smell of smoke.

"It looks like the fire started in your bedroom," Mr. Prisk said, po-faced, to Gerald. "The firemen think it may have been an electrical fault. It's fortunate that Mr. Fry came back from some errands in time to raise the alarm, otherwise we could have lost the building."

Gerald, Sam, and Ruby sat on a leather lounge in the center of the room. Fry stood by the window, his shadow long across the carpet.

"What happens now?" Gerald asked, the bewilderment that had dogged him when he arrived in England returning like a fog roiling across his brain.

"Well, you can't stay here," Mr. Prisk said. "The entire place will need to be cleaned, and there is major work to be done in your bedroom—it's gutted."

Mr. Prisk paused, which gave Sam a chance to speak. "Gerald could stay at our place," he said. "He could share my room. Till everything's fixed here."

Gerald's brain fog lifted. He beamed at Mr. Prisk.

"That's a great idea," he said. "I'd be out of the way."

Mr. Prisk adjusted his glasses and looked hard at the Valentine twins.

"That would not be appropriate," he said.

Gerald's shoulders dropped.

"Why not?" Sam replied, perhaps a little too sharply.

"Because, my boy, in case you haven't heard, Gerald is now the richest child in Europe. I hardly think any accommodation you could provide will have the privacy or the security he requires. I have no intention of allowing a repeat of this morning's circus."

Sam slumped, joining Gerald at the back of the couch.

"I have spoken with your parents," Mr. Prisk said to Gerald, whose face reflected his thoughts about that news. "And we all agree that you should spend the rest of your holiday at Miss Archer's house in the country. Though naturally, of course, it's your place now."

Gerald moaned.

"It's quite suitable and you'll have space to run around," Mr. Prisk continued. "Six thousand acres, to be exact. You can't get into too much trouble there."

Gerald lifted his gaze from the carpet.

"So I get to spend my holiday stuck in some backwater by myself. Terrific. And let me guess: Mr. Fry will be looking after me?"

A low sigh came from where Fry was standing by the windows.

Mr. Prisk studied Gerald's downcast face.

"All right," the lawyer ventured. "Let me see what I can arrange."

"What do you mean?"

"It's a lovely old place with plenty of room. There's a swimming pool and a tennis court, horses to ride, a stream for fishing, woods to explore. You could take your friends with you."

"That sounds fantastic!" Ruby said. "Where is this place?"

"The estate is called Avonleigh. It's about three hours' drive from here, just outside Glastonbury."

Gerald's head jerked up.

"Glastonbury?" he said. "It's not anywhere near Beaconsfield, is it?"

Mr. Prisk looked at Gerald in surprise.

"Why, yes it is," Mr. Prisk said slowly. "Avonleigh and Beaconsfield share a boundary. I'd say it would be a forty-minute walk down from the main house. How do you know about Beaconsfield?"

Gerald smiled. "Just keeping tabs on the new fortune, Mr. Prisk."

The lawyer raised an eyebrow. Gerald grinned back, trying to look as innocent as possible. Mr. Prisk excused himself to call the Valentines' parents, and Mr. Fry set off in search of a bucket and scrubbing brush.

Once Mr. Prisk and Mr. Fry had gone, Gerald led Sam and Ruby down a smoke-stained hallway toward his bedroom.

They stepped past piles of rolled-up, charred carpet that

were still smoking. Soot clung to everything: the singed wallpaper, the blackened chandeliers, and the paintings on the walls. Outside Gerald's room a fireman sprayed bursts of foam on the last of the embers.

"Not much left, I'm afraid," the fireman said, as Gerald poked his head around the door frame. "Looks like it took hold pretty quick."

Gerald gasped. His room was a blackened shell. The bed was a twisted mess: wrought iron bent like an enormous pretzel, the mattress a tangle of blackened springs. The furniture had been reduced to ash. The curtains were completely consumed. The ceiling was black, and water dripped everywhere. Gerald tiptoed into the room across to the closet. He reached into his pocket for the key but saw that the door was standing askew where the hinges had buckled from the intense heat. He tugged on the brass handle—it was still warm. With some effort he forced it open. Inside there was little damage, though his clothes stank of smoke. At the back of the closet, Gerald shoved the suitcase to one side and pulled up the corner of carpet.

He looked at the bare floorboards.

Sam and Ruby's heads popped around the closet door behind him.

"It's gone," Gerald said, stunned.

"What's gone?" Sam asked.

Gerald turned around, his eyes burning.

"The letter from Geraldine, all the papers, a bunch of envelopes I hadn't even opened yet. I hid them all under there this morning."

"Burned in the fire, maybe?" Sam said.

"No. The carpet isn't even singed in here."

Ruby wrinkled her nose.

"What's that smell?"

"Smoke, you idiot," Sam said. "I think there's been a fire."

Ruby ignored him. "No, that other smell."

Gerald sniffed the air, then looked down at his fingers. He rubbed the tips under his nose.

"It's like . . . bleach."

He picked up the corner of carpet again and smelled his fingers.

"That's what it is. Just like the smell from the—"

"Thin man!" Sam exclaimed. The fireman across the room looked up from his work.

"Ssshhh!" Ruby hissed.

"What?"

"Trust no one, remember?"

Sam gave his sister a "whatever" look and turned to Gerald. "What does it mean?"

Gerald looked at his friends. He had been ready to give up the search for the diamond and for the person who killed his great-aunt. But that smell of bleach . . .

He rubbed his ribs where the thin man's knife had

pricked his skin that morning.

"It means we're going to the major's party on Midsummer's Eve," Gerald said.

Gerald spent the night at a hotel nearby. In the morning he pulled on the clothes he'd been wearing the previous day, rushed his breakfast, and hurried downstairs to find Fry waiting on the street outside. Ruby and Sam were in the back of the Rolls. Gerald climbed in beside them.

"This is very nice," Ruby said, pushing her shoulders into the leather luxury of the backseat. "I could get used to this."

"I guess," Gerald said. "But it has its drawbacks."

Fry dropped into the driver's seat and slammed the door. He flung his cap onto the passenger seat and flicked a switch on the dashboard. His muttering was silenced when the privacy screen behind his head reached the ceiling.

Ruby tried to suppress a giggle.

"Who is that guy?" Sam asked. "He hasn't said a word to us since he picked us up."

Gerald shook his head. "You know how I inherited a bunch of stuff?"

"Yeah."

"Well, I got him as well."

The Rolls eased into the traffic and they started the journey out of London.

"So your folks were okay with you coming away?"

Ruby nodded. "Dad did some work with the Archer Foundation once. He spoke with Mr. Prisk and they were fine."

"You know how they are," Sam said as he fiddled with the switches on the back of the front seat. A panel slid aside, revealing a TV screen. "Always wanting to know where you are, who you're with."

Gerald had a vision of Vi and Eddie bolting from the church hall in a rush to board the jet to get to the super-yacht in the Caribbean.

"Nope," Gerald said. "Can't say I've noticed it."

"Are your parents missing you, d'you think?" Ruby asked.

Gerald chewed on this for a bit.

"At the moment I'm thinking of adopting your parents," Gerald said. "I'm part of the family, remember."

It didn't take Fry long to have them out of London, and soon they were cruising along country roads.

It was a brilliant sunny day and Gerald gazed out the window as hedgerows and stands of oak trees flashed by.

Ruby broke into his reverie.

"Major Pilkington is our bad guy, then?"

Gerald shuffled around to face her.

"Well, sure. He said he had the diamond locked away at Beaconsfield."

"I guess."

Sam looked at his sister.

"What do you mean 'I guess'?" he said. "How much more obvious can it get?"

"Maybe. But what about the thin man?"

"How do you mean?"

"Don't you think it's a bit odd that two people are looking for this diamond casket thing?"

"What are you saying?" Gerald asked. "That they're working together?"

"Why not?" Ruby said. "Maybe the major hired the thin man to do the rough stuff. You know, to be the muscle. He's after Gerald because he thinks Gerald knows where this casket is."

"I dunno," Sam said. "The major didn't come across as the type who'd hire someone to stick a knife in your ribs."

"Yeah," Gerald said. "But I can't figure out why the thin man isn't interested in the diamond itself. It's worth a stack of money."

"Because the major already has the diamond, dopey," Ruby said. "Don't you see? The major steals the diamond from the museum with what's-his-name? Arthur Chesterfield? But he doesn't have the casket. The buyer they talked about, he wants the diamond and the casket. So the major hires Creature Features to do whatever it takes to find the box. It's obvious!"

Ruby sat beaming at them, apparently waiting for applause.

"That doesn't explain why the thin man tried to burn the house down," Gerald said. "And it doesn't explain why Professor McElderry lied about the diamond casket."

Ruby was becoming impatient. "First, the thin man burns your house down to cover his tracks after nicking the package. And the professor? He hates kids. Simple as that." Ruby crossed her arms and waited for a response.

"Well, if you say so," Gerald said. "But I still don't understand what this has to do with me and Geraldine."

"What was in those envelopes?" Sam asked.

"I didn't even open half of them," Gerald said. "There was one marked Family Tree, and another had a bunch of scribbles on it and I can't even remember what was on the last one. Maybe there was something in there about the diamond casket."

"How did the thin man know where you'd hidden them?" Sam asked.

"You know what?" Gerald said. "I'd like to know the answer to that too."

They sat without talking, accompanied by the quiet hum of the car engine.

"That Alisha Gupta's a bit of a snoot," Ruby said at last.

Gerald raised an eyebrow. "Excuse me? Where did that come from?"

"I dunno," Ruby said. "She just struck me as being a bit snooty. All nose in the air. She might've said hello or something."

Sam laughed. "Just because she's prettier than you. Ow!" Ruby shook out her knuckles after scoring a good hit on Sam's shoulder.

"Maybe the Guptas are involved," Ruby said. "You know, in some insurance scam or something."

Gerald considered this. "What? Have someone steal the diamond for them, claim millions in insurance, then head home to India with the diamond and the insurance money?"

"Seems just as likely as anything else," Sam said, rubbing his shoulder. "And what about that police constable, Lethbridge? He was the last one with the diamond. Maybe it's like Mr. Gupta said—he staged the robbery and nicked it himself."

"And don't forget the professor," Ruby said. "If anyone had access to the diamond in the museum it would be him. And you have to admit, him pretending not to know about the diamond casket is suspicious."

Gerald totted up some numbers on his fingers. "Okay, that means we've blown out from a single suspect in the major to . . . uh, let's see . . . at least six or seven people working either alone or in teams, including—if you listen to Ruby—a sixteen-year-old criminal mastermind in a green sari, who goes to the top of the suspect list because she didn't say hello."

Gerald was quicker than Sam. He managed to duck out of the path of Ruby's fist.

"And we still have no idea what the diamond casket is," Sam said.

"Whatever it is, a lot of people are pretty interested in it," Gerald grunted.

The privacy screen behind the driver's seat slid down a fraction.

"We'll be arriving at Avonleigh in ten minutes," Fry said in a tone of dry indifference, not taking his eyes off the road.

"Finally!" Gerald said. "We're starving and—"

Before he could finish the sentence, the screen had risen back to the ceiling.

"What's he so grumpy about?" Sam asked.

"I guess it's the will," Gerald said. "He was with Geraldine for years and all she left him was a set of teaspoons."

"Teaspoons?"

"Apparently it's an old lady thing. So he got some silverware and I got, well, you know."

"You don't think he was expecting to inherit a huge amount, do you? You know, enough to want to knock her off?" Sam said.

"Sam!" Ruby snapped. "This is Gerald's great-aunt you're talking about."

"Well, it stands to reason," Sam went on, ignoring his sister. "Servant hopes to inherit a pile of cash, gets tired of waiting for the boss to kick on. Just the two of them in that big empty house. Easy enough for him to sneak up behind the old girl and—"

"Sam!"

"All right, all right. But think about it. Nothing like having an inside man on the job, is there? And who better to snoop around Gerald's room to find that package? I bet Fry even knew about that loose carpet in the closet."

Gerald frowned out the window at the passing countryside.

"Terrific. Add another name to the suspect list."

A few minutes later the Rolls turned off the main road and they found themselves driving along a narrow country lane, bordered by fields dotted with black-and-white cows. Summer was well underway in Somerset. The grass was knee high and the livestock looked well fed. The meadows along either side of the road began to feature the occasional barn, or suddenly played host to a blanket of yellow flowers standing bright against the blue sky.

A stone wall appeared on one side, rocks of various shapes and sizes pieced together in a giant jigsaw. Tall hedges blocked the view as they eased off the road to approach a gatehouse. The building was covered in thick ivy, but Gerald could make out patches of sandstone underneath. The car drew to a halt in front of a pair of enormous black iron gates, topped with gold-painted spikes. Set into the center of the gates was a sculpture of an archer encircled by a blazing sun—the same image that was painted on the tail of the jet that brought Gerald to London a few days ago.

Fry opened the driver's window and spoke into an intercom set into a mossy stone wall. There was a sharp click and the gates swung inward. Fry eased the Rolls through, the tires biting the gravel at the beginning of a long driveway lined with chestnut trees.

Gerald lowered the window to get a better view but all he could see was tree trunks and leaves.

After a few minutes the drive eased around to the left and then widened to reveal a broad avenue of conifers along an expanse of manicured lawns, leading down a gentle slope toward . . .

"Far out," breathed Sam.

"Look at that," Gerald said.

Ruby's eyebrows shot up. "Oh my."

At the bottom of the hill, at the end of the driveway, stood a vast mansion, its stonework the color of honey. The imposing building was like nothing Gerald had ever seen before. It stood four stories tall, but its pitched slate roof gave it the appearance of soaring far higher. Its facade was a masterpiece of stonemasonry and glasswork. Statues and carvings were set into the upper levels and gables. Expansive bay windows rose over two stories, the multipaneled casements a mirror to the blue sky above. Gardens and lawns stretched away either side of the north and south wings, lush in the warmth of summer. The place evoked an atmosphere of ancient wealth and power.

". . . nine, ten . . . eleven, twelve. That's at least twelve chimneys," Sam said. "It's enormous!"

Gerald banged his hand on the screen behind Fry's head, and the divider slid down.

"Yes?" Fry said icily.

"Is this it?" Gerald asked.

"Not to your liking, sir? Should I have the plans for the roller coaster brought forward?"

Gerald didn't reply. As the sheer scale of the house sank in, he couldn't speak. All this was his?

The Rolls crunched to a stop at the end of the drive. Gerald and the Valentine twins piled out and stood in awe, dwarfed by the colossal mansion. Gerald noticed two lines of people, one on either side of the steps leading to the main entrance. They were dressed in uniforms and it looked as if they were going to a fancy-dress party.

Gerald took some tentative steps toward the entry.

A woman stepped forward from the head of one of the lines. She was shorter than Gerald and her white hair was drawn into a tight bun. She wore a neat but plain gray tunic that almost brushed the ground. Her sleeves were buttoned at the wrist and her collar disappeared under one of several chins. She gave the impression of being slightly batty, an impression that was confirmed the moment she opened her mouth.

"Welcome, sir! Welcome to Avonleigh!" she trilled as she took Gerald by the hand and shook it with vigor. "It is an honor to have the new master with us. We are at your service."

Gerald stared at the woman as she beamed at him. He glanced across to the other people by the front doors. There were about fifteen of them, men and women, all dressed as if it was 1910. They dropped their gaze and bowed their heads to him.

"My name is Mrs. Rutherford, sir, and I am the house-keeper here at Avonleigh. I've been in the employ of the Archer family at this here house for forty-five years come Feb'ry and if you need anything at all you just ask me, sir."

Her face radiated, as if her life had been leading to this moment. Gerald eased his hand free from the woman's grasp.

"Um, thanks very much. But please, don't call me sir."

"Not call you sir, sir?"

"Yes."

"Well, what shall I call you, sir?"

Mr. Fry walked behind the woman, lugging Sam and

Ruby's bags toward the front door. "I could suggest a couple of things," he muttered.

"Just call me Gerald," Gerald said to Mrs. Rutherford, ignoring Fry's grumblings.

Mrs. Rutherford did not look convinced.

"By your first name, sir? That would not seem appropriate at all. May I at least please call you Master Gerald, sir?"

Gerald sighed. "Yes, that would be fine. And this is Master Sam and Miss Ruby," he said, redirecting Mrs. Rutherford's rapt attention to the Valentines. "They'll be staying here as well."

Mrs. Rutherford descended on Sam and Ruby and shook their hands. "If there is anything I can do for you . . ."

"Well," said Sam as he freed his fingers from her handshake, "we haven't had any lunch yet."

Mrs. Rutherford was aghast.

"No lunch! What has Mr. Fry been doing? You haven't eaten?"

She ushered Gerald, Ruby, and Sam up the steps to the front doors. Each servant bowed as they passed. "Mr. Pimbury, Mr. Partridge, see that the dining room is made ready. The master of Avonleigh is in residence!"

Chapter Fourteen

Sam scraped his spoon around the bowl one final time to round up the last of the custard and fresh berry pudding, then let it clatter to the bottom of the plate. He pushed himself back from the table.

"Well, that was pretty decent," he said.

Gerald and Ruby had already assumed the prone stomach-rubbing position in their chairs. Mr. Pimbury, hands in white gloves, whisked away the dirty plates and left the trio alone in the dining room.

Gerald, Ruby, and Sam sat at one end of an enormous table, large enough for twenty people. Silver candelabras, vases of freshly cut flowers, and gleaming crystal decanters ran the length of the table setting. There was a massive fire-place on one wall and, opposite, the room opened through

French doors onto a large paved terrace, which in turn overlooked an expanse of lawn that sloped down to fenced meadows and a house garden.

Ruby inspected a huge painting in a gilded frame above the fireplace. It depicted a bloody battle scene between some African warriors and British soldiers.

"What do we do now?" she asked. "Want to explore this place?"

"Sounds good to me," said Sam. "Once I can stand up again. I still can't believe all this is yours, Gerald."

Gerald sat silent, soaking in his surroundings: the red flocked wallpaper, the line of crystal chandeliers suspended from the oak-paneled ceiling, the intricate carving on the walnut buffet, the swirling pattern of the carpet.

"And what a pleasure it is to have the new master at home, sir." Mrs. Rutherford had entered the room and was fussing around the buffet, tidying and straightening.

"Please," Gerald said, "don't call me that."

"Begging your pardon, sir . . . uh, Master Gerald. Hard to give up the habit of a lifetime."

Gerald wandered across to the French doors and looked out over the rolling lawns bathed in the buttery afternoon sun.

"Mrs. Rutherford, how did my family ever get to own this place? I mean, look at it. It's good enough for royalty."

The woman glided over to Gerald, the hem of her gray

tunic sweeping the carpet. "This was the country seat of the last Duke of Avonleigh. The original house was built in the early 1600s, but His Grace the Duke made many modern changes to the place."

"When was that?"

"Oh, about 1862, I'm told. A bit before my time. He made some tremendous improvements. For instance, d'you see a village down by that hillock in the distance?"

Gerald was joined by Ruby at the terrace, but all they could see was a patchwork of fields and the odd sheep.

"Um, no."

"Exactly. His Grace had the village moved behind that hill. Spoiled his view, you see," Mrs. Rutherford said.

"He moved the village?" Ruby said in disbelief. "Bit extreme, isn't it? Just to get a view."

"Well, that's the rich for you," Mrs. Rutherford said. "Beggin' your pardon, Master Gerald. No offense meant."

Gerald stifled a grin. "None taken, Mrs. Rutherford." He was getting to like the strange woman.

"Anyways, it was your great-aunt's father, the late Mr. Dorian Archer, who bought the place from the duke's family. It was a far larger estate back then, but when His Grace passed on, his family had to split it into two properties and sell them to pay the death taxes. Mr. Dorian bought Avonleigh, and the Archers have been here ever since."

"But it must have cost millions. Where did the money

come from?" Gerald asked.

"Do you not know about the Archer fortune, Master Gerald?" Mrs. Rutherford said.

"Turns out I don't know much about my family at all," Gerald replied.

"Teabags."

"Pardon me?"

"The Archer fortune was built on teabags. Or rather, on the little staple that attaches the string to the bag."

"You've lost me. How does a staple become a twenty-billion-pound fortune?"

"Your great-grandfather Dorian Archer invented a process that made it safe for staples to be used in hot water. The old staples were made from lead and had a nasty tendency to poison people. So his invention revolutionized the tea business."

"Even so, it's only a staple."

Mrs. Rutherford raised an eyebrow. "Only a staple? Mr. Dorian licensed his invention to the industry. Every time someone uses a teabag, a fraction of a penny comes to you."

"And?"

"I believe that translates to about one hundred and fifty million pounds a year from England alone."

Gerald looked around the room and at the view across the terrace.

"A lot of teabags have gone into this place then," he said.

"Yes, Master Gerald. A lot of teabags indeed."

There was a sudden clatter of what sounded like a stack of frying pans falling down a flight of stairs, followed by a muffled oath.

Mrs. Rutherford darted from the room. They could hear her chiding one of the servants in the hallway.

"Take care, Mr. Partridge. I want those bags and boxes out of this house as quickly as possible, but without you hurling them down the stairs, if you please."

Her cheeks were flushed when she returned to the dining room.

"Terribly sorry about the inconvenience, Master Gerald," she apologized. "The removers' van is due any moment and I don't want delays."

"Removers? Who's moving out?"

Mrs. Rutherford became flustered for a moment.

"Didn't Mr. Prisk tell you? Your uncle Sidney and his—ahem—children have moved out of Avonleigh and into more appropriate accommodations in town."

Gerald looked surprised. "Sidney, Octavia, and Zebedee were living here?"

Mrs. Rutherford nodded, and shuddered. "And pardon me for being so bold, Master Gerald, it was a happy day when we got the call from Mr. Prisk to say you were coming.

Mr. Sidney is not a pleasant man, and as for Miss Octavia and Master Zebedee . . ." Mrs. Rutherford drew her lips in over her teeth as if she'd been sucking on a lemon. "Let's just say that a little bit of them goes a long way."

Ruby had been listening with interest.

"Octavia and Zebedee?"

"My cousins," Gerald said. "I met them for the first time at the funeral. Bit painful, actually."

Sam piped up from his seat at the dining table, still digesting his lunch. "Well, if I got kicked out of this place, I reckon I'd be pretty painful too."

Ruby looked thoughtful. "Gerald, what did your great-aunt leave Sidney in her will?"

Gerald frowned as he tried to recall the events from the church hall a few days before. "I remember he was really angry—he only got a million pounds."

"Only a million quid, eh?" Sam said, shaking his head. "No wonder he was cranky."

"Do you think your uncle expected to inherit this place?" Ruby asked.

"This place and a good sight more!" Mrs. Rutherford said sharply. "Beggin' your pardon, Master Gerald, but he is a most unpleasant man."

From the hallway came the chime of a grandfather clock.

"Goodness me, the time," Mrs. Rutherford said. "Master

Gerald, Mr. Prisk sent some clothes down from London seeing as yours are being cleaned after the fire. Allow me to show you to your room so you can change."

Twenty minutes later Gerald wandered down the crimson carpet of the main staircase and found Sam and Ruby in one of the enormous drawing rooms, playing a game of chess on an antique table.

Sam took one look at Gerald and burst out laughing.

Ruby covered her mouth with her hands.

"I guess Mr. Prisk picked these himself," Gerald said. He stood there with his arms outstretched, wearing a gray suit identical to the one worn by the lawyer, right down to the pressed white handkerchief in the jacket pocket, though Gerald did still have his runners on.

Ruby barely snuffed out a snicker. "I think we might take you shopping tomorrow."

"Yes," Gerald said. "That would be good. There's a wardrobe full of these things up there."

They spent the rest of the afternoon exploring the house and its surroundings. The swimming pool was still too cold, but the grass tennis court, set well away from the house and its servants, was the perfect place to while away a few hours.

Sam found some equipment at the back of a pavilion next to the court and soon the sound of tennis balls rebounding off strings echoed across the lawns.

Gerald discarded the jacket and rolled up his sleeves, but he still looked like someone from the 1920s as he dashed across the turf in his long pants, racket in hand. Sam and Ruby were on one side of the net taking great pleasure in running Gerald hard on the other.

"D'you reckon your uncle could be like Fry?" Sam grunted as he whacked a backhand over the net. "Y'know, killing Geraldine to get her money?"

"Maybe," Gerald said, flicking a high lob over Ruby's head. "He was really angry when he only got cash. But what about the diamond?"

"Maybe we've got it wrong," Ruby said, hitting the ball into the net. "Maybe the person who stole the diamond had nothing to do with Geraldine's death. Maybe there were two separate crimes."

Gerald joined Ruby by the net post.

"Let me get this straight. Even though Geraldine said in her note that she feared for her life because of the diamond, you're saying whoever killed her may not be connected with the diamond theft at all?"

"It's possible," Ruby said. "Think about it—the major has all but admitted that he stole the diamond. Remember what the professor said? It makes no sense for someone to nick the gem, then go and murder Geraldine. Maybe whoever killed Geraldine was only after her money. Her estate is worth two hundred of those diamonds."

"So where does the thin man fit in?" Sam asked, picking up a tennis ball. "He pretty much admitted killing Geraldine. Doesn't sound like he's family, hoping to inherit something."

"No," Gerald agreed. "But maybe he was hired by one of the family—or one of the servants."

Before they could give the problem any more thought a low dong rang out from the house.

Gerald checked his watch.

"Six o'clock. I guess that's dinner."

Mrs. Rutherford oversaw the running of the evening meal in the formal dining room. Much to Gerald's disappointment—and the Valentine twins' endless amusement—the serving was performed by Mr. Fry.

"Turkey."

"Excuse me?" Gerald said in surprise.

Fry's face was blank.

"Would sir like some turkey this evening?"

Gerald grunted a yes and Fry flopped some slabs of ivory-colored meat onto his plate among the roast vegetables.

"Thanks," Gerald mumbled.

"Moron," Fry said.

"Excuse me?"

"Would sir like some more on his plate? Or does he have sufficient?"

Gerald eyed Fry closely but the butler's face gave nothing away. Across the table Sam snuffled in his napkin.

"You've made a great friend there," Ruby giggled after Fry returned to the kitchen.

"Yeah, isn't he something?" Gerald glanced over his shoulder to make sure Mrs. Rutherford was out of earshot. She was busying herself at the buffet with a number of large crystal bowls containing desserts. "Do you wanna sneak over to Beaconsfield tonight? It'd be good to see what it's like before the major's party at the weekend."

Ruby leaned in. "Mr. Prisk said it was a forty-minute walk away," she whispered. "How are we supposed to find it in the dark?"

Then, to their horror, Sam called out, "Excuse me, Mrs. Rutherford. Can you tell us where Beaconsfield is, please?"

"Sam," Ruby whispered, her eyes bulging. "What are you doing, you idiot?"

"When in doubt, ask," Sam said to his sister before turning back to the housekeeper. "We're trying to get the lay of the land around here. You know, where town is, some of the other farms in the area. Mr. Prisk mentioned there's a place called Beaconsfield close by."

Mrs. Rutherford pushed a trolley laden with desserts across to the table.

"Yes, Master Sam. Beaconsfield is quite close. If you go down past the tennis court, across the lower meadow and over the rise, you'll find our lower boundary with Beaconsfield. Be quite a pleasant walk on a night like this."

Mrs. Rutherford doled fruit and custard into bowls, humming to herself.

"Um, Mrs. Rutherford," Gerald ventured, taken aback by her mention of a nighttime stroll. "Do you know anything about a party there this weekend?"

"Their annual midsummer's bash," she said in a matter-of-fact kind of way, placing the bowls on the table. "It'll be the same as every year, I expect. A lot of flash folk come down from London, get rolling drunk on Major Pilkington's wine, then go 'ooh' and 'aah' at the fireworks at midnight. Frightens every cow in the district, it does—and it's not just the fireworks."

Gerald dipped his spoon into a large serving of trifle and took a mouthful. Mrs. Rutherford was particularly helpful.

"So what's the major like?" Gerald asked.

"Major Pilkington? Oh, he and his mother have lived there forever, it seems. Mr. Dorian was always after the major's mother to sell the place to him, but she wouldn't budge. A very proud woman is Mrs. Pilkington. Though word in the town is that they could do with the funds, beggin' your pardon for sayin' so."

Ruby looked up from her damson-and-treacle pudding.

"What do you mean, Mrs. Rutherford?"

"Oh, you talk to the butcher and the grocer and you hear about bills being paid very late, if at all—that type of thing. I hear the place has become quite run down. Not what it used to be."

"Mrs. Rutherford?" Gerald said, not sure if he should press his luck.

"Yes, Master Gerald?"

"Do you know if there's any place around here called the peak of eternal light?"

Mrs. Rutherford considered the question.

"I know every hill and dale in this district as if they were me own children, Master Gerald, and I don't believe I have ever heard mention of such a place."

Gerald didn't ask any more questions but he had the distinct feeling Ruby was about to burst—she was shoveling food into her mouth in a rush to finish.

As they scoffed the last of the meal, Gerald felt a looming presence at his elbow.

"Nuts."

Mr. Fry plopped a silver tray in front of Gerald, sending half a dozen walnuts rolling across the linen tablecloth, then sulked off back to the kitchen.

Chapter Fifteen

Gerald skirted the hedges to keep out of sight of the house on his way to the tennis pavilion, his backpack bouncing on his shoulders. It was only three days before Midsummer's Eve, and the moon on the horizon was almost full. Sam and Ruby were already at the tennis court, discussing what had happened at dinner.

"Don't you see?" Ruby was saying, "The major and his mother are hard up at the moment. You heard Mrs. Rutherford—the unpaid bills, the house needing repairs—they're desperate for cash."

"Yeah, so what?" Sam said. "That doesn't make the major a killer."

Ruby groaned.

"Oh, don't be so thick. The major stole the diamond

so he can sell it. It's worth one hundred million pounds, remember?"

"Yes, I remember," Sam said. "I also remember the inspector saying it would be impossible to sell because it's so famous. Had you forgotten that?" He screwed up his face at his sister. "What do you think, Gerald?"

The sound of a dog barking echoed across the hills.

"I think I don't want to get into any family arguments. Come on, let's go."

Gerald hoisted his battered backpack and led the way down the hill toward the lower meadow. He had a bottle of water and some flashlights that he'd found in the pantry, but it didn't look like they'd be needed. The moon cast a ghostly hue over the landscape. They walked near a line of chestnut trees that ran down one side of the fields, making good progress through the ankle-high grass.

After a while, Sam prompted Gerald again. "You think the major is the killer?"

"No," Gerald replied. "I think the thin man killed Geraldine. But I think he was acting on someone's orders. And I don't think that someone is the major. There's something else going on here."

"Well, if you think the major's innocent, why are we doing a midnight dash over to his place?" Sam asked.

Ruby interrupted before Gerald could speak. "Oh, don't

be so gullible, it's because of the diamond box. The thin man is after the casket and so is the major. It's supposed to be hidden on this peak of eternal light, which the major reckons is on his property. Sam, you are so dim sometimes."

Sam stopped walking.

"You don't have to be nasty," he said.

"What?" Ruby pulled up and turned to face her brother.

"Just because I'm not thinking the exact same thing as you doesn't mean I'm stupid or gullible," Sam said.

Ruby took a breath. "I'm sorry, Sam," she said. "I get ahead of myself sometimes. I'm sorry if I've been mean to you." She walked back and took hold of his hands and squeezed. "I'll try to do better, okay?"

"Okay. Thank you."

"Good. Now, an interesting thing about the word *gullible*," Ruby said as they continued up the grassy slope. "It's the only word that's not in the dictionary."

"Really?" said Sam.

Gerald tried to catch Ruby's eye, but she had suddenly found the night sky intensely interesting.

At the top of the rise they stopped. They were looking into a small valley bathed in silver moonlight. On the far side they could make out a large house, fingers of smoke curling up into the night sky from the chimneys. A clock-face in a tower at one end of the building glowed a faint amber. They could just hear the chimes marking midnight. But most striking of all was not the house or the expanse of grounds or orchards around it, but the sight of an enormous conical hill in the distance. On the top of the hill, clear against the night sky, a lone tower stood sentinel over the valley.

"What do you make of that?" Sam whispered.

"Looks a bit like a lighthouse, doesn't it?" Gerald replied.

"Bit far inland for that, don't you think?" Ruby said. "And it's missing something if it's a lighthouse."

"What's that?"

"A light."

Gerald shouldered his pack and they set off into the valley. After twenty minutes of clambering over stiles and dodging cows and cowpats, they emerged out of some woods into a rose garden. A stone stairway at the far end led up to a large terrace. An enormous house loomed over them.

"You're kidding," Gerald whispered as he gazed up at the building. "It looks like Dracula's wedding cake."

The house at Beaconsfield was indeed a bizarre sight. It stood three stories tall and looked like it had been transplanted direct from Transylvania.

Ivy grew thick up the lower sections of the gray stone walls, twisting around ancient columns and tangling through moss-coated archways. The house was topped with spires, gothic turrets, and chimneys that probed the sky. Gargoyles clung to the ledges of the upper floors, and two enormous bats were sculpted into the walls, their mouths contorted in silent screams. An overwhelming sense of decay enshrouded the place. The pitched roof of what appeared to be a large chapel could be seen behind one wing of the house. At the other end of the building stood the clock tower, the amber eye of the clockface staring down at them. Sam tugged at Gerald's sleeve and pointed to the top of the tower.

"Look familiar?"

Gerald looked up. Atop the tower, clear in the moonlight, was a large weathervane. Not the traditional rooster, but a man with a bow and arrow—the same archer that stood guard at the gates of Avonleigh.

"What's that doing there?" Gerald said.

A breeze rustled the leaves of the rosebushes behind them. The archer didn't move, his arrow remained pointing resolutely west.

"This place is creep central." Ruby shivered. "Great place for a party, don't you—"

A light flickered on in one of the rooms above the terrace and spilled onto the expanse of tiles.

Ruby and Gerald stopped. Sam dropped to his hands and knees and crawled to the base of the stairs.

"Sam," Ruby whispered.

Her brother glanced back, then scurried up the stairs, stopping at the top to hide behind a large pot.

Ruby turned to Gerald. "What's he doing?"

Gerald shrugged, not taking his eyes off Sam. At the top of the stairs Sam signaled for them to follow. Then he disappeared onto the terrace.

"I take it back," Ruby fumed. "He is an idiot. Come on, before he gets into trouble."

They hurried up the stairs, ducked behind the large pot, and peered out from either side. The terrace was lit by the moon and the light shining through glass doors about twenty yards away. Gerald could see Major Pilkington inside, standing behind a desk at one end of a long room. At the other end, sitting in an armchair, was an elderly woman.

"His mother?" Gerald whispered.

Ruby nodded. "Where's Sam?"

Gerald scanned the terrace and finally spotted Sam, lying on his stomach behind a line of shrubs just a few feet from the major. He was resting his chin in his hands and idly waggling his feet in the air.

"He won't die from stress, will he?" Gerald whispered to Ruby.

Ruby muttered, "Come on, then."

They crept onto the terrace and scuttled across to join Sam, who looked up as they slid in beside him.

"What took you so—"

Ruby pressed her index finger to Sam's lips.

The sound of voices drifted onto the terrace through an open window above the glass doors.

"Think, Mother. You've lived here all your life. Surely you've heard of it." The major's voice rang out into the night.

Gerald had to strain to hear the reply.

"I've tried, dear. But it's no use. It doesn't sound familiar at all."

"Take another look at the map, then. The peak of eternal light."

Gerald motioned for the others to stay still and he poked his head out of the shrubbery. He could make out the major and his mother studying a large piece of paper on the desk.

"It's no use, Horatio. It doesn't ring any bells."

The major exhaled. "We've only got three days. It must be here. It has to be here."

"I'm tired, Horatio, and I'm going to bed. There's still a lot to organize for the party."

"Don't you understand? If I don't find this box there won't be any more parties. There won't be any more anything."

The major shook his head and followed his mother out of the room, switching off the light as he closed the door.

The terrace was silent for a few minutes as the Valentines

and Gerald waited. Light filled a window on the floor above and then it too was extinguished. From the clock tower came a single resonating bong—one o'clock.

Gerald, Ruby, and Sam crept across to the French doors.

Sam tried the handle but the door was locked. He glanced up at the window above the door. It was still open.

He turned to Ruby. "Think you can do it?" he asked.

Ruby studied the opening. It was about twelve feet off the ground.

"Yep." She nodded. "No problem."

Gerald blinked. "How are you going to climb up there? It's glass—there are no footholds."

Ruby winked at him. She took Sam by the shoulders and positioned him under the window with his back to the door.

"Ready?" she asked.

Sam bent his knees, cupped his hands in front of him and nodded. "Yep, ready."

Ruby walked halfway across the terrace, turned, and ran straight at her brother. A few paces away she leaped into the air, landing one foot hard into the stirrup of Sam's hands, the other onto his shoulder and then with her arms outstretched and palms together over her head she launched herself up and through the open window. Her feet just cleared the sill as she tucked into a ball and tumbled smoothly onto the rug inside the major's study. Seconds later she stood at the open French doors, a broad grin on her face.

"School gymnastics champion, three years in a row!" she puffed.

Sam and Gerald hurried inside and shut the doors behind them.

"That was awesome!" Gerald breathed.

"Well, I find chess boring," Ruby said.

Gerald handed them each a flashlight from his backpack.

They crossed to the desk and found the map still unrolled. Three flashlights shone down to show a detailed chart of Beaconsfield and its surroundings. Gerald traced his finger across the paper.

"Here's the boundary with Avonleigh, and this is where we came to get here. And this must be that hill we saw, the one with the tower on it."

Sam peered closer.

"Do you think that could be where the peak is?" he asked.

"Maybe, but by the sound of it the major has searched all over this area," Ruby said. "And the rest of these hills seem pretty small—hardly what you'd call a peak."

Gerald swung his torch around the room. The walls were hung with oils of gloomy landscapes and the occasional racehorse. The armchairs and couches all showed signs of age. The large Oriental rug that covered most of the floor was threadbare in several places. There was an oil heater in one corner and a grandfather clock stood by the door, its hands on midnight. Everything was covered in a fine layer of dust.

"Doesn't look like the cleaners have been through lately," Gerald said, directing his light onto the wall behind the desk.

A mantelpiece over a large fireplace was dotted with curios and keepsakes, souvenirs of a lifetime in the military. Gerald picked up a small wooden box with an elaborate inlaid pattern.

Ruby shivered. "Is it just me, or is it particularly cold in here?"

Gerald shone his flashlight into the fireplace. The grate contained an arrangement of dried flowers, which, like everything else in the room, was covered in dust.

"That's a bit odd, isn't it?"

"What's that?" Ruby said.

"Those flowers have been there forever. That fireplace hasn't been used for ages."

"It's summer. People don't light fires."

"But we saw smoke coming from a couple of chimneys when we were on top of the hill. And there's an oil heater over there in the corner." Gerald crouched down and ran his finger over the bottom of the grate. "No ash at all. This fireplace is the cleanest thing in the room."

"What are you saying?" Ruby asked.

"Well, maybe this fireplace is used for something other than fires. Maybe it's hiding something?"

"Like what?"

"I dunno. But it could be a good place to stash a stolen diamond."

Ruby looked at Gerald. "You want to look for a hidden passage behind a fireplace in a rundown gothic mansion in the middle of the English countryside?"

"Uh . . . yes."

"Bit of a cliché, don't you think?"

"It's only a cliché if you've heard it before," Gerald said. He shone his flashlight around the inside of the fireplace. "It's worth having a look."

Ruby rolled her eyes. "Oh yes, there'll be lashings of hidden passages around here. Then maybe we could go searching for smugglers. How wizard!" She watched scornfully as Sam and Gerald scoured the mantelpiece for any sign of a lever that might open a secret doorway.

"What are we looking for exactly?" Sam asked, as he ran his fingers along the length of the tiled backing behind the mantelpiece.

"I don't know—some sort of panel that slides out of the way or a button or something," Gerald said. "Anything that might—" He stopped. From outside came the squeak of a floorboard.

"Hide!" said Ruby in an urgent whisper. The flashlights flicked off. Sam flung himself behind a couch and Ruby disappeared into a dark corner hidden behind a hanging tapestry. Gerald didn't know which way to go. Across the room, the door opened. He dropped to the floor and rolled under the desk, just as the light came on.

Gerald lay on his side and pressed himself hard against the front of the desk. The squeak of floorboards came nearer until a pair of tattered tartan slippers came to a halt a yard from his head. The major turned on a lamp, then took something from the top of the mantel. Gerald edged forward to get a better look.

It was the wooden box that he had been looking at earlier. The major turned it over in his hands, then slid out a small panel that was part of the inlay. Under the panel was a switch, which in turn popped open another hidden panel on the other side of the box. The major shuffled the box in his hands, sliding panels and pushing buttons until at last there was a faint click and the top of the box opened.

From his hiding place under the desk, Gerald saw the major pull out a square of paper. But then his view was blocked as the major moved. For minutes all Gerald could see was a curtain of dressing gown. Then the major stood back from the desk, put the paper back in the box and returned it to the mantel.

The desk lamp clicked off, the tattered tartan slippers retraced their steps across the floor, and the room was returned to moonlight as the major closed the door behind him.

Sam was the first to emerge. Without a word he went straight to the fireplace, picked up the wooden box, and began pressing his thumbs across its surface.

Gerald popped up beside him.

"It's a Japanese puzzle box," Sam said, continuing to run his fingers over the sides. "Our grandma used to have one—she hid her jewelry in it."

"How does it work?" Gerald asked.

"Built into this pattern there's a number of sliding panels, see?" Sam slid a sliver of wood the width of his thumb out from one side of the box. "Some have buttons under them that trigger another panel to open. Look, this one has a switch on a spring. It acts as a key unlocking a different panel."

A light twang came from inside the box as Sam pushed the switch. "You need to do all the right moves in the right order to open the top."

"How many ways are there to do it?"

"Depends on how many panels in the box. This one looks like it might be about ten steps."

"So how long to open it?"

"You saw the major. If you know the combination it's just a few seconds."

"And if you don't?"

Sam continued to fumble with the box. "We could be here all night."

"Did you see what he put in there?" Ruby asked.

"A piece of paper, but I couldn't see what was on it."

"Another map?"

"Maybe. But it wasn't very big. Not like a page from a book or anything."

Something caught Ruby's eye. "Speaking of books—"

She shone her flashlight onto a bookcase next to the fireplace. It was lined with rows of books all bound in the same leather.

"What is it?" Gerald asked.

"Look at all these books," Ruby said. "They look like they've been bought by the foot. I don't think they've ever been opened."

"So? Maybe the major's not much of a reader."

"Except for this one." Ruby took down a volume; the spine was well worn at the top. She opened the cover. "Does Major Pilkington look like someone who'd be heavily into *The Odyssey*?"

Ruby looked up at the gap in the row of books. Without saying anything she pushed her hand between the volumes and felt for the back of the bookcase.

"Hello."

A hollow clunk sounded behind the grate and the back of the fireplace swung inward.

"Cliché ahoy!" Ruby winked at Gerald. "Let's go."

Sam reluctantly put the puzzle box back on the mantel. With their flashlights lighting the way, Gerald, Sam, and Ruby crouched down and disappeared into the passage behind the fireplace.

CHAPTER SIXTEEN

R uby was the last to crawl through the opening. As she got to her feet the fireplace swung shut behind her. She flashed her flashlight around the doorway but could see no way of getting back into the major's study.

"This better lead somewhere useful," she muttered.

Gerald, Sam, and Ruby found themselves in a gloomy corridor constructed from ancient bricks that formed a peaked arch above their heads. There were some rusted candleholders set into the walls that looked like they hadn't been used for years.

On the floor inside the corridor was a stack of cardboard boxes. Gerald folded back the top of the uppermost one and pulled out a bottle.

"Whiskey," he said, shining his flashlight on the label.

"Must be the major's private stash." But apart from the hoard of booze there was nothing to be found.

Gerald shone his flashlight deeper into the corridor and led the way. They had gone only a dozen paces or so when he stopped and swore.

"What is it?" Sam asked.

"There's a manhole here. I almost fell straight down it."

"Is that all? I thought you'd seen a rat or something."

Gerald swung his flashlight beam into Sam's face. "A rat?"

"I don't like rats, is all," Sam said, shading the light from his eyes. "There's nothing wrong with that, is there?"

"I guess not," Gerald said. He shone the flashlight into the manhole. An iron ladder ran down one side of a sheer vertical shaft. The light petered out before it reached the bottom.

"Waddya think?" he asked the others.

"I don't think we're going to find the peak of eternal light down there," Sam said.

Ruby leaned her chin on Gerald's shoulder to peer into the hole. "We've come this far—we may as well keep going," she said.

Gerald clenched his flashlight between his teeth and lowered his legs into the hole. The ladder rungs were cold on his hands and the scrape of his footsteps echoed into the blackness. Ruby followed, then Sam.

The descent seemed to take forever. With their flash-lights in their teeth, there was no talking, just the rhythmic song of shoes and hands on the metal rungs. After a few minutes Gerald's left foot made contact with the ground; it was so sudden that Ruby landed a shoe on his head.

"Hey!" Gerald protested, spitting his flashlight from his mouth. "Ease up."

"Sorry," Ruby said, dropping beside him. "Where are we?"

They shone their flashlights around to reveal an arched passage identical to the one they had left far above. Still on the ladder, Sam pointed his light into the musty darkness. "Seems to go uphill."

They trudged along the dank corridor. Sam aimed his flashlight at his feet and kept very close to the others.

"So what's with the rat thing?" Gerald asked, keenly aware that Sam was bumping into his back every second step.

"It's their feet," Ruby said before Sam could answer. "He hates the thought of their claws crawling across his skin."

"Shut up, Ruby!" Sam snapped. Then in a calmer voice, "I don't like them, all right?"

"You should see what happens when he sees one," Ruby continued to Gerald. "It's fireworks!"

Sam went into a silent sulk.

Finally the passage came to an end and they were faced with another ladder bolted to a wall, leading up into another shaft, this one about ten feet wide.

"We must be getting close to something interesting," Gerald said, and he pulled himself onto the lower rung.

This climb wasn't as long as the first but instead of opening into a passageway, the ladder stopped a meter short of a blank stone ceiling.

Gerald pulled the flashlight from his mouth and pointed it at the flagstones.

"What's the story?" Ruby called from further down the ladder.

"Dead end," Gerald said. "Shine your lights up here so I can get a better look."

Three beams lit the area by Gerald's head. There was no sign of an opening, no hint of an escape. Gerald was about to suggest they head back to the study and try to find an exit from there when the light caught something on the ceiling.

"Sam!" Gerald called. "Hold your flashlight out a bit and shine the light up from a different angle. That's it."

He flicked off his own flashlight and shoved it in his pocket. Hooking his right foot under a rung and holding onto the top of the ladder with his left hand, he leaned over the shaft and reached up to the ceiling.

"Careful!" Sam said.

"I'm all right," Gerald grunted.

"I'm more worried about who you'll hit on the way down."

Gerald traced his fingertips along a series of grooves in the ceiling.

"What is it?" Ruby asked.

"These lines in the stone, they don't look natural. It's some sort of pattern, I think."

"Like what? A map?" Sam asked.

"No, nothing like that." Gerald turned his head on an angle. "It's a picture, I think."

"A picture of what?"

"It's a picture, in three pieces. Like a jigsaw puzzle. I've got to—"

Gerald climbed another step up the ladder until his shoulders were pressed against the ceiling. He crooked his right knee over the second-top rung and reached behind his head, leaning out across the shaft, stretching both his hands as far across the ceiling as he could.

"Gerald!"

"Just . . . a bit . . . farther . . ."

With a final lunge he managed to hook three fingers into a small indentation in the stone.

"Got it!"

"Got what?" Ruby asked.

But before he could answer, the wrenching sound of metal straining against metal echoed up the chamber.

"What was that?"

Gerald looked down toward Sam's anxious voice but could only see the light from his flashlight wavering below.

"It's the ladder!" Ruby shouted. "It's coming away from the wall!"

With his fingers still wedged in the crack, Gerald fumbled into his pocket with his free hand and grabbed his flashlight. He flashed it against the bricks. Two large rusted bolts had almost pulled free from the wall. The ladder was beginning to move.

"Gerald! You've got to come back."

There was a second grinding creak and with a lurch the top of the ladder broke away from the wall. Gerald gasped. He kicked his right knee free and the ladder tumbled away beneath him. His fingers still clung to the cleft in the ceiling and his body swung back like a pendulum. The flashlight tumbled from his grasp and spun down into the blackness. His back thumped into the opposite wall and Gerald knew at once that he would fall to his death. His fingers couldn't possibly hold his weight. He closed his eyes tight.

Bolts popped like rifle shots from the bricks as the rest of the ladder pulled free. The sound of twisting metal tore into the darkness. But Gerald didn't fall. He opened his eyes and looked down in disbelief to find the balls of his feet balancing on a rung. The ladder now spanned the breadth of the shaft at a steep angle, its bottom still fixed at the ground, its top wedged into the bricks on the opposite side. Gerald was caught at full stretch, three fingers still clutching the crevice in the ceiling and his feet just reaching the rung. With his back hard against the wall, he grabbed another rung with his other hand and held on tight.

Gerald took a deep breath, but his relief shattered as he remembered Sam and Ruby. Had he killed them?

He peered down. The twins were six feet below him, clinging onto the ladder, dangling by their hands above the void. They had held on as the ladder fell, but the jolt when it hit the wall opposite knocked their feet from the rungs.

For a moment no one spoke. Ruby had dropped her flashlight and the only illumination came from the flashlight that Sam still held in one hand, his fingers wrapped around both it and the rung above his head.

Ruby breathed, "Sam, you've got to get your feet onto the ladder, then climb back around the side, like this." She swung a leg forward and hooked a shoe onto a rung. Then she smoothly pulled herself around until she was back on top.

"Okay, Sam, your turn," she panted.

Sam followed his sister's maneuver, hauling himself up, and soon they were both back on the ladder, but this time facing the opposite wall.

"Gerald, are you all right?" Ruby called.

Sam trained his light up onto Gerald's face. He was still stretched across the top of the shaft.

"Not on me," Gerald shouted. "Shine it on the ceiling."

Hands shaking, Sam turned the light back to where

Gerald's fingers were clutching the rock cleft. Gerald could see a series of lines and whorls in a circular pattern on the stone ceiling. He took a tentative step higher up the ladder, giving him the leverage to pull hard. A large doughnut-shaped section of the ceiling turned and clicked into place. Gerald's fingers were now next to another indentation in the stone: a bigger opening, into which he was able to squeeze his fist. He heaved his weight in the opposite direction and an inner ring slowly turned until it too clicked into place.

From below, the pattern on the ceiling was transforming into a distinct picture.

"I can see it," Ruby said. "Just the center piece to go, Gerald."

Rivulets of sweat were streaking across Gerald's face and running into his eyes. He wiped his brow on the sleeve of his outstretched arm.

For the third time, the shivering grind of metal echoed in the pit.

"Hurry, Gerald!" Ruby cried. "The ladder's not going to hold much longer."

Gerald took a deep breath. With the second ring slotted into place, another indentation lined up. He took another step up the ladder and hooked his right foot under a rung. He reached out his other hand to squeeze all his fingers into the space in the stone.

"Come on, Gerald!" Sam stammered. "Hold on."

Gerald dropped his head back and saw Ruby's anxious face staring up at him. He gave her a grim smile then twisted hard at the shoulders, swiveling the central piece until it lined up with the outer rings. Another deep click sounded. Gerald released his hands and, with his stomach muscles almost tearing under the strain, hauled himself back to the ladder.

He looked up at the ceiling. Where before there had been faceless rock there was now a clear image.

"What is it?" whispered Ruby.

"That," said Gerald, still catching his breath, "is the Archer family crest."

Carved into the rock were three forearms, each hand clasping its neighbor by the elbow to form a triangle, with a flaming sun in the center.

"What is that doing here?" Ruby asked.

"Don't know, don't care," said Sam. "How does it get us out of here?"

Gerald stared up at the image.

"That is a very good question."

He again braced his foot under the rung and leaned out across the shaft. He pressed a palm against the central carving of the sun. A thin line appeared around the outside of the crest and with only a little effort from Gerald, the entire centerpiece moved up and across to one side. The dull glow of moonlight filtered through the opening. Gerald flung his hands over the lip and kicked his legs free of the ladder, leaving him swinging.

"Gerald!" Ruby cried.

Gerald's face contorted and with a heave, he pulled himself up and out of the shaft.

"What about us?" Sam's voice rang up from below.

Gerald's face popped over the edge of the hole. "I guess this is here for emergencies." A rope ladder unfurled into the shaft and soon Ruby and Sam were climbing through the opening.

For a minute they sat there, oblivious to where they were, glad to be on a level surface.

"How did you do that, Gerald?" Ruby asked at last. "Holding on by your foot, that leaning out and clinging on by your hands—it was amazing!"

"There's a rock-climbing wall in the school gym back home," Gerald said. "I find chess boring too."

Sam stood and shone his flashlight down into the pit.

"I'm assuming the major doesn't open the hatch that way," he said. "I can't see him hanging by his toes over the top of a mine shaft."

Gerald nodded, wriggling his fingers to get the blood flowing again. "Maybe there's a hook on a stick or whatever; you know, to latch onto that hole in the rock," he said.

"You mean something like this?" Ruby picked up a short rod with a curved metal spike fixed to the end.

Gerald shook his head. "Yes, something like that," he said. "Fat lot of good it is on this side of the hole."

Sam swung the flashlight around them. They were in a small room, not much bigger than a walk-in wardrobe, with a single glass-paneled door. Apart from the rod with the hook, and the circular opening to the shaft below, the stone floor was bare.

"Let's see where we are," Sam said, moving to the door. He turned the handle, the door opened smoothly, and Sam walked through. Gerald and Ruby were still getting to their feet when Sam's cry broke the silence. It sounded like he was having a fit—his breathing was the staccato rattle of a machine gun. Gerald and Ruby bolted through the door. They found him lying on the ground outside the room. His arms were wrapped around his knees, clutching them to his chest. He was shivering and short, tight gasps wracked his lungs. His flashlight lay broken by his feet.

"Sam!" Gerald dropped to his knees. "What's the matter?"

Ruby remained on her feet. She clicked her tongue.

"Ignore him," she said, shaking her head.

"What? But he's terrified!"

Ruby bent down and cooed lightly in her brother's ear, "Sam? Sa-am." Then, to Gerald's astonishment, she slapped him hard across the face.

"Oi! Snap out of it!" Ruby said. "Honestly, it's pathetic."

223

Sam's eyes bulged and he continued to take sharp breaths, but the shivering subsided.

"Ruby! What'd you do that for?" Gerald said. "He's in shock!"

"He's dismal, is what he is." Ruby stood up and put her hands on her hips. "You saw a rat, didn't you?" she said accusingly at Sam.

"B-b-big r-r-rat," Sam stammered from the floor, extending a shaking finger and pointing across the room. "N-n-nasty hairy th-thing, with p-pointy nose and c-c-claws. Came right n-n-near m-m-me."

Ruby rolled her eyes. "To think we're related."

Gerald helped Sam to his feet.

"Quite a defense mechanism you've got there," he said.

"Th-th-thanks."

They were standing in a large, rectangular room. A barrel-vaulted roof of grimy glass allowed a good view of the moon high above. On either side were tall stone structures, like enormous gray building blocks. At the end was a set of glass doors and through them, at the top of a rise, was Beaconsfield, dark against the night sky.

"Where are we?" Gerald asked, stepping slowly down the middle of the room.

"There was a rat, you know," Sam said, by way of explanation, sticking close to Gerald. "A very big one."

"Oh, leave off about the rat, Sam," Ruby snapped.

"We're sick of hearing about it. All that fuss over a little rodent." She had Sam's flashlight and was smacking it into the palm of her hand, trying to get it to work again.

"Big rodent," Sam corrected her, holding his hands apart to demonstrate a creature the size of a small dog.

Ruby let out a loud *tsk* and smacked the flashlight into her palm again. "There! That's got it."

The torch flickered to life. It splashed light onto one of the stone structures by Ruby's head. Wedged into the block, a foot from Ruby's nose, was a human skull. Out of an eye socket writhed a snake, straight at her.

Ruby's scream woke every living thing at Beaconsfield.

Chapter Seventeen

The knife sliced through the soft pink flesh before hitting the bone beneath.

Gerald smacked his lips. "This steak is delicious, Mrs. Rutherford." He stabbed another piece with his fork from the china plate and popped it in his mouth.

"So is this bacon," Sam mumbled through stuffed cheeks. "Is there any more?"

Mrs. Rutherford stacked extra rashers onto Sam's plate beside some fried tomato and poached eggs.

"You two have woken with healthy appetites this morning," she said. "You must have slept well. It's the country air, you know."

Gerald and Sam didn't dare look at each other. Across the breakfast table, Ruby made heavy going of pouring herself a glass of orange juice.

"You're not hungry, Miss Ruby?" Mrs. Rutherford asked, bustling around the table to help her with the juice jug. "Not feeling poorly, are you?"

Ruby shook her head. "Maybe I'll have a small bowl of cereal," she said.

Ruby was still trying to recover from her encounter with the skull the night before. After the last of her scream drained from her lungs, Gerald had grabbed her by the elbow and dragged her toward the door. "They're carvings," he told her as they ran. The flashlight picked up details of other grotesque sculptures in the shadows—more skulls, snakes, howling demons, goblins, and other beasts. They had dashed into the night, the lights of Beaconsfield turning on behind them, the sound of dogs baying in the distance.

Mrs. Rutherford fussed around the sideboard. "Interesting chatter in the town this morning," she said, as if thinking out loud. "All manner of talk about a ruckus at Beaconsfield overnight."

The sound of cutlery scraping on china came to an abrupt halt. Sam stopped chewing, a sliver of bacon still poking out from his lips. Ruby glanced up, a spoonful of cereal halfway to her mouth. Gerald clutched a knife and fork in either hand by the side of his plate. "Is that right?" he said, in as innocent a voice as he could manage.

"What sort of ruckus would that be, Mrs. Rutherford?" Ruby asked, ignoring the snickers from Gerald and Sam.

"In the family crypt, so the butcher tells me. I hear the police are up there this morning having a look around."

"A crypt," Sam said. "That'd be full of some scary things, wouldn't you think, Ruby?" His sister ignored him.

"I've not seen inside it," Mrs. Rutherford said. "But I hear tell it's not for the fainthearted."

"I can imagine," Ruby said, keeping her eyes away from her brother.

"Mrs. Piggins from the baker's said there was a break-in. Some sort of midsummer's pagan ritual, she says. All manner of shrieking and caterwauling going on."

Gerald bit his lower lip. "Just a bit of screaming, was there?" Both Sam and Ruby took a sudden interest in the contents of their breakfast plates.

"She said it was the hippies what done it, but my guess would be local children. Always happens during school holidays."

"Sorry, did you say hippies?" Gerald said.

"Yes. This district has a reputation for ancient magic, and it attracts people who go in for that sort of thing." Mrs. Rutherford topped up their glasses with orange juice. "This place has been the center of all sorts of myths over time. For one thing, it's supposed to be the final resting place of the Holy Grail."

"The one King Arthur and his knights of the round table spent their lives looking for?" Sam asked.

"The very same. They say taking a sip from that holy cup will bring eternal life. Some people still believe it's buried around here somewhere. Avonleigh was named after King Arthur's fabled realm of Avalon."

They continued their breakfast in silence. The moment Mrs. Rutherford excused herself to attend to some matters in the kitchen, Sam and Gerald both started talking.

"D'you think the casket the major's looking for contains the Holy Grail?" Sam said.

"It's got to!" Gerald said. "The major's getting on. He probably thinks drinking from the cup would mean he'd live forever."

"Yeah, and maybe the peak of eternal light is actually something to do with eternal life. What did the major read from that piece of paper? The peak of eternal light will show the way? The way to what?"

"To how to live forever!" Gerald said.

Both boys turned to Ruby.

She sniffed.

"Bit far-fetched, don't you think?" she said.

"Waddya mean?" Sam protested.

"I mean really—King Arthur and the Holy Grail. Sounds like a story someone made up to get the tourists in."

"But it's a famous legend," Gerald said. "People have

been hunting for that cup for hundreds of years. Heaps of books have been written about it."

Ruby laughed. "You'd have to be pretty dim to believe a story like that."

"Did I mention that my sister has no imagination? Hey!" A bread roll bounced off Sam's head.

"I may have no imagination, but I am a very good shot," Ruby said with a self-satisfied grin.

Just then Mrs. Rutherford returned to the dining room.

"Mr. Fry will be ready to drive you into town in twenty minutes. Master Gerald, you'll find there aren't many clothes shops, but you should be able to find something more comfortable."

"Thanks, Mrs. Rutherford," Gerald said. Mr. Prisk's choice of suits and shirts was quite limiting.

"You'll enjoy town. It's very quaint—lots of old buildings and such. And of course, you'll climb the Tor."

Gerald looked confused.

"It's the big hill overlooking Glastonbury," Mrs. Rutherford explained. "There used to be a church up there. All that's left now is the tower—St. Michael's Tower. You can walk up there from the town. See the whole area from the top, right into Beaconsfield."

Not for the first time, Gerald gave Mrs. Rutherford a curious look. She seemed to have an eerie sense of knowing what they were thinking. She smiled back at him.

"This year the Tor's being used for the midsummer cele-brations," she said. "They're burning the witch up there, which'll be nice."

"Uh, burning a witch?" Ruby said.

"That's right, Miss Ruby. This year's special because it's the first time in a hundred years that the moon becomes full on the stroke of midnight on Midsummer's Eve. There's normally fireworks and bonfires and the like. The hippies dance around banging drums and having a bit of a sing-song. This year they're strapping a straw dummy to a big wooden wheel, setting it alight, and rolling it down the Tor. It's an ancient fertility ritual, apparently—meant to make the crops grow tall and strong. This'll be the first time they've done it for years."

"Really?" Ruby said. "Why did they stop?"

"Last time the wheel set Mr. Parson's barley crop on fire and wiped out half his apple trees."

Gerald stifled a laugh. "He can't have been too happy about that."

"No," said Mrs. Rutherford in a reflective tone. "I expect that's another reason the hippies aren't too popular."

During the short drive Mr. Fry was even more surly than he'd been the previous day. He pulled up at the start of a winding avenue of shops in the center of the town, and

Gerald, Sam, and Ruby piled out of the car.

"I guess we'll meet you back here in a couple of hours?" Gerald said. Fry mumbled a response and motored off.

"He keeps growing on you, doesn't he?" Ruby said.

"Yeah," Sam said. "Like a tumor. Come on, Gerald. Let's go shopping."

The street was starting to fill with an odd mixture of people. There were old ladies wearing old-style dresses and cardigans, despite the warm weather, trundling shopping trolleys and crisscrossing between the grocer, the baker, and the butcher. And there were clusters of young people with dreadlocks, wearing baggy clothes of every color, chatting on the footpaths.

Sam watched as a man strode past. He had braids in his long beard and a yellow jester's hat on his head, and he carried a wooden staff with bells and ribbons tied to the top. A bright orange cape billowed from his shoulders. "I take it that's a hippie, then?" Sam said.

They crossed the narrow roadway and wandered into the first clothes shop they came to. Gerald flicked through a few racks of assorted shirts and pants.

"There seems to be a lot of purple velvet, doesn't there?" he said.

Ruby shook her head. "And a lot of tie-dyed stuff as well. This might be harder than I thought."

After visiting half a dozen other shops and trying on

some hilarious combinations of New Age frockery, they emerged with an armful of bags. Gerald wore a standard set of jeans and T-shirt.

"That feels better!" Gerald said, stuffing the bags into his backpack. He spotted a charity bin in the grounds of a small stone church and dropped Mr. Prisk's suit inside. "I'm sure someone will appreciate this."

Sam clapped his hands together. "How about a walk up the Tor, then?"

In a few minutes they were well away from the town and wandering along a narrow tree-lined lane. The sun was warm on their faces and a few fluffy white clouds dotted a perfect summer sky.

Sam read from a pamphlet he'd picked up in one of the shops. "It says here that King Arthur's grave is in the grounds of Glastonbury Abbey. See, there's some truth to those old myths."

"Oh please!" Ruby scoffed. "The monks at those old abbeys relied on gifts from pilgrims and visitors to survive. You'd 'discover' King Arthur's grave too if it meant more tourists coming to town."

"There's not a poetic bone in your body, is there?" Sam said.

Ruby opened her mouth to reply, but Gerald interrupted, "Look!"

Rising before them was the Tor, a lone tower on top like

a candle on a birthday cake. The hill was bare of trees, and the grass was cropped short by a flock of sheep.

The walk to the top didn't take long, and near the summit, steps cut into the grassy slope made the final climb look easy.

"Come on," Sam said. "Race you."

They scrambled the final fifty yards to the top and collapsed on a broad stone area at the foot of the tower.

Catching his breath, Gerald gazed up at the last remains of St. Michael's Church. The square stone tower was stained with lichen and rose up high above them. With arched windows on each side and topped with a parapet, it was an impressive structure.

"Now that would be a rotten job," Sam said.

"What's that?"

"Carting all the stone up the hill to build this thing."

They walked through a tall arched doorway at the base of the tower and joined some tourists inside. They looked up to see the tower had no roof—the sky was clear above them. Sun streamed through the windows, illuminating the dust-filled air. Near the top, jutting out of the thick walls, were narrow stone ledges.

"They must have supported floorboards, I guess," Gerald said. "You'd get a great view from up there."

Back outside they scanned the horizon. The surrounding landscape was a mostly flat patchwork of hedged fields.

"There it is," Ruby said, pointing to a spot in the distance. "The house at Beaconsfield."

Gerald shaded his eyes and followed Ruby's extended arm. Sure enough, among the hodgepodge of orchards and meadows, the distinctive clock tower at Beaconsfield could be seen.

"Look how flat it is," Ruby said. "Where on earth would you find a peak of eternal light around here?"

Sam's voice carried across to them from the other side of the tower.

"Check this out."

They found Sam on a small grassy terrace on the other side of the hill, about twenty yards down from the base of the tower. He stood by a pile of sticks and branches. Below them, like a trail of ants, a line of people was snaking up from the bottom of the hill, carrying bundles of twigs and larger pieces of wood. Next to the pile was a large wooden wheel, like a cable drum, with what looked like a scarecrow tied to its side.

"Meet the witch!" Sam grinned.

Gerald stooped down and picked up a bucket, half full of thick black goo.

"They've covered it with pitch," he said. "This stuff will go off like a bomb when they light it."

Gerald, Sam, and Ruby watched the procession of colorfully dressed people carrying the wood up the hill, and joined the trail when it turned back toward town.

Then, out of nowhere, Ruby said, "Why would anyone have a secret passage to a crypt?" She shivered at the memory of the night before.

"Been weighing on your mind, has it?" Gerald chuckled. "I'm still trying to figure out why my family crest was in there."

They reached the spot where Mr. Fry had dropped them earlier that morning. Sam checked his watch.

"Still a bit before we get picked up. What do you wanna do to kill time?"

Gerald spotted a lane lined with small boutiques.

"What say we take a look down—"

Gerald stopped midsentence. He was staring at a girl walking up the lane toward them.

"You!" Gerald said in amazement.

Alisha Gupta looked at Gerald. She was dressed in designer jeans and top, a line of shopping bags strung up one arm, and a pair of large sunglasses on her head. She looked nothing like the demure daughter that they'd seen by her father's side at the museum.

Alisha looked at Gerald blankly. "Do I know you?"

"From the museum," Gerald said. "We were outside Professor McElderry's office when you and your father arrived the other day."

Alisha looked each of them up and down, paying special

attention to Ruby's runners. Ruby pressed her lips together, fighting the urge to say something.

"No," Alisha said at last. "I think I would have remembered if I'd seen you before."

"Oh," Gerald said, deflated. "What brings you to Glastonbury?"

Alisha let out a practiced sigh. "Some tiresome party that Father has been invited to. And I have to attend, apparently."

Ruby could contain herself no longer. "Oh, how terribly, terribly boring for you!"

Alisha spared Ruby a look of disdain. "Lovely to chat," she said. "But I have things to do. So, ta ta." She went to walk away, then paused. "Oh, by the way," she said to Ruby, laying a hand on her arm. "There are some lovely shoe shops back in there. Might pay to check them out, yes?" Then in a haze of jasmine scent, Alisha strode up the street like it was a catwalk.

"That little—" Ruby was incensed.

"Never mind," Gerald said. "Must be the major's party she's going to. Maybe her father's tied up in all this after all."

Sam glanced at his sister. He couldn't resist. "So, you gonna check out the shoe shops?"

"And why don't you go stick—"

Gerald stepped between them.

"There's a bookshop. Let's take a look."

A bell tinkled as they opened the front door. Then they were hit with the thick odor of decaying paper.

Gerald gagged as they went inside. "Get the feeling this place has been here for a while?"

The shop was a maze of tall bookshelves stuffed to overflowing. Books were piled everywhere: on the floor, on windowsills, on each step of a narrow staircase that disappeared up the back wall.

Ruby stepped carefully over a ragged bundle of magazines tied with twine. "Makes McElderry's office look like a library, doesn't it?" she said.

At the back of the shop, the counter and cash register were covered in rolls of paper.

Perched on a stool behind the counter sat a round man with a face like an enormous walnut.

"Hello, Gerald," came a gravelly voice. "Fancy a peppermint?"

Chapter Eighteen

"Mr. Hoskins!" Gerald said. "What are you doing here?" It was the first time he had seen the man since his great-aunt's funeral.

Hoskins shrugged. "Tryin' to make an honest living, sunshine. People aren't buying books like they used to."

Ruby glanced around the shop. "Can people find any books in here?" she asked.

"Of course they can," Hoskins said tersely. "May not be the book they was looking for, but they can find all sorts of good stuff if they take the time."

"Mr. Hoskins, this is my friend Ruby and her brother, Sam," Gerald said. "They're staying with me at Avonleigh."

Hoskins gave the Valentine twins a suspicious glare. "Yes,

I heard you'd moved in. Is my sister takin' good care of yer?"

Ruby stared at the man. "Mrs. Rutherford is your sister?" she asked. "But she seems so—"

"Bossy? Fussy? Nosy? Yes, I know all of that. Sisters, eh! But what can you do?" He gave Sam a knowing look. Sam opened his mouth to respond, but Gerald launched himself between them.

"Mr. Hoskins, I'd like to ask you something," Gerald interjected, keen to avoid further hostilities between Ruby and Sam.

"And what would that be?" Hoskins said.

"At the church, the day of the funeral, you said something about Geraldine. You said she had to keep away from me to protect something. What did you mean?"

Hoskins chewed hard on his peppermint.

"Not yet," he said at last. "You've still got to—"

The sound of a bell tinkling signaled another customer entering the shop. Hoskins glanced at the front door, and his manner changed in an instant. He grabbed Sam, who had been flicking through a stack of old comic books, and frog-marched him to the staircase.

"Looking for Christmas presents?" Hoskins asked. "Very wise. You'll find a good selection on the second floor."

"Christmas presents?" Sam said. "It's the middle of June."

Hoskins leaned in close. "I heard you weren't too bright—upstairs," he whispered hoarsely, delivering one final shove before ushering Gerald and Ruby after him.

As they disappeared up the rickety staircase, they could hear Hoskins's voice drifting up after them. "And a good morning to you, Major. Anything in particular you're lookin' for today, Major?"

The second floor was less messy than downstairs but not by much. Bookshelves snaked off into the shadows, looking as if they could collapse in a bookslide at any moment. Gerald, Sam, and Ruby hovered by the top of the stairs, straining to hear what was going on below.

"Who is that guy?" Ruby whispered.

"I met him at Geraldine's funeral," Gerald said. "Old friend of the family, apparently. He seems to know everyone."

"I can't believe he's Mrs. Rutherford's brother. Talk about opposites."

"Maybe they're twins." Sam grinned.

Before Ruby could return fire, Gerald hissed for quiet. "Ssshhh! Listen!"

They could just make out the major's voice.

"That book about the mythology of this area—the one I found here last month—I need it."

Hoskins's reply was short and to the point. "It's not for sale, Major. Wasn't then, isn't now."

"Then I'll just take a look at it. Upstairs, is it?"

The sound of advancing footsteps set Gerald, Sam, and Ruby into action.

"Scatter," Gerald whispered.

They each shot down a different aisle between the bookcases.

Gerald wound his way around towers of magazines. He checked left and right, looking for a bolt-hole to hide in. Without warning, his vision blurred in a haze of melting hues. He held out a hand to steady himself against a mountain of rotting newspapers. A bundle of magazines toppled onto the floor behind him as he gripped a shelf for support. Gerald shut his eyes but they were awash with whorls of color, like an oil slick spreading out across a lake. Then his vision cleared enough to see along one aisle. A small niche seemed to glow out of the shadows. He was drawn toward it. He stumbled, knocking more volumes to the floor, and found the tight nook on the bottom shelf of a broad wooden bookcase. He crawled in and crouched on a small pile of books, hugging his knees to his chest. Gerald shook his head and managed to clear his sight. He struggled to get his thoughts straight—he hadn't felt that way since the Reading Room at the museum. He had barely pulled his feet in underneath him when the major's stern voice rumbled close by.

"Haven't you heard of cataloging, Hoskins?" the major said. "This place is a shambles."

Hoskins was right behind him. "Course I have," he said. "Just introduced a new system—everything's arranged by color."

"What?"

"From red to violet. I like to call it the rainbow selection."

Gerald looked about him. It was true. Every book, magazine, and journal around him was the same color. He was in the indigo section.

"You order everything by color!" the major said. "How the devil are you supposed to find anything?"

"The same way you find anything worth finding, Major. Perseverance!" Hoskins said. "Best of luck." And with that, the man trotted back downstairs.

Gerald sat in his alcove, not daring to move. He was surprised when he heard a second set of footsteps making its way through the stacks. Then a familiar voice piped up.

"So what color is this book, Major?"

Gerald's eyes widened. It was Pinstripe Trousers from the Rattigan Club. Arthur Chesterfield.

"Don't remember," grumbled the major, his voice coming ever closer to Gerald's hiding place. "Blue, maybe? It's in French. *Mythologie de l'Angleterre régionale*, or something like that—*The Mythology of Regional England*."

Chesterfield sniffed. "Sounds dreadful."

Book covers slapped against each other. Then Chesterfield called out again. "How do we know it's here?"

"It's got to be here," the major grumbled. "The page that described the peak of eternal light—I tore it from that book. There must be more information in there."

Gerald was startled as the major's legs came into view only feet away. He was even more startled when he glanced down at his own feet. Poking out from under one grubby shoe, embossed in faded gold, was the word *Mythologie*. Gerald's eyes bulged wide.

The major hesitated in his tracks, then slowly turned in Gerald's direction.

"Maybe down here."

The brown shoes came to rest by Gerald's feet. Then, to Gerald's dismay, the major squatted down and started searching through a pile of books right next to his shoulder. He stared aghast at his own face reflected in the major's glass eye. The only thing between him and discovery was the major's bulbous red nose. Gerald stopped breathing. His heart thumped inside his chest. He could feel his pulse pounding in his temples. His eyelids peeled back and his chest tightened. Just as his vision was turning white, Chesterfield called out, "What about the police, Major? Have you heard from them since the club?"

Major Pilkington paused in his search and his glassy stare lifted out of view as he stood up. Gerald sucked cool welcoming air in through his nostrils and let his head fall back in relief.

"No," the major said. "They don't suspect a thing. They'll be searching for clues in that Tube station for months. Those kids did us a favor."

"You must be joking!" Chesterfield said, tension clear in his voice. "If a bunch of kids could track us down, the police won't be far behind."

"That was luck."

"Luck's a fool," Chesterfield snarled. "We need to find a permanent solution to those three—and sooner rather than later. There's too much at stake."

The major paused and Gerald could sense the friction between the men.

"Let's find this diamond casket first," the major said. "Then we can take care of the kids."

For the next ten minutes the only thing to be heard was the sound of books being shoved around, then Chesterfield groaned, "This is hopeless. We're never going to find anything here."

The major muttered a violent oath and the two of them retreated down the stairs. Gerald sucked in a lungful of air and rolled out of his hiding spot onto the floor. He scrambled around to grab the book he'd been sitting on. The front was covered with dusty prints from his shoes, but there staring at him was the title: *Mythologie de l'Angleterre régionale* by Camille Flammarion.

He opened it up right there on the grimy floorboards. Ruby appeared and leaned her chin on his shoulder.

"How did you find that?" she gasped.

"Dumb luck, I think." He didn't feel like explaining the weird vision that had led him to the book. He flicked to the index.

"Oh no. It's in French." He turned to Ruby. "Do you speak French?"

Ruby shook her head. "Only if you want to order a coffee with milk."

"Take a look. You never know."

Ruby ran her finger down the page. "Hmm," she muttered. "*Très difficile*. Look. There's a chapter on Somerset—that's the area around here." She thumbed through the pages and turned up a section of dense text. There was a rudimentary map of the district, with the Tor at the center and a series of circles emanating outward, like ripples on a pond. Each one was marked with a number.

"This map must be a couple of hundred years old at least," she muttered, poring over the detail. "Look, the town's shown here and that must be the abbey."

Gerald shifted to get a better look. He and Ruby hovered shoulder to shoulder.

"There's no sign of any peak of eternal light?" Gerald asked.

"No, but look. This must be where the major tore out the page. You can see where it's come away from the spine."

Gerald flicked back to the map and traced his index finger out from the Tor.

"This must be about where Beaconsfield is," he said, tapping the page. "What do you reckon these numbers are?"

"Distance from the Tor maybe? A lot of maps show that if there's a central point of interest," Ruby said.

"Maybe." Gerald studied the page. "But look at how far apart the circles are from each other. The distance is the same, but the numbers don't go up by equal amounts. They're all over the place."

"Well, if they're not distance markers, what are they? Height above sea level or something?"

"Or," Gerald suggested, "they could be page numbers."

Ruby looked at the map. The number on the circle that ran through Beaconsfield was 337.

In a tangle of hands and a flurry of paper they flipped the pages until the book lay open at page 337.

"Oh my," said Ruby.

Gerald gazed at the page, then said, "Where's Sam? He should see this."

On page 337 was a black-ink drawing. Gerald ran his fingers down the paper. "This is starting to freak me out," he said.

The drawing depicted a landscape with St. Michael's Tower on the left and the clock tower at Beaconsfield on the right. Dominating the picture were four identical images, joined by a diagonal line running down the page from left to right. The images were each of a triangle formed by three forearms clasped hand-to-elbow with a blazing sun in the center.

"Your family crest is turning up in some interesting places, Gerald," Ruby said.

Gerald shook his head. The crest on the far left, the highest on the page, appeared to be suspended in the sky. The next one sat squarely on the top of St. Michael's Tower, and a third hovered above the Beaconsfield clock tower. The last crest, on the far right of the drawing, was on the ground. Printed under the sketch was a single line of text: *Pleine lune du solstice de l'été.*

Gerald dragged a hand across his forehead. "What on earth does all this mean?" he groaned.

Suddenly, Sam's head popped around the corner. He was holding a silver-gray sphere slightly smaller than a volleyball.

"The question isn't what on earth," he said, holding up the ball. "It's what on moon."

Ruby gave him a look. "What are you on about?" she said.

"I'm on about the peak of eternal light, dimwit," he said. "Remember—the thing that's going to show us the way. We've been going about it all wrong."

"Oh yeah? How?"

"Well, think about it. Is there any place in the world that has eternal light—where the sun never sets? Not around here, that's for sure."

"So where is it, Einstein?" Ruby said.

Sam held up the gray sphere in front of him. "It's on the moon, actually." A grin spread across his face.

Gerald and Ruby looked blankly at Sam.

"What did I tell you?" Ruby said at last. "A complete idiot."

"What do you call this then, genius?" Sam thrust out the gray ball. Gerald took it and saw that it was a globe, not of the earth but of the moon. Sam pointed to a spot at the top. Near the north pole and by an enormous crater was written: "Peak of Eternal Light."

Ruby was dumbfounded.

"Where did you find this?" she asked.

"I hid in a cupboard in the green section," Sam said. "Among a bunch of atlases, maps, and stuff. This was in a box."

Gerald took the globe and tossed it in his hands.

"A place on the moon where the sun never sets . . . in eternal light," he said. "But how does that show the way to the diamond casket?"

Ruby picked up the book and studied the drawing again.

"Look at this crest, the one that's hanging in the air," she said. "What if that's the moon?"

"The moon?"

"What say the peak of eternal light beams down from the moon onto the Tor—that's the crest on top of St Michael's Tower. And it's then reflected onto the clock tower at Beaconsfield, where the next crest is."

"Then what?" Gerald said.

"From there it's reflected onto the place where the diamond casket is hidden. The four crests are like points of light, marking a path from the moon to the Tor, to the clock tower and then to the hiding place. *Pic de la lumière éternelle indiquera le chemin*—the peak of eternal light will show the way."

"Gee, I dunno," Gerald said.

Sam looked over his sister's shoulder. "Come on, Gerald. You said St. Michael's Tower looked like a lighthouse—maybe this is the light. And look at the name of the major's place—Beaconsfield! That's gotta stand for something."

Gerald looked unconvinced. "But we were there last night. The moon wasn't shining any spotlights."

Sam took the book from Ruby. "Look what's written here. *Lune* is French for moon, you know, as in lunar. And *solstice* is midsummer. I bet this means something about a full moon during the summer solstice."

"What did Mrs. Rutherford say?" Ruby chimed in. "It's the first time in more than a hundred years that there'll be a full moon on the stroke of midnight on Midsummer's Eve. Remember? The hippies are getting all excited about it. Maybe the position of the moon has to be just right for this to work."

"And maybe that's why the major kept going on about running out of time," Sam said. "If this happens only once every hundred years you don't want to be waiting for the next one."

The Valentines stared at Gerald. He looked from one to the other.

"Light has to reflect off something," he said at last. "Like a mirror or glass."

"The weathervane on top of the clock tower," Sam said with a snap of his fingers. "Remember? It didn't move, even though there was a breeze. It held its position as if it was pointing somewhere specific."

Gerald looked at the moon in his hands, then back at his friends.

"All right, let's say that's what's meant to happen. The full moon on the stroke of midnight on the longest day of the year beams onto the Tor, bounces off St. Michael's Tower and onto the weathervane on the clock tower at Beaconsfield, which then miraculously guides us to the diamond casket. But we still have no clue what the diamond casket is or why everyone under the sun—"

"And the moon," said Sam.

"Yes, no idea why everyone under the sun and the moon is looking for it."

Ruby shrugged. "Sounds as good a theory as we're going to get."

"That's settled then," Sam said. "We just need to be somewhere near the clock tower at Beaconsfield at midnight tomorrow night. And we'll see where the light takes us."

Gerald shook his head. "I thought you didn't have any imagination," he said to Ruby.

Ruby smiled. "Only when everything else fails."

Chapter Nineteen

Downstairs, the bookshop was deserted. A handwritten sign saying BACK WHEN I FEEL LIKE IT hung on a peg on the inside of the front door.

Out on the footpath, Gerald, Ruby, and Sam formed a huddle.

Ruby spoke first. "What do you think that Chesterfield bloke meant when he said he wanted a permanent solution?" It sounded like she didn't want to hear the answer.

"Whatever it is, it can't be good," Sam said. "Reckon we should go to the police?"

"And tell them what?" Gerald said. "That we've been handed our second death threat in a week? They'll laugh even harder than last time."

"You're right," Ruby said. "Especially since it involves

the major. It's not like we've been too convincing in that department so far."

"Okay," Sam said. "No police."

Ruby grabbed Gerald's wrist and looked at his watch. "Mrs. Rutherford asked me to pick up a few things from the grocer's," she said. "Wait here for Mr. Fry and I'll be back in a few minutes." She disappeared into the crowd of morning shoppers, leaving Gerald and Sam outside the bookshop.

"How is it that grown-ups only ever ask girls to run their errands?" Gerald said to Sam.

"Good arrangement, if you ask me," Sam said.

They watched the passing parade of locals, hippies, and tourists meandering down the cobbled streets, in and out of shop doors. Gerald was about to suggest they duck off to find a drink when he noticed someone coming out of a liquor store across the road.

"I don't believe it," Gerald said to Sam. "It's Uncle Sid."

A large man lumbered onto the footpath, a bottle of whiskey in each hand. He was followed by a boy and a girl.

"Look, it's the pig's arse—uh, Octavia," Gerald said.

Sam studied the trio. "And the kid who looks like he's constipated. That'd be Zebedee?"

Gerald was about to reply when Sid looked up. Their eyes met across the street.

"Oi!" Sid called. "Wilkins!"

"Uh-oh," Gerald mumbled.

Before he could do anything, Sid had stamped across the road, Octavia and Zebedee following close behind.

"Moved in, have you?" Sid demanded as he towered over Gerald, casting a broad shadow across him. "You all comfy in my house, are you?" The menace in Sid's eyes was electric, like a starving dog denied a bone.

Gerald retreated a step.

"I didn't know you were living at Avonleigh," Gerald said. "There was a fire in London. Mr. Prisk said I had to come down here and—"

"And boot us out of our home," Zebedee said, his lip curling into a snarl. It was like looking at a boiled-down version of his father. "Whatsamatter? Didn't you inherit enough houses?" He shoved Gerald in the chest.

"Hey!" Gerald protested as he stumbled backward and fell onto the footpath.

Sid advanced on him, a smirk greeting his son's thuggery. "That house was mine, Wilkins. Geraldine all but promised it to me. That and a whole lot more."

Sam helped Gerald up. "I didn't know any of this was going to happen," Gerald said. "I didn't even know Geraldine."

"Then why did she leave the sodding lot to you?" Sid demanded. He raised one of the bottles above his head like a caveman wielding a club.

"No!" Sam shouted. Gerald shut his eyes.

A gloved hand wrapped itself around Sid's raised arm.

"Your usual breakfast shopping, Mr. Archer?" It was the cool voice of Mr. Fry. He wrestled the bottle from Sid's grip.

"Mr. Fry!" Gerald said in amazed relief, still half expecting to wear a bottle of Scotch across his forehead.

"I trust there will be no more unpleasantness," Fry said to Sid. "Or perhaps you would rather I call the police again."

Sid stared daggers at Gerald.

"Leave off, Fry," he muttered. "What Wilkins and I have to talk about is of no interest to you."

"Rest assured, Mr. Archer," Fry said with a sniff, "anything you have to say is of no interest to me. Now if you'll excuse us, we are expected for lunch at Avonleigh. I understand Mrs. Rutherford has prepared a particularly magnificent spread today."

Fry ushered Gerald and Sam into the back of the Rolls. The car cruised past Gerald's uncle and his cousins. Sid's face was contorted in purple rage.

"You'll get yours, Wilkins!" he bellowed at the vehicle, spittle flying in all directions. "I'd watch my back if I was you!"

Gerald looked through the rear window at the man screaming on the footpath. The list of people who had it in for him seemed to be growing.

"Mr. Fry?" Sam asked, leaning his elbows on the back of the driver's seat. "Does this car have bulletproof glass?"

Fry allowed himself a thin smirk. "Naturally. This is a bespoke Rolls-Royce—custom-built for Miss Archer. There are four inches of ballistic steel encasing the driver and passenger cells. You have nothing to worry about from Sid Archer." Fry thought for a second. "At least not while you're in the car."

"I never thought I'd say this," Gerald said, "but I was glad to see you back there."

Fry stared unblinking at the road ahead. "Young sir may be a royal PITA, but sir is the master of the house."

Sam sniggered. Gerald looked at him curiously. "Who's Peter?"

"P-I-T-A," said Sam with a grin. "Pain in the arse."

Gerald rolled his eyes. "And I thought he might have stopped hating me."

Up ahead, Ruby emerged from a grocer's shop carrying two bags. She waved as she spotted the Rolls.

"You'll never guess who I just saw," she said as she clambered into the back. "Professor McElderry!"

"What?" Gerald and Sam chimed. "What's he doing here?"

"I have no idea," Ruby said, catching her breath. "He went into that pub."

"So everyone on our suspect list is in town," Gerald said, shaking his head. "Major Pilkington and Chesterfield, the Guptas, and now Professor McElderry. Not to mention my uncle Sid."

"You saw your uncle?" Ruby asked.

Gerald described the scene outside the bookshop.

"That was close," she said. "Lucky Mr. Fry came back."

Sam clicked his fingers. "And there's another suspect! Don't forget Fry. He could have been the inside man for the fire at Gerald's place, remember?"

There was an awkward silence. Ruby coughed into her hand and pointed a discreet finger over Sam's shoulder. Sam turned to see the back of Fry's head only inches away. The privacy screen was open.

"Ah-hah," Sam breathed.

Without a word, Fry leaned forward and flicked a switch on the dashboard. The screen slid silently into place.

Dinner that night consisted of a three-bird roast: a goose stuffed with a chicken stuffed with a pheasant.

"I know it's not Christmas, but I couldn't resist," Mrs. Rutherford trilled as she piled their plates with second help-ings.

Ruby soaked up some gravy with a forkful of mashed potato. "I can see why your uncle was angry at moving out of here," she said between mouthfuls. "I don't ever want to leave. This is delicious!"

Gerald waited until Mrs. Rutherford had returned to the kitchen before taking a folded sheet of paper from his pocket.

"I've tried to make some sense of this whole thing," he said, spreading the paper. "I've drawn up a list of who's who and where they all fit in."

On the paper was an elaborate matrix with all the suspects listed across the top. Boxes ran down the page, labeled Motive, Opportunity, and Alibi. Inside each box Gerald had scribbled notes.

"What's that next to everyone's names?" Ruby asked from the end of the table.

Gerald blushed. "Um, just sketches of the suspects."

Sam inspected the page. "They're good."

"Thanks," Gerald said. "I get bored easily."

"Okay then. Who done it?" Ruby asked.

Gerald cleared his throat. "I think we're all agreed that Major Pilkington and Chesterfield have the diamond. I heard them say so at the Rattigan Club."

"What about the major's alibi?" Sam said. "Wasn't he having dinner with Lord Fungus-guts at the club the night the diamond was stolen?"

Gerald nodded. "That's right. But only one of them needed to be inside the elephant statue to steal the diamond. Dinner at the club was the perfect alibi for the major. He helped seal Chesterfield in the elephant statue, then winched him up into the Reading Room sometime before Lethbridge came on duty. Then he scooted back in time for dinner."

Ruby settled back into her chair. "Okay, that sounds reasonable. But what about the thin man? Where does he fit in?"

"This is where it's a bit of a leap," Gerald said. "I reckon this diamond, this Noor Jehan, came with the casket as a set, and they're worth more together than separately. You remember the professor saying he'd heard rumors of a diamond casket, then Sam finds a drawing of it on his desk. The thin man was more interested in the casket than he ever was in the diamond. And the major and Chesterfield are desperately searching for the casket even though they've already got the diamond."

"So the casket is worth more than the diamond, you think?" Sam said.

Gerald hesitated. "I think the two together must be pretty special."

Ruby thought a moment before turning to Gerald.

"Then how does Geraldine come into it?"

Gerald frowned, concentrating. "It's all tied to the diamond casket. I think the thin man was hired by someone to find that casket, no matter what. He must have suspected that since Geraldine helped bring the diamond out here she must have known about the casket. Then she paid the price."

"So who hired the thin man to find the casket?" Ruby asked.

"It could be any of them," Gerald said. "It could be Gupta, trying to find the partner to his diamond. It could be the professor trying to find it for the museum, or for himself. It could be the major and Chesterfield. It could even be Lethbridge."

"Lethbridge?" Ruby said with surprise. "He doesn't seem smart enough to be tied up in all this."

"Who better to find a crim to do the dirty work than a copper," Sam said. "They spend half their lives with villains."

Ruby lowered her voice. "What about Mr. Fry?"

"There's every chance the thin man bribed him to get into Geraldine's house," Gerald said. "Those stolen envelopes must contain some answers."

"Do you think Fry heard me in the car?" Sam asked.

"Gee, I dunno," Ruby said. "He must have been all of three inches away when you opened your fat yap."

"That's unfair," Sam said.

"Let's assume he heard something," Gerald said. "And hope that he's not in touch with the thin man."

Sam grumbled to himself and toyed with the food on his plate.

"Anyway, if you look at motive and opportunity, I reckon the thin man killed Geraldine and it was the major and Chesterfield who stole the diamond," Gerald said.

"And everyone is looking for the diamond casket," Ruby said.

"Yep." Gerald nodded. "Including us. And that brings us to tomorrow night. This idea that the moonlight is going to show us the way."

"Yeah, what about it?" Sam said.

"Don't get me wrong, it sort of makes sense. There's plenty of examples where people in ancient times used rocks and towers to track the phases of the moon."

"And?"

"Well, I can imagine the weathervane on the clock tower at Beaconsfield acting as a reflector. That tower must be hundreds of years old, so I can buy that someone stuck the weathervane up there as a beacon," Gerald said.

"So what's the problem?"

"It's the Tor. I can't remember seeing anything on the top of that thing that would reflect light to Beaconsfield, or anywhere else for that matter."

Sam looked at Gerald, then at Ruby and back at Gerald again. "I have no answer for that," he said. "I really have no idea."

"Maybe there's another weathervane on top of St. Michael's but you can't see it from the ground," Ruby suggested. "It's not like we were actually looking for any-thing when we went up there."

"Yeah, maybe," Gerald said.

There was a long pause as they contemplated what lay ahead. Gerald broke the silence. "Tomorrow will be a week since the robbery at the museum," he said. "And almost a week since Geraldine was murdered."

He suddenly felt very tired. It had been a long week.

Summer had well and truly arrived in rural Somerset. The sun held its heat throughout the days and only a few clouds blotted clear skies. Bees droned like overloaded cargo planes; butterflies and dragonflies flitted across the meadow tops; and the perfumed air carried the lows and whinnies of cows and horses enjoying the magnificence of it all. Gerald, Ruby, and Sam, however, were completely unmoved. With a day and a half to go before Midsummer's Eve they were climbing the walls.

"Another hit of tennis?" Ruby asked without any enthu-siasm.

"No!" the others replied. They were stretched out on their backs on the manicured grass outside the tennis pavil-ion in the shade of an oak tree. They had polished off a Mrs. Rutherford lunch and were exhausted by the effort of digestion.

"This is worse than waiting for Christmas," Sam moaned,

dispatching a ladybug that had crawled onto his knee with a flick of his finger. "Can't it hurry up and happen?"

Ruby stretched her arms wide and slapped the others on the shoulders.

"Come on," she said, summoning some energy. "Let's do what everyone does when there's nothing better to do."

"What's that?" Gerald asked.

"Go shopping, of course!"

Fry may as well have been a reanimated corpse driving them back into town that afternoon. He didn't utter a word. He barely acknowledged Gerald's request to pick them up outside the bookshop in an hour.

"Good to see everything's back to normal," Gerald grunted as the Rolls pulled away from the curb. "Okay, Ruby, where do you want to go?"

The town was a lot quieter than the day before. Ruby tilted her head and scanned the streetscape. She pointed over Sam and Gerald's shoulders. "I think we should go into the shop that Professor McElderry went into."

Gerald and Sam swung around. "What?"

"He just crossed the road and went in there."

They scooted along the footpath to a dusty shopfront. Above the door, suspended from a rusted iron frame, was a faded sign: YE OLDE GLASTONBURY ANTIQUE SHOPPE. On display in the window was a mishmash of shoddy tat for tourists. They could see the professor through the grimy window, talking with a wizened man at the back of the shop.

Gerald mouthed, "Come on," and pushed open the door. They hurried across to a glass cabinet of Arthurian trinkets and were able to hide within earshot of the professor.

"How did you come by this, Jervis?" McElderry asked the man behind the counter. "I need to be sure of its provenance."

The man let out a wracking cough.

"It turned up in the barn of old Glenn Crowther. He passed away a few months ago, but I only got the call to look over his things this week," the man said.

He peeled back a layer of black cloth on the countertop and the professor peered down at what it contained.

"It has the markings on it, just like you described," the man said.

"So I see," the professor murmured. He bent low to the counter, squinting close through his glasses. "It certainly looks the goods. How did this Crowther fellow get hold of it?"

"He was the oldest stonemason in the district," the man said. "He would have worked on every major building in this area."

"Including St. Michael's Tower?"

"Yes, including St. Michael's. It's not unknown for tradesmen to take, shall we say, souvenirs," the old man said.

The professor's red whiskers pulled back into an approximation of a smile. "Then this must indeed be the one," he said. With a grunt, he hefted up a large brass weathervane in the shape of an archer.

From behind the glass cabinet, Gerald gasped.

The professor placed the weathervane back onto its velvet bedding and turned to the shopkeeper.

"We agreed five hundred pounds," the professor said, eager to complete the transaction.

"Cash," the man said, revealing a gap-toothed grin.

"What?" the professor said. "I don't carry that much around."

The man extended a bony finger toward the door. "You'll find a cash machine around the corner."

In a flurry of swearing and a promise to be right back, the professor bustled out of the shop.

A look of determination crossed Gerald's face.

"Come on," he said to the Valentines. He rushed up to the counter and surprised the old shopkeeper.

"Hello," Gerald said cheerily. "I couldn't help noticing the weathervane you were showing that man."

"Yes," the man said, his eyes narrowing at the young stranger. "What about it?"

"I'd like to buy it, please."

The man's eyes narrowed further. "Sorry, sonny," he said. "It's already sold."

Gerald took out his wallet. He slapped a fistful of notes onto the counter.

"I'll give you two thousand pounds for it."

The old man didn't blink.

"Can I wrap that for you?" he asked.

Chapter Twenty

Three empty tins of brass polish lay on the terrace at Avonleigh. The weathervane rested on a large tarpaulin, and Ruby knelt beside it, a blackened rag in one hand.

Gerald let out an exaggerated yawn and stretched his arms wide.

"What do you reckon the professor said when he got back to that antique shop?" he asked. "I don't suppose he was too happy." Gerald and Sam reclined on deck chairs in the warm afternoon sun, enjoying the sight of Ruby sweating over the weathervane as she tried to extract a shine.

"It'll be nothing compared to what I'll be saying to you two unless you come and help," Ruby said, wiping a dollop of polish from a cheek with her sleeve. "This thing is a mess."

Gerald and Sam hauled themselves onto the tarp and each took a rag from a selection that Mrs. Rutherford had found for them. "I can get Mr. Pimbury to do this for you, Master Gerald," she had said. "It's really not the done thing for the lord of the manor to be shining the brass!" Gerald had waved away her offer. But now he was having second thoughts. The sun bit into his neck as he leaned over the archer, rubbing hard.

Ruby sat back on her heels and dabbed her forehead with the back of her hand.

"Gerald, can I ask you something?" she said.

"Sure. What's up?" he replied, adding more polish to his rag.

"Back in the bookshop, when we were looking for places to hide—"

"Yeah?"

"Well, you suddenly peeled off down an aisle and just happened to find a spot right on top of the book that everyone was searching for."

Gerald stopped polishing and rested on his hands and knees.

"You know, I have no idea why I went down that aisle. It was just like that day in the Reading Room at the museum. It was like a movie was playing inside my head and I went along with it. I can't explain it."

Ruby looked at him curiously. "Is there something

you're not telling us?"

Gerald picked up the tin of polish. "No. What's to hide?" he said, avoiding Ruby's eyes.

She looked at him for a second. "Let us know if it happens again," she said.

It took another hour of polish and perspiration before the brass archer lay gleaming in the afternoon sun.

The last color of the day was draining from the evening sky by the time Gerald, Sam, and Ruby were ready to set off for the Tor. They had told Mrs. Rutherford that they wanted a good view of the fireworks from the hill overlooking Beaconsfield and promised to be back straight after midnight. She packed them a picnic of sandwiches and fruit in an old cake tin, which Gerald stowed in his backpack.

Sam hoisted the brass weathervane, wrapped carefully in its black cloth, onto his shoulders and they started down the grassy slope.

They made good time across the fields. The evening was perfectly still, and the sound of crickets and night birds filled the air. As they broached the crest above Beaconsfield the last of the twilight melted away, and across the valley, another body was making an appearance.

Gerald and the Valentines paused under a chestnut tree.

"Will you look at that!" Sam breathed. A golden sliver

appeared along the horizon. Within minutes an immense full moon was clear of the treetops and on its way into the night sky. A Swiss cheese of craters pocked its face.

"Do you reckon the peak of eternal light is up there?" Ruby asked, her face bathed in the moon's glow.

"Better be," Sam grunted, shifting the weight of the weathervane on his shoulders. "This thing weighs a freaking ton."

Gerald checked his watch. It was just after ten o'clock.

"Come on," he said. "We better hurry."

St. Michael's Tower stood a silent sentinel in the distance as they crossed into the shadows of the valley.

By the time they reached the base of the Tor, the full moon was well into the heavens, giving the tower a huge glowing halo.

Sam adjusted his heavy load and looked up.

"Bit spooky, eh?" he said.

"We better take the path that goes up around the back of the tower," Gerald said. "Don't want to let the world know we're here."

They climbed in silence. As they approached the top of the hill, a yellow glow appeared from the opposite side of the tower.

"What's that?" Gerald whispered, surprised at how loud his voice sounded.

They hurried to the foot of the tower and pressed

themselves against its side. Ruby motioned for the others to stay put and skirted to the corner. She glanced back at the boys and held an index finger to her lips. With a skip she disappeared around the side in the direction of the glow.

"What's she doing?" Gerald breathed.

Sam shrugged.

Almost immediately, Ruby reappeared.

"It's the bonfire," she said, with relief. "There's a couple of hippies lying down next to it. Looks like they're asleep or drunk or something. Come and see."

Sam and Gerald followed Ruby around the corner. About twenty yards down the other side of the hill was the bonfire that they'd seen being prepared a few days before. Flames licked high into the air. The effigy of the witch was nearby, strapped to the large wooden wheel, which was wedged against a rock. On the ground next to it was a petrol tin, its lid off and lying on its side. Two men in bright clothes were stretched out by the fire. The space around them was strewn with beer cans and wine bottles.

"I guess the excitement got too much for them," Sam said, twisting his shoulders under the weight of the weathervane. "We better get this thing into position."

They ducked inside the tower and Sam tipped the archer from his back and laid it on the stone floor.

"Right," he said. "Who's going up?"

Gerald and Ruby spoke at the same time.

"I am," they both said.

Gerald gave Ruby a dubious look.

"I think you'll find I'm better at this type of thing," he said. He pulled a coil of rope from his backpack and looped one end around his hips.

"Yes, we were all impressed with the rock-climbing exhibition the other night," Ruby said, grabbing the other end of the rope. "But I think the poise and balance of a gymnast might be more useful here." She tied a knot around her waist.

Gerald stared at her.

"You're joking, right?"

Ruby fixed him with an equally determined glare.

"Not even slightly. I'll climb up, throw the rope over the beam at the top of the tower and you two muscle men can hoist the weathervane up to me."

Gerald looked at Sam for support, but he simply shrugged. He'd clearly been on the receiving end of too many battles of will with his sister to bother arguing.

"Okay," Gerald grumbled. "But once we've hauled the weathervane to the top, I'll climb up and help put it into place."

Ruby grinned. "Sure. If you feel you need to prove yourself."

Before Gerald could respond, Ruby wedged a foot into a crevice between two stone blocks and hauled herself off the floor. Soon she was feet off the ground.

"Make sure you have three points of contact at all times," Gerald called up. He gave Sam a meaningful look.

"Oh, right," Sam mumbled. He cleared his throat. "Way to go, sis! Woo-hoo. You're my new hero!"

"Get knotted, both of you," Ruby grunted back, not looking down.

Ruby made steady progress up the inside of the tower, the rope hanging from her waist like an enormous rat's tail. She reached the first level of empty window casements in a few minutes.

"This is easy," she called down. "But there's a lot of pigeon poo up here."

She continued climbing, searching for cracks between the ancient stones. But the higher she went, the longer she was taking to find footholds.

"Come on!" Sam called up to her. "We haven't got all day."

From the ground they saw Ruby fumble with her right hand as she stretched high to grab a narrow ledge.

"It's getting a bit thin up here," she said. Her voice was strained.

Sam gave Gerald an uneasy glance.

"She's not too good with heights, actually," he said. "Should have mentioned that earlier, I guess. She just wants to show she's as good as you."

Gerald tilted his head to look up. Ruby was about two-thirds of the way up the tower, with nothing but sixty feet of air between her and the stone floor. He suddenly felt sick. One wrong move and . . .

"Ruby," Gerald called out. "There's a stone jutting out from the wall a few feet up to your right. Can you see it?"

Ruby froze.

"Yeah?"

"If you can get to that, then it's a clear path to the next line of windows. You can have a rest and it's only a meter or so to the top."

Ruby paused. "Waddya mean if?"

"What?"

"You said if I can get there. What happens if I can't get there?"

Gerald swallowed. "Let's concentrate on the stone, okay?"

Ruby extended her right hand. Her fingers sought out a nook in the rocks, like a spider seeking shelter. She eased her way up the stone face. All the while the rope snaked longer and longer down to Gerald on the ground. Finally she was able to wrap her fingers around the protruding stone and swing both hands up to cling on tight.

She breathed. Then she stuck her foot onto a narrow ledge and pushed up hard.

Without warning, a section of stone gave way. Ruby

dropped face first into the wall, landing a heavy blow to her chest. Her full weight dragged on her fingers. Her body twisted as her feet flailed in the air, trying to find support.

"Ruby!" Gerald and Sam cried in alarm, as a shower of stone and mortar rained down. "Hold on!"

Her knuckles white, Ruby flung her right foot to the side and jammed her toe into a tight cranny. With one foot and two hands clinging to the wall, she took a deep breath, her left leg searching the air.

"You all right?" Sam called to his sister.

She didn't answer.

With another breath, Ruby pulled herself up. Her dangling foot found a ledge and soon she was grunting her way to the top. She threw a leg up and straddled the window as if it was a stone horse. She beamed down at the boys.

"Ta-dah!" she called out, waving a hand in the air.

Gerald and Sam gave Ruby a slow round of applause.

"Yes, well done," Sam called. "Now how about finishing the job?"

Looking up, Gerald saw Ruby stiffen on her perch.

"What's the matter?"

Ruby's face had tightened in alarm. "B-b-behind you!" she shouted.

Gerald swung around. In the shadows, a few yards away, stood the thin man.

With alarming speed, the black figure covered the

distance between them. He raised a gloved hand and swatted Sam's face with a cruel backhand blow. Sam smacked into the wall, knocking his head against the stone, and his body slid senseless to the floor.

Ruby's scream filled the narrow void. The thin man barely glanced up. He snatched the rope from Gerald's hand and gave it a mighty wrench. The force of the heave yanked Ruby from the casement, flipping her over the ledge. She clung to the stone shelf with her arms, her legs thrashing over the sheer drop.

Before Gerald could move, the thin man had him by the shoulder and lifted him clear off the floor.

The vice grip shot lightning bolts into Gerald. And again, the overwhelming stench of bleach filled his nostrils.

"The time for subtlety is over," the thin man snarled. He ground a thumb deep into Gerald's shoulder. "You will tell me what I want to know!"

Gerald's cries soared to the top of the tower.

"Waddya want?" he screamed in agony. "Let me go!"

The thin man flung Gerald to the floor. He lifted a pointed black boot and drove it hard into Gerald's ribs. Gerald rolled across the flagstones trying to escape, but again and again the boot found its mark, ripping the breath from Gerald's lungs.

Then it stopped. Gerald lay gasping for air. The thin

man glared from behind his sunglasses. Not so much as a bead of sweat showed on his alpine skin. Then he crouched, took a fistful of hair and reefed Gerald's head back.

"Where is the diamond casket?" he demanded.

Gerald peered back at him through half-closed eyes.

"Tell me," the thin man snarled, "or this birdie is going to fly." He reached out and tugged hard on the rope. High above Ruby yelped in alarm as she was yanked dangerously close to the window's edge.

"It's at Beaconsfield," Gerald gasped. "Somewhere at Beaconsfield."

The thin man twisted his hand, tearing out clumps of Gerald's hair.

"I know that!" he hissed. "Tell me where!"

"We don't know," Gerald said through the pain. "That's why we're here . . . trying to find out."

He stared back at the skeletal creature. Even with all the menace and the violence, the thin man's face still didn't register an emotion.

At last, the thin man spoke: "I killed your great-aunt."

Gerald clenched his teeth and stared straight ahead.

"And those two filthy beings lying out by the fire—I killed them as well."

A slow grinding realization was forming in Gerald's brain.

"And I'm going to kill you. You know that, don't you?"

Gerald blinked back tears. But he shook his head.

"You w-won't kill m-me," he stammered. "If you do, you'll never find the casket."

The thin man's mask broke. A broad sneer spread across his face.

"Mr. Wilkins," he derided, "unless you want to watch your friend fall to a cruel and painful death right before your eyes, you will tell me where the casket is." He lowered his mouth level to Gerald's ear. "And then I will kill you."

He gave the rope another violent tug. Gerald could hear Ruby scrambling to hold on—a muffled cry tumbled down. Without a sound, the thin man slid a long thin blade from his sleeve, the same one that he'd thrust into Gerald's back at the museum a week before. The point pressed into the skin at the base of Gerald's exposed throat. A bead of blood formed at its tip.

"Killing the old woman brought me no joy," the thin man breathed. "There's no challenge in killing the weak." He licked his lips, a sharp colorless tongue wiping across the equally colorless mouth.

"What do you and the major want this casket for?" Gerald blurted out, fire in his eyes. "What's so special that you have to kill for it?"

The thin man opened his mouth and cackled.

"The major?" he spat with contempt. "And me?" The cancerous laughter returned. "That old buffoon has no idea what he's dealing with." He tilted his head like a bird of prey and studied Gerald's pale face.

"And neither do you, I suspect," he said. "Such a shame for someone to die and not know the reason why, or what could have been." The thin man twisted the tip of the dagger.

"The carotid or the jugular?" he mused. "Each just as effective."

Gerald's eyes shone wet. Thoughts and visions flooded his brain. Of his mother and father sunning themselves on an island half a world away, oblivious to his pain. Of his friends back home on a snowboarding holiday, friends he would never see again. Of this cursed inheritance that would surely end his life. Of Sam standing behind the thin man with the brass weathervane held high over his head . . .

Gerald's eyes snapped back into focus. The thin man sensed movement behind him but turned too late. Sam swung the sculpture like an almighty pendulum, holding the long rod attached to its back, and caught the thin man square across the face. The impact lifted the vile creature off his feet and sent him sprawling across the flagstones. The air was filled with a tremendous bong as the archer resonated with the blow. The dagger flew from the thin man's hand and clattered into the shadows.

The thin man regained his feet but could not stand upright. His sunglasses had been shattered by the blow, exposing two red eyes like sinkholes in the front of his face. Dazed, he brought a hand up to his head. As he withdrew it, Gerald saw it was covered in blood. The dark figure stumbled forward. But again Sam advanced, swinging the brass weapon, this time hitting the thin man hard across the chest. He flew spread-eagled backward into the night, as if he'd been yanked out by a rope around his waist. Gerald jumped to his feet and followed Sam out the door. Sam's eyes were wide, his jaw set tight.

Outside the tower, they found the thin man on his hands and knees, sucking in air. He lifted his face to them. With his head silhouetted against the bonfire, the red eyes almost glowed in the dark. A thick trail of blood streamed from one ear. He spat onto the ground.

"You are all dead now," he muttered.

The thin man's hand disappeared inside his coat. It was halfway out, clutching a shining silver blade, when Sam strode forward, this time wielding the archer like an Olympic hammer thrower.

The night air was rent by another mighty toll as the archer struck under the thin man's chin, snapping his head back and sending him flying off the terrace toward the bonfire.

Sam dropped the weathervane and picked up a stick the size of a baseball bat. He struck the thin man again and again as they skirted the bonfire, shouting in time with each blow, "Don't. You. Ever. Hurt. My. Sister. Again."

The final strike sent the thin man cartwheeling through the air, a whir of black-clad arms and legs. He landed on the straw witch, his limbs snared in firewood and pitch. The impact knocked the wheel from its mooring and set it rolling—straight toward the bonfire. The thin man was stuck fast, snared in the witch's embrace.

"Quick!" Gerald shouted.

He and Sam made a dive for the wheel but it had picked up too much speed. It bounced past the thin man's two victims and into the heart of the flames. The pitch-covered witch exploded as the wheel emerged at the other side, a blazing ball accelerating down the hill. The thin man's screams disappeared as the wheel shot over a dip, sparks flying.

Gerald and Sam stood in silence until the wheel reappeared at the foot of the hill, still burning and rolling toward a distant apple orchard.

Gerald glanced at Sam.

"You all right?" he asked.

"Yeah," Sam panted. "You?"

"I think so. And thanks."

"No problem."

Gerald eyed the weathervane, lying on the ground where Sam had dropped it. "I thought you said that thing weighed a ton?"

Sam grinned. "Amazing what you can do when your blood's up."

The quiet was broken by a wail from the top of the tower. Gerald and Sam looked at each other in alarm.

"Ruby!"

They raced back into the tower, the bonfire behind them crackling bright, the full moon rising higher into the night sky.

Chapter Twenty-one

Ruby's arms and face were covered with scratches. Sitting astride the parapet, she concentrated on steadying the weathervane. Gerald, perched next to her, shunted the support rod toward a hole that they had found in the stonework. The opening was in the center of an archer etched into the rock. Despite centuries of pigeon poo, there was no mistaking the outline.

"Is this going to work?" Ruby asked.

"As long as Sam didn't whack it out of shape too much, we should be okay," Gerald said, nudging the rod along the stone with his shoulder. He paused. "Um, Ruby, did you see?"

Ruby shivered. "I don't want to talk about it."

Gerald nodded and went back to work. "There." The

weathervane dropped into place. "That's it."

From their position at the top of the tower, feet dangling either side of the wall, they gazed out into the evening and across the valley. The archer's arrow pointed at Beaconsfield. The night was clear and the clock tower glowed in the distance. The first chimes of eleven o'clock rang up the vale on the back of a gentle breeze.

"You ready for this?" Gerald said to Ruby. He studied the scratches on her face, a line of dried blood on one cheek. "You've had a bit of a day."

Ruby grinned without humor. "I think we've all had a day," she said. She placed her hand on Gerald's neck where the thin man's knife had drawn blood.

"You're hurt."

Her touch was warm.

"I'll be all right," Gerald said. "Let's see this thing through, okay?"

He tied the rope around Ruby's waist and put her arms over his shoulders. Then, with a grunt of "Hold tight," he pushed off from the wall. By the time Ruby opened her eyes again they had rappelled to the ground.

Ruby hugged Sam, and then the three of them ran out into the night.

Major Pilkington's party was in full swing when they made it to the bottom of the stone stairs at Beaconsfield. Above them on the terrace, at least two hundred people talked and laughed raucously. The place was festooned with colored party lights and decorations. Against the backdrop of the vampire's castle that was Beaconsfield, it was an extraordinary sight—like a New Year's Eve party at a morgue. Waiters with trays of drinks moved through the crowd, and judging by the racket on the terrace, they had been busy all night.

"How are we going to crash this party?" Gerald asked the others.

"Are you kidding?" Ruby said. "They're all tanked. We could be starkers and they wouldn't notice. Come on, let's have a look."

They crept up to the top step and peered over the edge. The terrace was overflowing with immaculately dressed revelers. A set of speakers blared from the far end, but the music was almost drowned out by the noise emanating from the party guests. Men and women, middle-aged to elderly—the throng teemed in a constant swirl of laughter and champagne. Ruby nudged Gerald and pointed toward the house. Standing outside the study were the major and Arthur Chesterfield. The major appeared to be talking forcefully to the younger man. He consulted his watch, then with a jab of a finger dismissed Chesterfield, who hurried off across the terrace and into the night.

"Should we follow him?" Ruby asked.

"No point," Gerald said. "I've lost sight of him already and—"

"Look!" Sam interrupted, pointing into the crowd. "It's Gupta."

Standing apart from the crowd and looking uncomfortable with the drunken revelry was Mr. Gupta, the owner of the missing diamond. He was dressed in a black dinner jacket with matching frown. His daughter, Alisha, wearing a purple sari embroidered with jewels, stood beside him. Her hair was pulled into an elegant plait that fell down her back, and she wore an orchid behind one ear. An expression of world-weary boredom was fixed on her face.

Ruby smirked. "Well, looks like she's having a great time."

"You don't like her, do you?" Sam said.

"That's not true," Ruby replied. "She's a bit of a princess, that's all."

"For all we know she is a princess," Gerald said. "I think she looks kind of nice."

"I think she looks kind of hot!" Sam said.

Ruby groaned. "Can we concentrate on the task, please? It's almost midnight."

Gerald glanced up at the clock tower. The archer weathervane stood overlooking the terrace and the party guests. Away in the distance St. Michael's Tower was set against the night sky. And above them, the full moon rose ever higher.

Sam grabbed Gerald by the arm. "It's still ten minutes till midnight," he said. "I want to check something." Without looking back, he leaped onto the terrace and jogged across to the study door.

"Sam!" Ruby hissed. "He is pure idiot, I swear." She grabbed Gerald's hand. "Come on."

She dragged Gerald onto the terrace. A waiter holding a tray of soft drinks stood at the edge of the terrace, not doing a lot of business that night. Ruby rolled down her sleeves to cover her scratched arms, waltzed up and smiled at the waiter, taking a glass in each hand. "Here," she said to Gerald, shoving a drink at him. "Act like you own the place."

Ruby sauntered in the direction of the study, Gerald close behind. They were a few feet from the door when Ruby stopped and turned to face Gerald. He pulled up just short of her. "Quick," she said, taking his hand again and yanking him into a knot of boisterous partygoers. "It's Inspector Parrott!"

They hustled into the cover of the crowd. Peeking around a large woman in a long clinging dress, they could see Inspector Parrott, deep in conversation with the major's mother. He seemed to be enjoying himself.

"What are we going to do?" Ruby yelled into Gerald's ear, trying to be heard above the din. "If Parrott sees us here we're dead meat!"

"Dunno," Gerald replied. Then, in an urgent voice, "Look! It's Constable Lethbridge. Over there by the bar."

On the far side of the terrace, dressed in a dirt-brown suit, stood Lethbridge, a pint glass in each hand.

"What is this? An open house?" Ruby said. "Come on. Parrott's tied up talking to the major's mother. Let's make a dash for the door."

They strode across the terrace toward the house. Checking over their shoulders to make sure they weren't spotted by the inspector, they narrowly avoided running into the back of a large red-headed man. Gerald gagged at the sight of Professor McElderry inches away. Eyes bulging, Gerald spun on his toes and with Ruby in hand danced clear just as the professor turned around. Gerald didn't breathe again until they were inside the study with the door shut behind them. The curtains along the windows overlooking the terrace were drawn, and the only light came from the lamp on the major's desk.

They found Sam sitting in the chair, his feet on the desk, fiddling with the Japanese puzzle box.

"Oh, hello," he said. "What took you so long?"

Ruby fumed. "Are you nuts? What are you doing in here? We've just seen the inspector and Lethbridge, out there."

"Yes, I know," Sam replied, not taking his eyes off the box. "The professor too. And Gerald, I think I saw your mad uncle."

"Sid?" Gerald said. "Why would he be here?"

"He and the major were neighbors, weren't they? Could be friends."

The concept of Sid having friends threw Gerald for a second before he remembered time was tight.

"We should be outside," Gerald said.

Sam continued to fumble with the small wooden box, flipping switches and sliding panels, but it remained shut. He smiled.

"Time to think outside the box," he said. He lifted up a heavy Bakelite telephone from the desk and brought it down on top of the container in a crash of splintering wood and twisting springs.

Ruby was incredulous. "What did you do that for?"

"What?" Sam asked as he picked through the remains. "Gerald was keen to get a move along."

Gerald reached over Sam's shoulder and grabbed the folded paper that the major had consulted the first time they'd been in the study. He brushed the broken box bits aside and laid the paper on the desk. Three heads converged above it.

On the page was a detailed drawing of a long rectangular casket, its sides set with hundreds of jewels. The lid was decorated with an intricate pattern of suns and moons. In the middle was the profile of a bare-chested archer. And set into the archer's muscled torso was an enormous diamond.

Sam traced his finger under some text at the bottom

of the page. "*La boîte des diamants . . .* that must mean the diamond box," he said. "*L'une des trois.* One of three!"

"There are three of these things?" Ruby said, raising her eyebrows.

Gerald checked his watch. "Well, in five minutes we'll be closer to finding one of them. We better get back outside, it's—"

"What are you doin' in here?" A flat droning voice interrupted them.

Gerald, Sam, and Ruby froze. Standing in the open doorway to the terrace were the unsmiling figures of Octavia and Zebedee.

"Oh no," Gerald groaned. "What do you want?" He folded the paper and slid it into his back pocket.

Octavia scowled. "We'd like our home back, for a start," she said.

Gerald threw his hands in the air in frustration. "Look, we haven't got time for that now," he said, marching toward the door. "It's got nothing to do with—"

Zebedee stepped across and blocked Gerald's path, pushing him back into the room.

"Hey," Gerald said. "Will you stop doing that?"

Octavia smiled grimly. "Waddya reckon, Zeb? Break and enter? Destruction of property? Should be enough for time inside. And with him out of the way, maybe we can get our home back."

Gerald's mouth tightened.

"You little—"

Octavia snubbed her nose at her cousin. "Zeb, go get Dad." She seemed used to giving the orders. Her brutish brother took a step toward the door.

"Wait!"

It was Ruby. She moved quickly across to Octavia. "If you go now you're going to miss out."

Gerald was stunned. What was she up to?

Zebedee paused in the doorway.

"Miss out on what?" he asked.

"I shouldn't tell you this. It's about that diamond, the one that was stolen from the museum in London."

"What are you telling them that for?" Sam protested.

Ruby turned to her brother and shrugged.

"Oh come off it, Sam," Ruby said. "The whole reason we're down here. Why Gerald inherited that house. They were always gonna figure it out."

"Figure out what, princess?" Octavia asked, hands on her hips.

Ruby didn't miss a beat. "That the stolen diamond is hidden in this room."

She crossed to the bookcase and removed the beaten copy of *The Odyssey* from the shelf.

"Come see for yourself if you don't believe me."

Ruby buried her arm deep between the neighboring

books and a clunk sounded behind the fireplace. Octavia and Zebedee looked at each other, then scurried across. They peered into the dark opening behind the grate.

Ruby snatched Gerald's backpack and pulled out a flashlight, handing it to Octavia.

"It's hidden in a chest inside."

Octavia glared at Ruby but curiosity won out. She flicked on the flashlight and led her brother through the fireplace to the tunnel. The moment they crossed the threshold, the panel snapped back into place, sealing them inside.

"That oughta hold them for a while," Ruby said in a satisfied tone. "Come on, you two. Time's almost up."

They left the muffled sound of fists beating on metal and ran outside.

The party had moved onto the lawn on the other side of the rose garden, about fifty yards away from the house. Apart from a few waiters collecting glasses, the only person on the terrace was an elegantly dressed man leaning on a cane. Alerted by the sound of three sets of feet scuttling across the flagstones behind him, he turned.

"Sir Mason!" Gerald called out as he skidded to a stop, the others bundling into the back of him.

Sir Mason Green, his silver hair shining in the moon-light, gave a surprised smile.

"Gerald, I didn't expect to see you here," he said. "Come to watch the fireworks? The others are down on the lawn—my leg slows me up these days."

"Sir Mason," Gerald blurted out. "I think we know where the diamond is!"

Green stared at him. "Oh, really?"

He listened intently as Gerald poured out the events of the past few days: the mystery of the diamond casket and the peak of eternal light, the missing weathervane, the attack by the thin man at St. Michael's Tower, and the two people he murdered. Green's eyes widened at the description of the thin man trapped in the burning wheel, rolling down the Tor.

"Extraordinary," he said. "We must inform the police at once. This is a very serious matter."

Before any of them could move, the first haunting toll of midnight rang down from the clock tower. The full moon was now directly overhead.

"This is it," Ruby said. "Midnight on Midsummer's Eve!"

The bell tolled again. The revelers on the lawn started a countdown.

"Ten . . . nine . . ."

"This better work," Gerald muttered.

". . . eight . . . seven . . ."

The moon above them was so bright, so clear, the craters on its surface so vivid.

". . . six . . . five . . ."

Ruby grabbed Gerald's arm and squeezed hard.

". . . four . . . three . . ."

The archer atop the clock tower seemed to grow in stature, a dull glow emanating from its torso.

". . . two . . . one . . ."

The night sky exploded in a firestorm of blazing light. The squeals of delight at the fireworks from the partygoers on the lawn were in stark contrast to the speechless awe that gripped Green, Gerald, Sam, and Ruby. Directly above them, the moon shimmered. A shaft of brilliant white light scored down from the heavens, splitting the sky and striking like lightning the upper battlement of St. Michael's Tower. A beam seared across the valley, making a direct connection with the weathervane atop the Beaconsfield clock tower. The archer juddered, emitting a high pitched hum that cut through the squeals from the lawn and etched itself into the heads of the four people on the terrace. They clapped their hands to their ears as the hum grew to a deafening intensity. Green's cane clattered onto the tiles. The archer shook at its moorings, and Gerald felt sure it would explode when, from the tip of the archer's arrow, a sharp bolt of blue light shot into the grounds of Beaconsfield.

"Come on!" Gerald yelled. "That's the spot!"

Sam and Ruby set off with Gerald as he rushed into the night, leaving Green hobbling after them as best he could.

The blue bolt cut a path across the property, past

overgrown gardens and long abandoned greenhouses. Sam and Ruby caught up with Gerald and together they vaulted a wild hedge, still following the blue light across the grass. Then they pulled up short. The light disappeared through the open door of . . .

"The crypt," Gerald breathed.

Ruby blanched. "I'm not going in there," she said, shaking her head. "There's no way."

Sam took her by the elbows. "We're all in this together," he said. "There's nothing to worry about."

"You say that like those two statements are somehow related." Ruby scowled at her brother. "You remember what was in there."

"It's up to you. You can come or stay out here, by yourself."

Ruby grimaced. "Okay," she said. "But I hope we don't see any rats."

Sam flinched but didn't say a word. The three of them stepped inside the crypt.

The interior was awash with light. A bank of portable floodlights set up against the left wall illuminated the room. The bizarre carvings and sculptures that lined the walls looked less threatening, but even Ruby didn't pay any attention to them. The blue beam from the archer's arrow shot through the door, across the room, and into the eye of a snake carved in the side of a sarcophagus. The beam then reappeared out the snake's gaping mouth and shot into a large round hole in the wall in the center of a mosaic showing an enormous serpent attacking a man.

Under the hole in the wall was a pile of rubble.

"Get the feeling we're not the first ones here?" Gerald said.

He reached into his backpack and pulled out three headlamps. "This time I came prepared," he said. They strapped the lights on and poked their heads through the opening. A metal ladder disappeared into an absolute blackness. Even with the lamps there was no sign of the bottom. Gerald clambered onto the ladder and led the way down.

They went deeper and deeper, far further than the pit underneath the major's study, the lights from their headlamps cutting into the darkness around them. At one point the surrounding walls changed from the dull red bricks they'd seen under the house to bare stone. The air was cooler than on the surface, and a rank musty odor surrounded them. Finally the narrow shaft opened into an enormous cavern.

It was still about a hundred feet to the ground, but Gerald stalled on the ladder, marveling at what lay beneath him.

They were at the edge of a colossal open space. Even from his vantage point on one wall, Gerald couldn't see the top of the cavern, which disappeared into the rocky shadows. The area must have been at least a hundred yards across at its widest point, possibly more. Near the bottom of the ladder were two racks of floodlights similar to the ones they'd seen back in the crypt. Gerald reached up and patted Ruby on the ankle. He pointed to a large block of sandstone near the lights and motioned for her and Sam to follow.

They reached the ground and scurried across to the block, falling to the ground behind it.

"What is this place?" Ruby whispered into Gerald's ear but he shook his head, his eyes urging her to remain silent. They poked their heads around the edge.

Ten yards away was a tall marble column, one of several that formed a ring inside the perimeter of the chamber. Large white marble blocks capped the tops of the columns, forming an unbroken band. About fifteen yards further in was a circle of about thirty identical statues—life-sized archers, standing about fifteen feet apart, each resting a crossbow on his shoulder. They all faced the center of the chamber, where, on a mosaic floor and right at the heart of the cavern, there stood a large rotunda, its gold roof glinting in the floodlights. The roof was supported by four marble pillars that also appeared to be made of solid gold. Then they all saw it.

In the center of the rotunda was a black marble plinth. And, even though it was a good forty yards away, clearly visible on top of the plinth was a rectangular box, maybe three feet long, glittering with jewels.

"That's it," Sam whispered. "It's just like in the drawing—"

Gerald clamped his hand over Sam's mouth and with a jerk of his head indicated across the chamber.

Standing beside one of the marble columns were the major and Chesterfield. They were studying a sheet of paper. Sam's eyes bulged.

The major straightened up and clapped Chesterfield on the shoulder.

"Ready, Arthur? Watch out for the snakes."

Major Pilkington strode between the columns toward the center of the chamber, leaving Chesterfield trotting behind. He passed the archers and without breaking stride he was across the mosaic floor and up the three steps into the rotunda. Chesterfield joined him moments later.

Gerald craned his neck to see. One of the columns was blocking his view. He nodded at Sam and Ruby and together they scampered over to the nearest pillar. They peered around the edge but still couldn't see what was happening in the rotunda. Gerald dropped to his belly and commando-crawled the ten yards to the nearest statue. He sat in a tight ball with his back against the base. His heart beat hard, echoing in his ears. He glanced back at Sam and Ruby, peeking out from behind the column. He took a deep breath and ducked his head to see around the corner. The rotunda was only fifteen yards away. Inside it, the major and Chesterfield stood on either side of the black plinth, staring down at the glittering diamond casket.

"Beautiful, isn't it, Arthur?" the major said, running his hands over the top of the box.

Chesterfield snorted. "For what the buyer's paying, it'd want to be!"

The major hesitated. "Whatever's in here must be worth a blind fortune."

"We've discussed this already."

"We tell the buyer we couldn't find it and we keep it for ourselves," the major said. "Or find a second buyer and get some bidding going."

Chesterfield stared at the major.

"We're talking hundreds of millions of pounds, Arthur. Each! Think of it."

Behind the statue Gerald was joined by Sam and Ruby.

"We may as well see what's inside," Chesterfield said, tempted by the major's argument. "No harm in looking."

The major smiled.

"Quite right, my boy," he said. "No harm at all."

The major reached into his jacket and pulled out a black velvet pouch. He loosened the drawstring at the top and tipped it up. Into his outstretched palm slipped a diamond, the size of a duck's egg.

"Look at it, Arthur," the major said, holding the gem up between his thumb and forefinger to catch the light. "Noor Jehan—the light of the world—the greatest diamond in history."

Chesterfield reached out and took the gem.

"One hundred million pounds' worth. And if this is only the key, imagine what's inside the casket!"

Back behind the statue, Gerald whispered to himself. "The diamond's a key?" His great-aunt had been murdered for the key to a box.

Chesterfield cupped the gem in his hand.

"Ready?" he asked the major. The major didn't need to reply; his eyes said it all.

Chesterfield placed the diamond into a recess in the top of the box. It was a perfect fit.

The moment the gem was in place, Gerald heard a faint click above his head. He glanced up at the statue. Slowly, the crossbow lowered from its resting place on the archer's shoulder and snapped into place. Gerald looked around. Every one of the thirty archers now aimed a crossbow into the heart of the rotunda. His eyes darted to the ground and by his hand there was a sharp piece of stone, shaped very much like a . . .

A grunt from the rotunda swept his eyes back to the

major. Chesterfield was trying to turn the diamond in the casket lid.

"It won't budge," he fumed. "It's stuck tight."

The major edged around to help. "It hasn't been opened for seventeen hundred years—it's bound to be a bit stiff."

Chesterfield twisted hard on the diamond. It shattered into a million pieces in his hand. He looked at the major, dumbfounded.

"What the deuce?"

In an instant Gerald swung back behind the statue and snared Sam and Ruby by their shirt collars, hauling them on top of him in a tangle of limbs, squeezing them in as tight as he could. He opened his mouth to scream a warning.

But before he could make a sound the circle of archers let fly a volley of arrows. They flew through the rotunda and slammed into the statues opposite, sending shards of stone shrapnel into the air. Round after round of arrows dropped into the archers' crossbows. They zipped either side of Gerald and the Valentines, just missing them. Harrowing shrieks echoed out from the rotunda, where the major and Chesterfield had been standing. Gerald clutched his friends ever tighter as they all struggled to make themselves as small a target as possible. But then, as quickly as it began, the attack was over. The screams dissipated up into the shadowy ceiling, and the deadly crossbows returned to their resting places on the archers' shoulders, their task done.

Gerald peeked out from between Ruby's arm and Sam's neck. The chamber was silent. "A booby trap," Gerald said, his heart racing. "I saw some old arrowheads on the ground but couldn't warn them."

"Not your fault," Sam said, his eyes wide. "No way you could have known."

Ruby sat clutching her knees and gulping in air. "Do you think they're d . . ."

Gerald's hands were shaking. "I'll take a look."

"Don't!" Ruby shouted, then checked herself. "D-don't leave this spot. There could be more traps."

Gerald nodded. He eased his head around the corner of the statue. The ground between him and the steps to the rotunda was littered with broken stone and shattered arrows. He scanned the area at the base of the black plinth. Chesterfield was slumped on the floor, at least eight arrows in his lifeless body, a stream of blood snaking its way to the top step. Gerald looked around for the major and saw a pair of tweed-trousered legs on the floor on the far side of the rotunda. There was no movement.

Gerald crawled back around the statue's base and sat facing Ruby and Sam.

"No" was all he said.

For a moment they sat there, too shocked to move.

Ruby still clutched her knees and stared down at her feet. Her arms quivered. Sam pulled his sister in tight.

"Someone's gone to a lot of trouble to protect whatever's in that box," Gerald said. He looked around the chamber nervously. "What other surprises are in here?"

Sam shook his head. "You heard Chesterfield. If they used a priceless diamond as the key, imagine what's hidden inside?" He sat upright. "Hold on! I thought diamonds were the hardest things in the world?"

"They are," Ruby said, wiping away a tear. "So what?"

"Then how can a diamond shatter?" Gerald said, echoing Sam's thoughts.

The answer came from a composed voice behind them.

"When it's not a real diamond."

They swung around to see Sir Mason Green leaning on his cane between two of the columns at the edge of the chamber. They rushed to him.

"Sir Mason," Gerald said. "The diamond exploded in Chesterfield's hand."

"Then the arrows got them," Sam broke in.

Sir Mason looked at them, concerned.

"But you're okay? That's what matters." He glanced at the rotunda and frowned. "I'm afraid for the major and his young colleague, though, the news is not so good."

Gerald looked into the man's face. "What is this place, Sir Mason?"

Green ran a hand down his pointed chin and cast his eyes around the cavern. "It appears to be some form of Roman burial chamber," he said. "I was going to say Roman ruin, but judging by the fate of the major and young Chesterfield I'd say it's in perfect working order. The Romans often set up elaborate traps to protect objects of great value."

Sam shook his head in wonder. "We should go and find Inspector Parrott."

Green, lost in thought, gazed around the cavern. "Yes," he said absently. "I expect so."

Ruby spoke next.

"Sir Mason?" she asked. "Did you know Major Pilkington very well?"

Green seemed surprised by the question. "Well, Miss Valentine, I expect I'd describe him as an acquaintance. Why do you ask?"

"It's just that you're both members of the Rattigan Club, and seeing as there's only three hundred members, I would have thought you'd be a bit more surprised, or even upset, at him dying like this," Ruby said.

Green looked sideways at Ruby. "What makes you think I'm a member at the Rattigan?"

"The tie you're wearing," she said. "It is quite distinctive."

Green pressed his hand to his chest but didn't look down at his tie—a rich maroon with a pattern of neat gold *R* symbols. He smiled.

"Most observant, Miss Valentine," he said. He peered at the twins. "Tell me, which of you two is the fastest runner? I expect it would be Mr. Valentine, yes?"

Sam stepped forward. "I can beat her over any distance."

Green nodded. "Yes, I thought as much. Now, stand over here, please?" He ushered Sam to a spot next to one of the columns. Sam shrugged and turned back to face the others.

"Excellent," Green muttered. "Now—"

In a blur of movement, Green lifted his cane and whipped away its outer covering to reveal a long silver blade. He lunged forward and slashed the razor-sharp sword high across Sam's thigh. Sam dropped to the ground, yelling in pain. He grabbed at his leg as a thick stain of blood seeped through a cut in his jeans. His face reflected his horror.

"Sam!"

Ruby dived to her brother, sickened at the blood on his fingers.

"What are you doing?" Gerald rounded on Green but the old man was too fast. In a blink he had flicked the tip of the blade under Gerald's chin, a droplet of Sam's blood still fresh on its point.

Green spoke calmly, not taking his eyes off Gerald.

"Miss Valentine, you must place pressure on the wound

to stop the bleeding. I have cut your brother's femoral artery. Unless the wound is held shut, he will bleed to death within minutes."

Gerald gasped. Ruby was kneeling by Sam's side, her hands out, lost as to what to do.

"Ruby!" Gerald cried. "You have to hold the wound shut."

Ruby threw her head around to Gerald. A steely resolve spread in her eyes. She tugged at the slit in Sam's jeans and yanked hard on the cloth, tearing a larger opening to expose the wound. Then she grabbed her brother's T-shirt and whipped it over his head, wrapping the cloth around her hand. She pressed down hard on the gash in Sam's leg. He cried out in agony, but the pressure seemed to have the right effect. The flow of blood eased, then stopped.

Green still stared into Gerald's eyes.

"Has the bleeding stopped, Mr. Wilkins?" he asked.

Gerald went to nod, but the point of the blade dug into his throat. "Yes," he replied.

"That is good news," Green said with a trace of a smile. "If Miss Valentine maintains pressure on the wound, then her brother should survive. But I suggest she doesn't move from her position. I don't want to kill you or your friends, Mr. Wilkins. But rest assured, if you give me cause, I will not hesitate."

Gerald glared back. "Sam!" he called out. "You okay?"

Sam sat slumped against a column, his chin on his chest and his eyes squeezed tight. "I'll be right," he said.

"See?" Green said. "Everyone is fine—and nicely occupied. No one is going to alert the police, and Mr. Wilkins, you are free to help me."

"Help you!" Gerald said.

"Yes. It's time to collect my bounty or, more precisely, for you to collect my bounty."

Gerald squared his shoulders. "Why are you doing this? You're worth billions. Why do you need more money?"

Green raised his eyebrows in surprise. "Why, Gerald, who said anything about money?"

Now it was Gerald's turn to look surprised. "But the diamond, and whatever treasure is in that box."

Green smirked. "This is the bit where the villain explains his brilliant criminal caper, is it? Well, I expect you deserve some answers," he said. "After all, I couldn't have found this place without you."

"What do you mean?"

Green turned the sword in his hand, its tip half an inch from Gerald's chin.

"When I said on the terrace that I was surprised to see you, I was genuinely surprised," Green said. "You were supposed to be dead."

Gerald didn't flinch.

"You see, my underfed associate was supposed to make

sure you secured the beacon on St. Michael's Tower, then dispose of you."

Gerald gasped. "The thin man was working for you?"

"Of course," Green said. "A person in my position doesn't go around monstering old ladies and setting fire to London houses—even the fashionable ones. He's an odd fish, my slender confederate. Obsessed with hygiene. He seems to think humanity is infested with bugs, which does make him an effective killer. Though it appears removing you was a task too far."

"Too right!" Sam's eyes were open and they blazed at Green.

Green let out a sharp *tut*. "You are hardly in a position to be making noises of bravado, Mr. Valentine. If you value your pretty sister's life, I suggest you shut it!"

He whipped back to face Gerald. "My man was set the simple task of locating the diamond casket. I assumed your great-aunt would know but, sadly for her, she wasn't cooperative."

"So you had her killed," Gerald shouted in disbelief.

Green appeared almost chastened. "No need to be harsh, Gerald. The instruction was to extract the location of the casket. The hired help just went a bit far. But what can you do? After that, my attention turned to you."

"How would I know where it is? I never even met my great-aunt."

Green smirked. "Yes, that was a surprise. Turned out you didn't know the big family secret after all."

Gerald blinked. "What? The location of the casket?"

Green laughed with delight. "Mr. Wilkins, you have no clue, do you? The casket is not the prize—it is merely a checkpoint along the way." He nudged Gerald with the sword. "Enough talk, you have a task to perform." Green motioned for Gerald to walk to the rotunda.

Gerald stumbled as he went. "But I can't open the box," he protested. "Didn't you see? The diamond shattered."

"Yes," Green said, prodding the blade into Gerald's ribs. "That diamond was most certainly a fake. But the one in my pocket is most decidedly real."

"You have the diamond!"

Green smiled. "Mr. Wilkins, I have had the diamond from the day it arrived in England."

Gerald's brain reeled back to the plane and the picture in *Oi!* magazine.

"Of course," Gerald said. "The photo of Geraldine at the opening of the museum exhibition—that was you with her!"

"Well done, Mr. Wilkins. I had a replica of Noor Jehan made a year ago, the moment we convinced Mr. Gupta to loan the diamond to the museum. The fake cost me a small fortune, but it was perfect in every detail, except, of course, it wasn't a diamond. I swapped it with the real one the night that photograph was taken."

"So the major and Chesterfield stole the fake one!"

"Yes, I hadn't banked on that. But then I overheard the major and Chesterfield talking at the Rattigan one night. Both drunk and bemoaning the state of their finances. Then the major mentioned he'd found an old book that had details about a diamond casket hidden somewhere at Beaconsfield. I saw my opportunity."

"What do you mean?"

"Mr. Wilkins, the diamond by itself is of no value to me. I own several diamonds. But the casket—that is another matter. I had my thin assistant contact the major and offer him a significant sum if he could locate this sacred container."

"You're the buyer?"

"I didn't care who found it, as long as I possessed it. But I needed to retrieve the fake diamond as well. If it was exposed there would be too many questions."

Gerald shook his head, trying to take it all in.

"After you, Mr. Wilkins," Green said, prodding Gerald onward. "But take it easy. We are in the snake's lair, and you've seen how it can bite."

Gerald took a step toward the center of the chamber. They were about halfway between the outer columns and the ring of stone archers. Green followed, his sword at Gerald's back, the scabbard in his free hand.

They had moved only a few feet when Green's foot

touched a paving stone and there was a distinct click.

"Don't move!" he cried.

They both froze.

"What is it?" Gerald asked, still staring at the rotunda and the ring of archers ahead of them. The last time he'd heard that click . . .

"I have stepped on a trigger stone," Green said. "The moment I take my weight off it the trap will be sprung, whatever it is."

Gerald scanned the stone archers. Their crossbows were resting on their shoulders. "What is this place?"

"I told you; this is the serpent's lair. The traps are to stop grave robbers." Green looked about him, searching for something. "Gerald!" he snapped. "Put your foot on the paving stone next to mine. Okay. Step down firmly. That's it. Now, I'm going to walk away."

Gerald recoiled. "What? And leave me here in the middle of some booby trap?"

Green paused. "Well, better you than me." He lifted his foot. High above them a deep rumble emerged from the shadows. Before Gerald or Green could move, an enormous iron-barred cage crashed over the top of them, capturing them like bugs under a cup.

"Now what?" Gerald asked, trying to remain calm. He looked left and right for flying objects.

From high above came a faint rustling sound.

"I think we're about to find out," Green said, waving his sword in front of him.

With a rush of air and a dumping sound as if the heavens were breaking apart, a great white blur descended.

Green and Gerald both saw it coming. They flung their arms over their heads and braced themselves. When it hit, it was like being pelted with a barrel of tooth picks.

Gerald opened an eye. Scattered around his feet were thousands of what looked like small white sticks. They were in his hair, on his shoulders, on his backpack, down his shirt.

Green was covered in them too. He picked some off his jacket and inspected them.

"Snake bones," he said.

"Snake bones!" Gerald said in astonishment. And sure enough, little snake skulls with tiny fangs, snake vertebrae and snake ribs were everywhere.

Green surveyed the top of the cage.

"When these were alive that would have been a pretty nasty death," he said. "A thousand snakes dumped on your head."

Gerald snorted. "Well, that's what you get when your booby traps are a couple of thousand years old." The bones crunched under his shoes as he stepped over to the cage bars. Skulls and ribs turned to dust. He grabbed a bar in each hand and shook. Two long sections broke away in his grip, leaving an easy exit.

"Robbing old tombs might not be so hard," Gerald said.

"Don't get cocky, Gerald. Or have you forgotten the major's fate?"

Green motioned with his sword and Gerald continued. They came to the ring of archers and paused. The floor between them and the rotunda was an ornate mosaic. For the first time Gerald had a good look at the pattern: it was a nest of writhing snakes.

"A popular theme," he muttered. He looked at Green. "You sure you want to do this? Still time to run away, you know."

Green shook his head. "Watch where you're walking."

Gerald took a tentative step onto the tiles. He checked the floor ahead. It was only ten to fifteen yards to the first step of the rotunda. But after the trap—and the arrows—it looked as long as a football field. What was it that Green had just said? To watch where he walked? Gerald took another step, placing a foot softly on a tile snake's belly. Watch where he walked! Terrific advice. From the guy who set off a trap dumping a million snake bones onto them.

Gerald paused, glancing at the rotunda. The major's legs were sticking out from behind the black plinth. Poor Major Pilkington. Nobody deserved to die that way. Gerald took another step, treading on a snake's tail. And what was it the major had said to Chesterfield as they'd set off across the floor? "Watch out for the snakes"? Pity they hadn't watched out for the arrows. Gerald took another step and a snake bone dislodged from a crease in his jeans and tumbled onto the floor. It was a skull, the upper fangs still intact. It bounced on the tiles and came to rest in front of him on the head of an open-mouthed mosaic serpent. Gerald froze, his foot just inches off the snake's head. Watch out for the snakes, the major had said. What was the most dangerous part of a snake? The part to avoid at all cost?

"Stop!" Gerald yelled to Green, spinning on his back foot to face the old man. "Don't step on the snakes' heads, they're—"

It was too late.

Green's foot landed squarely on the head of a serpent. This time there were no clicks, no falling cages. The floor beneath Gerald dropped open, and he fell into a gaping chasm.

Chapter Twenty-two

Gerald was falling backward, his feet high and his arms flailing in the air. The pit was fifteen feet deep and the bottom was studded with rows of stakes, points upward.

Like a cat falling from a tree, Gerald twisted in midair. He had only a fraction of a second to coil around to avoid a bloody meeting with a stake thrusting up from the ground. He half turned his torso, legs and arms moving as counterweights, but it wasn't enough. He landed on a stake that stood two feet out of the ground. Its tip pierced his backpack. A sharp stab rammed between his shoulder blades. This was the end.

Gerald opened an eye. Judging by the pain in his ribs, he was still alive. He opened his other eye to find himself lying on his side on the pit's stony floor, face-to-face with a human skull. It was skewered ear-to-ear on one of the deadly stakes. Gerald yelped. He went to sit up but his shoulders were pinned down. Desperate, he wriggled from side to side but couldn't budge. He craned his neck and saw that his backpack was impaled on a spike. Reefing his arms free of the straps, he scrambled upright. He stared wide-eyed at what was left of his pack.

By all the laws of physics, Gerald should now have a wooden stake emerging from the front of his ribs. He yanked the bag free and rummaged inside, pulling out a metal lid with a colossal dent in it—the cake tin containing Mrs. Rutherford's midnight picnic! Gerald held up the lid in amazement. He stuck his fist through the hole in his pack, and let out a low whistle. The stake had pierced the backpack then smashed into the cake tin and glanced off the lid. So instead of becoming a human shish kebab, he had thumped onto his side, winded but skewer-free.

Gerald looked around him. There were at least five skeletons, in a variety of contorted positions, impaled on stakes. This trap had been sprung more than once over the centuries. And then he saw something quite unexpected. Bending back and forth, its razor-sharp point stuck fast between the flagstones of the floor, was Sir Mason Green's sword. Gerald had forgotten about Green. He raced through the thicket of spikes and tugged the sword out of the ground. He held it in his outstretched hand, looking for any sign of the old man. There was nothing but old bones and wooden stakes. Only then did Gerald think to look up. Suspended over a corner of the pit, clutching the scabbard of his sword that had wedged into some rocks, was Sir Mason Green. One foot flailed in the air and the other was jammed against a ledge, just holding his weight.

Gerald was stunned. The only thing holding the trap-door open—the only thing preventing it from springing back into place and sealing him inside—was Sir Mason Green.

"Don't move!" Gerald yelled. "If you fall we'll both be trapped!"

Green's reply was to the point. "You need to help me then. I can't hold on for much longer."

"Okay. Don't move."

Gerald searched the sides of the pit. The lower ten feet of the walls were vertical featureless marble. Above that there were enough nooks in the rock to allow him to climb back to the top. He had to find a way to scale the bottom section. Still clutching Green's sword, he crossed to the wall closest to where he had fallen and ran a palm across the smooth face.

Gerald swore to himself. His foot kicked up against something and he glanced down at another skeleton. He kept sweeping his hand across the marble facing, but then he took a second look. There was something different about this collection of bones. This one wasn't stabbed through with a stake. It was lying clear of the deadly spiked forest. This one must have survived the fall, like he had, and then couldn't get out of the pit. Gerald gulped. Then he noticed something else. He knelt down to take a closer look. The bones were pitted with hundreds of tiny teeth marks. Something had been gnawing on this guy's bones!

Things weren't looking good. A moan from above drew his eyes.

"Do something, Gerald!" Green's strength was waning.

Gerald scoured the pit, desperate for escape. His mangled pack lay on the floor a few yards away. He looked at it curiously. Was there something moving inside his backpack? He took a step closer and placed the tip of the sword under a corner of torn fabric and lifted. Three giant rats leaped from the hole, squealing as they fought over the remains of Mrs. Rutherford's picnic. The rodents slashed at each other with their teeth in a feeding frenzy. Gerald jumped back, disgusted. Then immediately he wished he hadn't moved. The largest of the three rats lifted its head from the cake tin and eyed Gerald across the floor. Gerald retreated a step, but now the rat was interested. It left the other two to squabble over the last of the fruit and scuttled toward him. Gerald moved backward but the rat kept at him. Its body was at least a foot long; its lean frame and crazed eyes betrayed its hunger. Without warning, it launched itself from the ground, its mouth wide, and soared straight at Gerald.

Gerald didn't have time to think. He sliced the sword through the air and connected with the rat, sending it skidding across the floor and into the wall. Then the other two rats looked up. They sniffed the air, left the backpack and moved toward Gerald. They split left and right and came at him slowly, stalking their prey. Gerald raised his sword and tensed. Then the first rat released a dying squeal. The other two stopped, looked at Gerald through black eyes, then scurried over to gorge on their dead companion.

Gerald knew he had to get out. He ran to his backpack and picked up the cake tin. It was still intact; the lid had taken the brunt of the stake. He placed the tin on top of a spike closest to the wall near where he had fallen in. Then he ran to the opposite side of the pit. He glanced at the rodents in the corner, their faces wet with fresh blood. Gerald knew he would only get one shot at this. He sprinted as hard as he could toward the wall, clutching the sword with the point to the ground. At the sudden burst of movement, the rats abandoned their feast and set after him. When he was three feet short of the spike, he thrust the sword into the ground and pushed off hard as he leaped up, driving a foot onto the cake tin. He launched himself into the air, flinging his hands high. Gerald hit the wall hard, but he wrapped his fingertips over the top edge of the marble and hung there. He breathed hard and pulled, the muscles in his arms screaming. He raised himself just enough to swing a foot onto the rock face. With a cry of determination, Gerald hauled himself higher and clawed his way up the wall, finally rolling back into the cavern, a sweat-soaked mess.

He struggled to his feet and limped to where Green still clung to the scabbard.

"Hurry, Gerald," the man breathed, his face contorted in pain. "Give me your hand."

Gerald didn't move.

"Ruby," Gerald called out. "How's Sam?"

"He seems all right," Ruby answered, her hand still pressed hard against her brother's leg. "But we've got to get him out of here."

Sam coughed. "Don't worry about me. Just deal with him."

Gerald turned his dark gaze back to Green.

"Hurry, please!" Green implored.

Gerald narrowed his eyes. "Why should I help you? Why shouldn't I kick this stick away?" He tapped the end of the scabbard with his foot.

Green went pale. "No!" he yelled. Down in the pit the rats circled.

"Tell me why not!" Gerald fumed.

Green lifted his head and locked eyes with Gerald. "You won't do it, Gerald, because you can't do it," he said.

"And you know you can't."

Gerald was unmoved. "You don't think so? You don't think I could do this?" He stamped down onto the end of the scabbard. It shunted perilously close to the edge of the pit.

Green clung on for his life.

"Gerald!" There was panic in Green now. "Is this who you are? A killer?"

Gerald's heart was closed. "You had Geraldine killed. You stabbed my friend. You ordered that man to murder us! What does that say about you?"

Green shifted his hands, running out of strength. "You're right, Gerald. I've done wrong, but you can't do this. We'll . . . we'll go to the police. Let them do their job. Please."

Gerald grunted. Then stamped down on the scabbard again. Green's hands juddered. The foot that was balancing on the rock ledge slipped, and Green was left dangling full length above the pit.

A scream of "No!" filled the chamber.

But it wasn't Green.

"Don't do it, Gerald!" Ruby shouted. "It's murder!"

Gerald stared hard at the man who had ordered them dead. A sick feeling of rage built in his gut. How easy would it be to kick that scabbard away? And who would blame him if he did? Gerald raised his foot.

Green tried to meet Gerald's eyes. "Ask yourself," Green

pleaded. "Who are you?"

Gerald answered with a hard kick of his foot, knocking the scabbard from the corner of the pit. In the same instant, Gerald dropped to the ground, flat on his chest, and latched onto the man's wrist. Green swung over the pit as Gerald clung to his arm. Their eyes locked.

"I don't know who I am," Gerald said to Green. "But I know I'm nothing like you."

Green opened his mouth, but this time words would not come. His terror was complete.

Gerald gritted his teeth and strained hard. He pulled with all his strength and heaved himself back onto his knees. The sudden movement sparked Green into action. He lifted a knee over the edge of the pit. Gerald lunged forward and grabbed Green's belt, then swung the old man over the lip and onto the cavern floor.

The scabbard fell and the trapdoor swung back into place. Green lay there, panting. "Thank you, Gerald, thank you."

Gerald looked at him with loathing, his breathing hard. "I'm going to get some help for my friend," he said. "And you're coming with me."

Green picked himself up from the floor. "Yes, of course," he stammered. "But first, I need to collect what's in that casket." From his boot he slid out a long silver dagger, identical to the one used by the thin man.

"How can you do that?" Ruby screamed from across the chamber. "Gerald just saved your life."

Green wiped sweat from his forehead and ushered Gerald at knifepoint toward the rotunda. "Yes," Green said. "He's a far better man than I."

They traversed the mosaic floor, avoiding the snake heads. At the rotunda steps, Gerald saw the damage done to Arthur Chesterfield; the lifeless body was sprawled in front of the black plinth. And behind it lay the major. He had been hit by a single arrow to the front of his head. Gerald looked away.

Green rushed to the diamond casket. He seized it in both hands, but it was stuck fast to the plinth. He reached into his jacket and took out the Noor Jehan.

"See this, Gerald," Green said. "The most fabulous gem in the history of all creation. A maharaja killed his mother so he could possess it. Now who would use a thing of such beauty, of such perfection, for so mundane a task as a key?"

Gerald eyed him with distaste. "Who cares?"

Green ran a hand across the surface of the casket. "Wilkins, you're new at this thing of wealth. When you've got money—real money—it can only buy you so much. How many houses can you live in? How many yachts can you sail? The true curse of wealth is that no matter how much you've got, it's never enough. And the more you get, the more you want. There are other things worth striving for."

"Worth killing for?" asked Gerald.

"Of course," Green said. "People have been killing each other to get hold of this casket for centuries."

Green held the diamond above the box. "These two objects haven't been together for over fifteen hundred years. It's time for them to be reunited."

Green placed the diamond into the recess in the casket lid. It sat in place seamlessly. Then to Gerald's horror, a series of clicks sounded, and a circle of crossbows lowered into position.

"The archers!" Gerald called out in panic.

"They will only be triggered if the wrong key is used, and there is only one Noor Jehan," Green said. Then he paused. "But I didn't get this close by being careless, so, Gerald, you can have the honor of opening the casket."

Green crouched at the base of the black plinth, beneath the archers' firing line, still pointing the dagger at Gerald. "Turn it."

Gerald checked the circle of statues. Every crossbow held a fresh arrow and every arrow pointed at him. He looked across to Sam and Ruby—both wide-eyed in horror. And finally he looked down at the diamond nestled in the casket. It was beautiful. He took a breath, placed both hands on the gem, and turned it.

The mechanism moved smoothly. A series of clicks

rang around the circle of statues and all the crossbows lifted back onto the archers' shoulders.

Green jumped to Gerald's side. He lifted the lid, which came away with ease, and shoved it at Gerald. Green peered inside the casket, his face alive. Then he reached inside and removed a gold rod. It was about a foot and a half long and decorated with intricate filigree. Green clutched it in both hands, his face suffused with light.

"At last," he murmured. He turned to Gerald. "Do you have any idea what this is? What it can do?"

Gerald took a step back.

"You of all people should know," Green said. Then a strange expression settled on his face, one of intense curiosity. "Gerald, tell me what happens when I do this—"

Before Gerald could move Green had grabbed him by the back of his head, yanking down hard on a fistful of his dark hair. Then with something approaching tenderness, he laid the golden rod across Gerald's brow.

Gerald thought he was going to die. His eyelids peeled open and his pupils contracted to pin pricks. His mind exploded in a phosphorescent blaze of imaginings. It was as if every vision he'd ever had, every daydream, every escapist moment, every sweat-soaked nightmare, was combined, squeezed and condensed into a single electric pulse. Two beams of white-hot light burst out of his eyes. It was like all the beasts of his sketchbook had come to life. Blood-caked monsters hacked at him. He was flying, floating, falling. Suns exploded, spears struck his forehead, waves dashed onto rocks beneath towering castle walls, cities lay in darkness, in ruins, faces melted. Twisting . . . turning . . . falling . . .

For an instant, Gerald saw everything. He was everywhere.

Then he stopped breathing.

All was black.

The first thing Gerald noticed when he woke was the headache. It was a complete toe curler: a triple-sledgehammer-between-the-eyes, joy-throttling migraine.

The next thing he noticed was the number of people around him. They were sitting in shabby lounge chairs, standing in small groups, and leaning against the corner of the major's desk.

The major's desk!

Gerald tried to cut through the haze in his head. He was lying on a leather couch in the major's study at Beaconsfield. Despite there seeming to be dozens of people milling around, no one was paying him any attention. It was as if he wasn't there. Constable Lethbridge, his notebook out and his pencil dancing in his hand, was taking down information from Professor McElderry. By the lamp in the corner was Mr. Gupta, a smile on his face so wide that

Gerald almost didn't recognize him. And what was Mrs. Rutherford doing here, chatting with Ruby by the French doors? Was that Sam, sitting in one of the wing-backed chairs, drinking a glass of water while someone wound a bandage around his leg? (That's good, Sam's okay.) And who was that sitting talking with Inspector Parrott? Was it old Major Pilkington?

"The major!" Gerald yelled.

All conversation in the room ceased. Every eye turned to Gerald, who was sitting bolt upright as if he'd seen a ghost.

Ruby was first to reach him.

"Gerald! You're awake," she cried. "You've been unconscious for ages."

Gerald grabbed Ruby's forearm and jabbed a finger at the major.

"What's he doing here?" he gabbled. "Last time I saw him, he was—"

"Dead?" Inspector Parrott said.

"Well, yes," Gerald said. "There was a flipping great arrow in his head."

The inspector bent down and picked up something from the floor. He held it up so Gerald could see. It was an arrow with what looked like a deflated Ping-Pong ball on the end. The major swiveled in his seat to face Gerald. He was wearing a black eye patch.

"It appears the major had a lucky break," the inspector said. "The arrow hit his false eye and knocked him over. He hit his head on the way down and slept through your adventure."

Gerald shook his head in confusion. "What about Chesterfield? Surely he's—"

"Yes, I'm afraid Mr. Chesterfield is no longer with us," the inspector said. "But the major has been most forthcoming about this whole affair."

Ruby patted Gerald on the shoulder. "It's all right," she said. "It makes sense when you hear it—well, mostly."

Again Gerald shook his head. "What happened down in the chamber? Last thing I remember was Green grabbing me by the hair."

Ruby frowned. "Yeah—there was some sort of struggle. All we could see was Green's back. It only went on for half a minute or so and then you must have passed out. Green dumped you and bolted past us and back up the tunnel. We knew you were okay because you kept moaning like you were talking in your sleep."

Gerald rubbed a spot on his forehead. "I don't remember any of that."

Actually, he had complete recall of everything that happened up to the moment where Green laid the golden rod across his forehead. And he knew he would never forget the vision that followed, no matter how hard he tried.

"How did we get back here? What happened to Sam?" Gerald turned to look at his friend. "How's your leg?"

Sam shifted in his chair, wincing at the movement. "The doctor thinks I'll live."

A middle-aged man with graying temples, who must have been a guest at the major's party, made some adjustments to a white bandage on Sam's thigh. "It's a nasty cut, but not too serious. A little to the left, though, and it would have severed the artery. Then it would have been a different story. If he stays on crutches, he'll be right in a week or so."

"See," Sam said. "Take more than a raging nutbag with a secret sword in his walking stick to put me down."

Gerald grinned. "How did we all get back here? It's not like Sam or I could walk or climb that ladder."

Ruby tried her hardest to stop a smile breaking out across her face.

"You'll have to thank Mr. Fry for that," she giggled.

"Fry?"

Then Gerald saw him, standing in a corner by the French doors, looking at the dusty surrounds of the major's study as if they made his skin itch.

"Mr. Fry turned up in the chamber about twenty minutes after Green did a bolt—he must have only just missed him coming out of the crypt," Sam said. "We were arguing about whether or not I could look after myself while Ruby

330

went for help. Then Mr. Fry turns up. He carries you over his shoulder and up the ladder, then comes back, bandages me up, and does the same."

Gerald looked at Fry with a new appreciation. He opened his mouth to speak.

"Don't thank me!" Fry said. "I couldn't stand it. I was only following Mrs. Rutherford's instructions to look for you when you didn't return to the house."

Gerald checked his watch. It was almost four in the morning! Mrs. Rutherford crossed the room and put her hand on Gerald's forehead.

"We were all very worried about you," she said with a crinkly smile. "I've rung your parents."

"Really?" Gerald said. "Are they coming back?"

Mrs. Rutherford coughed into her hand. "I understand they're sending flowers."

Gerald rolled his eyes.

Inspector Parrott stood up. "From our investigations it is clear that Sir Mason Green was at the center of this entire affair. We've put out an alert to Interpol. He won't get far."

Gerald muttered to himself, "I wouldn't count on that."

Inspector Parrott motioned to Lethbridge. "Constable, bring us up to date."

The policeman flicked through the pages of his notebook. "Well, Major Pilkington has been experiencing some financial difficulties of late. A year back he was in the bookshop in town and found an old book that described a relic that was supposedly hidden on his estate. He then set about trying to find it with a view to selling it."

All eyes turned to the major, who was sitting disconsolate in the corner.

"It's true," he said. "We were going to lose Beaconsfield. The cost of running this place is ruinous. So when I discovered there could be something valuable hidden here, I jumped at the chance. The diamond casket was to be our ticket out of debt. I owed poor Arthur Chesterfield's father a significant sum, and I thought this would be a way to pay him back."

Gerald piped up. "And then you were contacted by a buyer, weren't you? Someone who would pay a lot of money for that casket."

"That's right," the major said. "I thought all our problems were solved. Then I read further into that book and discovered the link between the casket and the Noor Jehan diamond and—"

"And you got greedy," Gerald said.

The major's head dropped. "Yes, we got greedy. The Noor Jehan was going to be on display at the museum. I couldn't believe our luck. During the Blitz the underground station beneath the museum was used as an air-raid shelter. I knew the place like the back of my hand, including that hidden entrance into the Reading Room. It was Arthur who came up with the elephant statue idea."

Lethbridge suddenly tensed. "You mean it was Mr. Chesterfield who stole the diamond, who shot me in the—"

"Fake diamond," Gerald interrupted. "Green stole the real one when it arrived at the museum."

"Excuse me, Major?" Ruby said. "I thought you served in Africa in that war. How would you know so much about an air-raid shelter in London?"

The major's face fell even further. "I may have . . . um . . . exaggerated a touch. I was a teenager during the war. I've never even been outside Britain."

"But what about the Battle of Bilghazi? What about your eye?"

"I lost my eye when I left a teaspoon in my cup and took a sip," he mumbled. The major's humiliation was complete.

Gerald whispered to Ruby, "I don't think the Rattigan Club is going to like this at all."

Ruby snuffled back a laugh.

Lethbridge flicked some more pages. "We followed up on the information from Miss Valentine about an attack at St. Michael's Tower. Local police found the bodies of two men but have had no success as yet in locating a large wooden wheel or anyone who might have been attached to it."

Inspector Parrott drummed his fingers on the desk. "I have some questions about this mysterious thin man, Mr. Wilkins."

"He was Green's hired thug. He killed my great-aunt and he almost killed us," Gerald said.

The inspector shook his head. "Sir Mason Green, a thief. Who would believe it? Still, we have the diamond. So that crime is solved at least. And don't you worry about Green—Interpol will catch him soon enough." With that, the inspector wished them good night and left.

Sam hobbled across and joined Gerald and Ruby on the old leather sofa.

Mrs. Rutherford fussed over him, fetching extra cushions.

"You've all had quite the adventure," she said. "Let me arrange for Mr. Fry to get us home before the sun comes up."

She turned to go, then hesitated. She looked at Gerald from over the top of her glasses.

"Your great-aunt would have been very proud of you, Master Gerald," she said. "She placed great stock in those who stand by their friends."

Gerald smiled. "Mrs. Rutherford?"

"Yes, my dear?"

"Do you know why Aunt Geraldine left her estate to me?"

Mrs. Rutherford considered the question. "When the time is right, that is a question you will be able to answer for yourself." She looked at Gerald and his friends, sitting exhausted on the old sofa. "Miss Archer was right," she said. "Not everything of value has a price tag attached."

When Mrs. Rutherford went to find Fry, Ruby turned to Gerald. "What do you think that golden rod was? Green was carrying it like a relay runner's baton when he went past us."

"Dunno," Gerald said, again rubbing his forehead. "But I'd like to find out."

"There's another thing," Ruby said. "As Green ran past, he turned back and said something."

"What?" Gerald asked, half knowing the answer.

"He said he'd be back to ask you what you saw."

"What d'you reckon he meant by that?" Sam said.

"I have no idea," Gerald replied.

Sam shifted in his seat. "So what happened when you fell into that pit?"

"Well," Gerald began. "There were these three rats . . ."

Sam went white. "Stop! Stop right there. Don't need to know anything else, thanks."

Gerald's nose twitched. He caught the scent of a familiar perfume. He looked up to find a wave of purple fabric before his eyes. It was Alisha Gupta. And she was smiling at him.

"Hello," she said.

Gerald stood up clumsily. "Oh . . . hello."

She dipped her head and gazed at him through upturned eyes.

"My father asked me to come and thank you," she said. "I'm Alisha."

"I'm Sam," said Sam, jumping up from the couch on his good leg and wedging himself between Gerald and the girl.

"Oh, hello," she said.

"And I'm Ruby," Ruby said, resolutely seated on the couch. "Hi there."

"Hmm, yes," Alisha said, then turned back to the boys. "My father wanted to say he thought you were very . . ."

"Brave," Sam said. "It was nothing, really, and this wound will heal quick as—"

"No," Alisha said. "Foolish. My father thought you were both very foolish to risk your lives for a mere gem. But he is grateful for your actions."

She rose up on her toes and kissed Gerald's cheek. For the second time that night, fireworks sparked in Gerald's brain. He watched in a wide-eyed stupor as Alisha Gupta waved a smiling good-bye and sashayed back to her beaming father.

"Oh puh-leese," Ruby sniffed from behind them. "Laying it on a bit thick, aren't we?"

"Where's my kiss?" Sam said, incredulous. "I'm an injured hero too."

"Don't worry," Gerald said, his eyes still dreamy. "They always ignore the one they like the best."

Ruby snorted. "Ha! If that's the case, Sam must be the most popular boy in England."

There was a commotion by the door. Sid Archer burst into the room, his face glowing bright red and a vein throbbing across his forehead.

"Where are they?" he demanded. "Where are my flippin' useless kids?"

Gerald turned to Sam. "Octavia and Zebedee!" he said.

They both looked at Ruby, who had gone a little pale.

"Well," she said, as she hurried across to the bookcase behind the major's desk. "Serves her right for calling me a princess, doesn't it?"

Epilogue

In the week after the events at Beaconsfield, the warm sunny days continued; the locals couldn't remember the last time they'd seen such a stretch of good weather. Sam and Ruby's parents drove to Avonleigh to stay for a few days and enjoyed getting to know Gerald, as well as exploring the Somerset countryside with their children. They even made Gerald an honorary Valentine, which pleased him no end.

Sam's leg was almost fully recovered and he abandoned his crutches. It was agreed that a summer at Avonleigh was just as likely to hasten his recovery as returning to London. So after three days, Sam and Ruby's parents hugged and kissed them good-bye. There was no sign of Gerald's parents, but true to their word, they did send flowers. Mrs.

Rutherford placed them in a large crystal bowl on the dining-room sideboard. Vi and Eddie phoned a few times, but the calls stopped after three days, and Gerald accepted that as his lot and got on with having fun with his friends.

One day Mr. Fry drove them back into town to the bookshop. But for some reason Mr. Hoskins had taken an extended holiday and the CLOSED sign hung yellowed on the inside of the door. Mrs. Rutherford was vague about her brother's whereabouts, only saying that he had some business abroad.

Gerald's testy relationship with Mr. Fry didn't improve, but it didn't get any worse, either. Mr. Prisk, the lawyer, came to visit one morning. But even he—Great-Aunt Geraldine's closest confidant—could shed no light on the "big family secret" that Green had mentioned down in the cavern.

About five days after midsummer, Professor McElderry arrived at Avonleigh and spent the afternoon with Gerald, Sam, and Ruby. Over a cup of tea and some homemade scones and jam, he explained all he could about Noor Jehan and the diamond casket.

"Sorry I wasn't upfront with you about the casket when you asked," he said, biting into a jam-laden scone. "Say! These are good. There had been a bit too much interest in it and I didn't know if I could trust you."

"How do you mean, a lot of interest?" Gerald asked.

"Your skinny mate—the one that smelled like a mop bucket and looked like death—came around the week before the robbery. Said he was doing some research on ancient locked boxes and asked a lot of questions about this one. We had a few phone calls too—I'm guessing they came from Arthur Chesterfield. The old myths surrounding this box are pretty fanciful, you know. And as I was very close to finding it myself, for the museum, I wasn't about to provide any tips to some newbies. When you lot rolled up asking questions, I clammed up."

"What type of myths?"

"You name it—from relics linked to ancient doomsday cults to Julius Caesar's baby teeth—that box was said to contain all manner of stuff."

Gerald nodded and took a breath. "How about the . . . um . . . Holy Grail?" he asked.

McElderry almost choked on his scone. It took a minute for his combined laughter and coughing to stop. "No one believes that exists," he guffawed.

"What was the golden rod that Green took off with, then?" Ruby asked.

McElderry's mood darkened. "That I don't know," he rumbled. "But I've got the casket now. It's covered in ancient symbols and there were carvings all around the rotunda. That chamber dates to the end of the Roman Empire—at least 400 AD. It was probably constructed by a religious cult, using the midsummer solstice as a location device. Then, over the centuries, Beaconsfield was built over the top of it. Once we've disarmed all the traps we'll be able to find out more."

Gerald shook his head in wonder.

"What kind of cult would go to that much trouble to protect some gold rod?" he asked.

McElderry licked a dollop of cream from his fingers. "Gerald, what do you know about your family crest?"

Gerald shrugged. "Not much. Mr. Prisk said it was pretty old."

"Well, from my inspection of the records it looks like the original property here—the combined Avonleigh and Beaconsfield—was once owned by a very ancient ancestor of yours. It looks like your family crest is directly tied to the cult that built that burial chamber."

Gerald nodded. "That'd explain why the crest keeps popping up everywhere. Mrs. Rutherford said my great-grandfather was always at Major Pilkington's mother to buy Beaconsfield from her."

Professor McElderry brushed some crumbs from his whiskers. "Dorian Archer may well have known about the existence of the diamond casket and wanted to secure it," he said.

Sam put down his cup and reached across the table for the plate of scones. "So what's the story with you and the archer wind vane? How come you were looking for that?"

McElderry bristled. "The major wasn't the only one with access to old books. I work at a museum, remember? My research had shown the casket was somehow linked to the solstice. I'd asked old Jervis to keep an eye out for a vane that matched the one at Beaconsfield. Every antiquarian worth his salt knew about the diamond casket—I was just closer than anyone else to finding it."

"Except for us," Sam said. "And to be fair, Major Pilkington and Mr. Chesterfield did get there first, and—"

McElderry pushed his chair back from the table and grabbed his hat. "Did I mention that you might well be the stupidest boy in the entire world?"

He left without thanking Mrs. Rutherford for the afternoon tea.

The next morning as Gerald, Ruby, and Sam sat down to another magnificent breakfast, with plans for a swim in the pool straight after, Mrs. Rutherford delivered a letter to the table.

"This morning's post, Master Gerald," she said.

"Who's writing to you?" Sam asked through a mouthful of scrambled eggs.

Gerald tore open the envelope and removed a

single sheet of paper. He looked over the contents, then laughed.

"What is it?" Ruby said.

"A credit-card bill," Gerald replied. "For a lot of pizza and coffee." He glanced at the twins' matching confused faces. "Long story, but it's how I got to meet you and start this adventure."

"Is it just the start?" Ruby asked. "Do you think we'll see Sir Mason Green again?"

Gerald had taken his wallet from his pocket and was idly spinning the black plastic card in his fingers.

"He said he'd be back."

Sam shoveled another forkful of egg into his mouth. "A guy with that much money could disappear for a long time. He'd have cash stashed all over the place."

Gerald slipped the card back into his wallet and took out the photograph of his great-aunt and the small mirror that she'd left him. He looked first at Geraldine, then at his own eyes in the mirror.

He still had no idea why his great-aunt had started him on this journey. And he never wanted to see Sir Mason Green again. But there was a gnawing feeling in his gut.

Gerald looked at Sam and Ruby, who had resumed an argument from the night before about who was the strongest left-handed (it had ended in an arm wrestle and a shock victory to Ruby). He smiled. If there was ever to be a showdown with Green, he hoped Sam and Ruby would be there with him.

"Come on, you two," he said. "Race you to the pool!"

Three chairs tipped back as they tumbled out onto the terrace and into whatever else the summer could throw at them.

EXTRAS

THE BILLIONAIRE'S CURSE

THE ARCHER LEGACY ◆ BOOK ONE

A Conversation with Richard Newsome

The Truth Behind the Fiction

A First Look at *The Emerald Casket,*
The Archer Legacy, Book Two

A Conversation with Richard Newsome

How did you come up with the idea for the Archer seal? Did it spring from your research? Does it have any hidden meaning or historical reference?

The Archer seal plays a pretty significant part in the mystery. It provides a vital link between Gerald and his past, and goes to the very core of why Gerald's life is in danger. It's also a nod to the power of a trio—a three-legged stool will never wobble, and the triumvirate of Gerald, Sam, and Ruby is intensely strong, provided they stick together. The image of the three arms forming a triangle just popped into my head about three seconds after I sat down and thought, *Right. What's this family seal going to look like then?*

Are the characters in *The Billionaire's Curse* based entirely on your imagination? Or are some of them inspired by people you know?

There's a real mixed bunch in there. The characters of Ruby and Sam are loosely based on my two oldest children, though they have been melded with a few other folks as well. Mr. Fry, the butler, has several of my neatness flaws in his personality (I am an obsessive sweeper . . .). Probably the only character who doesn't have some real DNA in him is Gerald. He is just Gerald.

Was the Noor Jehan based on a real diamond? Is there any truth to its story?

I wanted a diamond that would be awe-inspiring. I have always been fascinated by the big-gem stories; they always carry such a weight of legend and intrigue. And for something that is essentially useless, big-gem diamonds do make people go berserk. The Koh-i-Noor (meaning the "Mountain

3

of Light") diamond has such a fantastic history to it (it has been a prize of war for centuries and now resides in the British Crown Jewels in London) that I needed something to match it. I thought the "Light of the World" sounded like a good name and I asked a Hindi- and Urdu-speaking work colleague for a translation. So the entirely fictitious Noor Jehan was born.

The story is (literally!) filled with Archers. What does the symbol of the archer mean to you? How did your research impact your decision to give the archer such a prominent place in this book?
Rather more of the story than you might suspect is based on research surrounding old myths and legends. I spent many months camped out in my old university library, exploring the stacks for accounts of ancient times. I can't give too much away without ruining the ending, but the archer does play a role in the final resolution of the mystery.

Mrs. Rutherford tells Gerald that the Holy Grail is reputed to be buried somewhere in the vicinity of Glastonbury. Did you stop in Glastonbury during your travels? Did you visit King Arthur's grave? What kind of research did you do there?
I spent a few days wandering around Glastonbury, in England, when researching the book. The Grail legend is bread and butter for the local tourist trade, as is the Arthurian myth. There is a spot where King Arthur is supposedly buried, but there is so much conjecture as to whether he even existed that I doubt highly the grave site is legitimate. But the Tor and St. Michael's Tower most certainly do exist and it was while climbing up that magnificent hill that much of the final climax to the book began to form in my mind.

Was Avonleigh based on a real place?
Avonleigh and Beaconsfield are both based on actual houses in Somerset. Avonleigh is modeled on Montacute House, while the Major's rotting ancestral pile of Beaconsfield is based on the magnificent Tyntesfield in Wraxall. I completely fell in love with Tyntesfield on my research trip. It is such a sensational folly of gothic design—all spires, towers, and gargoyles. I knew at once that it had to be the setting for the climax of the book. And there is no way on earth I would ever wander around the place at night!

What were your inspirations for drawing on ancient Roman culture?
It is almost impossible to divorce early British history from the impact of the Romans. I have been fascinated by the Roman Empire since I was about eleven, when I saw the BBC television series *I Claudius*, which was based on the book by Robert Graves. The chance to revisit that era was too much of a temptation.

You have had a number of careers to date—why is writing books your favorite?
It beats working for a living! Actually, that's not true. I've always been a dedicated worker and put in 100 percent in all my jobs. This authoring caper is by far the most difficult thing I've tried to do professionally, but it is also the most personally rewarding. I've had a mother thank me for being the reason her teenage son started reading books again. Can there be any greater satisfaction than that?

How did the original idea for *The Billionaire's Curse* come to you? Was it an opening line that struck you? A plot point? A character?

Bizarrely, the ending for the entire trilogy came to me in a dream. I woke with a start and the vision from the dream was still sharp in my mind. I knew it would make a great finish to a story. I just had to come up with the beginning and the middle. I also knew it would be just too big to squeeze into a single volume, so the trilogy gave me sufficient scope to properly explore the yarn.

What would you do if you inherited the Archer fortune?

There are two answers to that question: the right one and the fun one. The right one would be to set up a foundation that supported education, health, and the arts. The fun one would involve a large yacht and six months sailing around the Greek and Turkish islands.

What were you like when you were Gerald's age?

At the age of thirteen, I was having a ball at school. I threw myself into everything I could: rugby, cricket, basketball, debating, drama . . . even trombone in the school band. I was mediocre at them all, but had a great time giving them a go. Life's too short to live on the sidelines.

Anything else we should know about you?

I can violently wiggle my ears. I can juggle. I write all my first drafts longhand, in pencil—with the same pencil: a mechanical one I bought in a stationery store in New Zealand more than ten years ago. If I lose that pencil then . . . well, let's not even contemplate what might happen. It wouldn't be pretty.

Can you give us any clues about the next two books in the series?
Of course. Turns out that Sir Mason Green is actually Gerald's father! It is going to so totally shock everyone. It will be such a surprise. Oh, wait a minute. . . .

Do you have advice for aspiring writers?
Stick at it. *The Billionaire's Curse* was turned down thirteen times before it found a publisher. It took a decade from first word to finalization. But perseverance and a good dose of luck can work wonders. Oh, and read heaps too.

The Truth Behind the Fiction

There really is a . . .

Peak of eternal light on the moon. Recent studies by researchers at Johns Hopkins University identified four peaks on the moon that could qualify as peaks of eternal light—that is, places where the sun never sets. They could play an important role for any future moon base, being ideal places to site solar power stations.

Ghost Tube station at the British Museum. One of the first books I ever bought on Amazon was *Abandoned Stations on London's Underground*. Not exactly a riveting read, but interesting anyway. According to its author, J. E. Connor, the British Museum Tube station opened on July 30, 1900, and was closed on September 25, 1933. The station was used as an air-raid shelter in World War II, protecting Londoners during the height of the Blitz.

History of rolling flaming witches down hills. Midsummer celebrations across Europe have long been associated with bonfires. In some towns, a straw witch was strapped to a wheel and set alight. The flaming wheel would be pushed down a hill and if it stayed alight all the way to the bottom a strong harvest would be expected.

Magnificent Reading Room at the British Museum. Don't just take my word for it. Go and visit the place. Some of modern civilization's greatest writers and thinkers have paced and pondered around its cavernous insides. And there really are fake bookshelves used as doors to the stacks.

Huge amount of tea consumed in Britain each day. The United Kingdom Tea Council says 165 million cups of tea are consumed in Britain each day. If Gerald's family received a royalty of just a quarter of a penny for each teabag used (and 96 percent of Brit tea drinkers use tea bags), that would produce more than $150 million a year for Archer Corporation. And that's just from the UK!

A first look at

THE EMERALD CASKET,

The Archer Legacy, Book Two

CHAPTER ONE

The canvas sack landed against the oak doors with such a judder it threatened to knock them off their hinges. Two more followed, each stuffed to bursting point. One of the doors opened inward and a tall, barrel-chested man, dressed in a dark suit, peered down at the pile of bags. They were stenciled with the words ROYAL MAIL. The man's nostrils flared a millimeter. His eyes narrowed. Then, with an exhalation that reeked of resentment, he bent down and dragged the first of the sacks into the house.

The volume of mail delivered to the mansion at Avonleigh had been growing steadily for a fortnight. The post office in the village High Street had tacked a HELP WANTED sign in the window. Three postal carriers had called in sick that week alone. Back strain. The local chiro-practor was advertising for an assistant.

"It's jolly good for business, is all I can say," Mrs. Parsons from the post office told Mrs. Rutherford when she dropped in to mail a letter to her brother. "Better than Christmas."

Mrs. Rutherford nodded. "Yes, Avonleigh has come to life in the past few weeks. We couldn't be happier up at the house."

"So will he be coming to town soon?" Mrs. Parsons asked, her eyes wide. "You know, to meet a few of the locals? It would seem appropriate."

Mrs. Rutherford pursed her lips. "He's a little tied up at the moment. I don't think he'll be making any social calls for a while."

There was an uncomfortable silence.

"That is disappointing." Mrs. Parsons sniffed. "A new lord of the manor has obligations. Even if he is Australian. Mister Gerald should be reminded of that by those who ought to know better." She gave Mrs. Rutherford an icy glare.

"He prefers *Master* Gerald," Mrs. Rutherford said. "And I'm sure he'll meet everyone who is worth meeting in good time. A good day to you, Mrs. Parsons."

Mrs. Rutherford fixed an AIR MAIL sticker to the front of her envelope, marched from the shop, and dropped the letter in the post box out front. She consulted the list she'd written in the kitchen at Avonleigh that morning, checked the basket on the front of her bicycle to make sure everything was there, then settled onto the seat and trundled up the cobblestones. She'd only gone twenty yards or so when Mrs. Parsons stepped from the post office and onto the footpath.

"You can't keep him to yourself forever, Mrs. Rutherford!" she cried.

The woman on the bicycle smiled to herself and continued on her way, pedaling through the winding backstreets and onto a country lane, clicking and clacking over every bump and rut in the road.

It had been like this ever since the new master of Avonleigh had taken up residence. The first week or so had been quiet enough. Master Gerald had been able to wander in and out of town with his friends, still unrecognized. But after the events at Beaconsfield, and all the excitement in the newspapers and on television, it seemed the whole world wanted to know Gerald Wilkins.

The locals in Glastonbury were at Mrs. Rutherford every time she came to town.

"When will we get to see him, Mrs. Rutherford?"

"Is he as nice as they all say, Mrs. Rutherford?"

"Would he like to meet my daughter, Mrs. Rutherford?"

That last question in particular had become more frequent and more insistent. It coincided with the enormous increase in the volume of mail delivered to the mansion. As she was the housekeeper at Avonleigh, Mrs. Rutherford had also taken it upon herself to act as gatekeeper for the new master. He did have a few things on his mind. After all, it isn't every day a thirteen-year-old boy wakes to find he has inherited a colossal fortune from his great-aunt.

Well out into the countryside, the bike came to a halt outside a large set of iron gates. In the center of the gates was the image of an archer at full draw, his muscled torso set against a blazing sun. Mrs. Rutherford pressed a button on an intercom recessed into a mossy stone wall. The gates swung inward. She coasted through the opening and down a gravel drive lined with chestnut trees, the branches forming a canopy over her head.

Summer hung heavy in the air and Mrs. Rutherford took a deep sniff of the perfumes of the Somerset countryside—the loamy soil, the aroma of freshly cut grass, a blizzard of pollens. A team of gardeners tended to a hedge and flowerbeds as Mrs. Rutherford rattled past on her bicycle, sending them a cheery wave. She curved past the rose garden and the topiaries, beyond the croquet lawn and the turnoff to the old stables and the greenhouses, and was presented with the full Elizabethan splendor of the mansion at Avonleigh.

At the bottom of a gentle slope stood the main house, a four-story monument to the stonemasons' craft. Hewn from golden rock and assembled by artisans, the building stretched upward and outward, a palace fit for an emperor. Manicured lawns, weed free and splendid, spread out on either side of the house.

Mrs. Rutherford wheeled her bicycle into a stone alcove and emerged with the wicker basket over her arm. She wandered around the end of the south wing. She reached an expanse of grass, took a look over her shoulder, then kicked off her shoes and took girlish delight in scrunching her toes into the velvet lawn. When she finally walked off the terrace and into the main drawing room, her cheeks were pink with life.

"Morning, Mrs. Rutherford." A girl of about thirteen sat cross-legged in the middle of the floor, surrounded by piles of envelopes and packages. "You're looking happy this morning."

Mrs. Rutherford placed her basket on a side table and brushed her hands down the front of her dress, a simple gray uniform that almost reached the oriental carpet at her feet.

"I am very happy this morning, Miss Ruby," Mrs. Rutherford said. "It is a beautiful day and one worth celebrating. I have plans for a particularly spectacular dinner this evening, if I do say so myself. Now, is there any sign of Master Gerald and your brother?"

The girl slit open an envelope with a silver letter opener. "They're mucking around outside," Ruby said. "I thought

I better make a start here. Most of it's left over from yesterday."

A door banged open and the tall man in the dark suit entered. He dragged a mailbag across the carpet and added it to the stack in the corner.

"Are there any more, Mr. Fry?" Mrs. Rutherford asked. Fry was massaging his right shoulder.

"That's the last of them," he said, without a jot of enthusiasm.

"Excellent. You'll be happy to hear the post office is starting an afternoon delivery as well."

"Marvelous," he said, and trudged out of the room.

Ruby stifled a giggle. "He's not too happy today."

Mrs. Rutherford clicked her tongue. "He is never a bundle of joy at the best of times," she said. "But ever since Miss Archer's death—well, he's been even more unpleasant than usual."

"Has Mr. Fry worked here for a long time?" Ruby asked.

"Let me see. I'd been here twenty years when he started with Miss Archer, so that would make it some twenty-five years that we've had the pleasure of Mr. Fry's company."

"Wow. And did she leave him anything in her will?"

"A set of teaspoons, I believe. Quite nice ones. None of your tat."

"And she left the entire estate to Gerald?"

Mrs. Rutherford busied herself with a bowl of flowers

on the mantelpiece. "That may explain why Mr. Fry hasn't been overjoyed since Master Gerald's arrival. Most inappropriate, I think, begging your pardon for saying so."

Ruby brushed aside a few strands of hair and retied her ponytail. "And Gerald is now the youngest billionaire in the world. It's all a bit fantastic, isn't it? One day he's at school in Sydney and the next he's flying to London to inherit twenty billion pounds."

"I understand there's a prince in Dubai who may be worth a touch more," Mrs. Rutherford said. "But Master Gerald's landed in it, that's for certain."

Ruby looked up at the housekeeper. "Do you mind if I ask what Gerald's great-aunt left you, Mrs. Rutherford?"

The woman smiled. "Not at all, Miss Ruby. Miss Archer left me the memory of a kind and generous soul, whom it was a pleasure and honor to know. And that is all any of us should ever hope to receive."

Ruby picked up another pile of envelopes. "So not quite like Gerald's mum and dad, then?"

Mrs. Rutherford sucked on her lips. "I'm sure I don't know what you mean, Miss Ruby. Master Gerald's parents are touring the Archer estate's global holdings of luxury properties to ensure that all is in order."

Ruby grinned. "So will they be back from that Caribbean island anytime soon?"

"Not while the gin holds out," Mrs. Rutherford said

under her breath. "Begging your pardon for saying so."

At that moment two bodies rolled into the room, a wrestling tangle of limbs across the carpet. Among the flurry of arms and legs it was possible to make out blond hair—Sam Valentine with his broad shoulders and summer tan. He slammed his opponent onto the floor, straddled his chest and pinned him to the rug.

"There!" he declared, "I win."

The other boy stopped struggling. His unruly mop of dark hair, plain T-shirt, and blue jeans gave no hint that this was the richest thirteen-year-old on the planet.

"Go easy," Gerald said. "Leg feeling better, is it?"

"That? Yeah, it's pretty much right."

"And how about the morbid fear of rats? How's that going?"

Sam flinched as if his worst nightmare had just walked through the door. In a blink Gerald flipped him over and sat on top of him, knees pressing his shoulders into the rug.

Sam howled, struggling to escape.

Gerald rolled off and the two of them got up from the carpet, laughing and breathing hard.

"Boys," Ruby said.

Mrs. Rutherford shook her head. "And they don't improve with age, believe me."

"Morning, Mrs. Rutherford," Gerald said. "Just showing Sam who's boss."

"Yes, I'm sure," Mrs. Rutherford said through lemon lips. "Now, you three are to deal with this correspondence today. I'm interviewing for a secretary to handle the mail, but for now it is your responsibility. Hop to it while I see how morning tea preparations are progressing." She bustled out of the room.

Gerald and Sam flopped down on either side of Ruby.

"Not fair using rats against me in a fight," Sam said to Gerald.

Ruby leaned across and patted her twin brother on the knee. "Then you should try being less of a wuss around them, shouldn't you?"

Sam muttered something about a medical condition and picked up the nearest pile of letters. Ruby slapped him on the wrist.

"Mitts off," she snapped. "I've already sorted those. Look, it's quite straightforward. Even for you. The colored envelopes go over here. That's the greeting cards and pathetic love letters from stupid girls. All the long white envelopes go here—that's the begging letters. The parcels go over by the fireplace and anything with a window in the front goes into this stack for Mr. Prisk to look at. Clear?"

Sam rubbed the back of his hand. "What's this pile then, Miss Frustrated Librarian?"

Ruby glanced at a mound of square buff-colored envelopes, constructed from expensive-looking parchment.

"That's invitations to opening nights, parties, and sporting events," she said.

Gerald scooped up an armful of envelopes. "This is ridiculous. Why are so many people writing to me?"

"Because you're richer than the queen," Ruby said. "They're all from people wanting something."

Sam held up a letter in one hand and a photograph in another. "This one wants locking up. Take a look at that." He handed the photo to Gerald, who inspected it with alarm.

"'Dearest Gerald,'" Sam read from the letter, "'I know you're the one for me. Ever since I heard about your brave escape from that awful Sir Mason Green at Beaconsfield I knew we were destined to be as one. Promise me your eternal love. Or I'll hunt you down and hurt you.'"

"What?" Ruby said. "You're making that up."

She snatched the photograph from her brother and took a look. Her eyebrows shot up.

"She just wants a new friend, that's all," Ruby said with a slight shudder. "She would have seen the news reports on TV—us recovering the stolen diamond, our run-in with Sir Mason Green—and she thinks we're worth knowing."

Sam laughed. "Not you and me, sister. No one wants to be friends with Sam and Ruby Valentine. All this is addressed to one person: Gerald Wilkins, care of Planet Gazillionaire. Population: one. It's about money, pure and simple."

They spent the rest of the morning going through the post.

Ruby upended another sack of mail across the rug and Sam groaned.

"Are you sure there's nothing in here for me?" he said. A handful of envelopes slipped through his fingers and onto the floor.

Ruby looked at him. "Who would write to you out here in rural Somerset?"

"Oh, I don't know. There might be a letter for me. From India, maybe. A little thank-you note. Or something."

Ruby laughed. "Sam, Alisha Gupta is not the least bit interested in you. She's not going to take time from her oh-so-busy social life to stick a stamp on an envelope for your sake."

Sam bristled. "Just because you two hate each other. Her dad was really happy we got his diamond back from Mason Green. And Alisha thought I was pretty brave."

"I seem to recall the word she used was *foolish*. Or maybe it was *grossly stupid*. Anyway, it was Gerald she was drooling over, not you."

Sam looked to Gerald for support, but he was sitting boggle-eyed on the floor, amid a mountain of love letters.

"They don't even know me," he said. "I could have fangs and drink blood for breakfast for all they know."

Sam flicked through a wad of photographs. "They'd

probably find that attractive."

Gerald surveyed the piles that surrounded them. "I didn't think being a billionaire would involve so much paperwork."

He plucked a letter from a bright pink envelope, releasing a perfumed shower of glitter. Then, out of nowhere, he asked, "Do you think Sir Mason Green will resurface?"

The once-respected businessman, philanthropist, and chairman of the British Museum Trust hadn't been far from Gerald's thoughts since the incident at Beaconsfield a fortnight earlier. Sir Mason Green was now an international fugitive, wanted for ordering the murder of Geraldine Archer—the very act that had paved the way for Gerald to inherit the Archer fortune.

"We won't see him again," Ruby said. "He found what he was looking for. Why would he come back?"

Gerald hoped that was true. He still found it difficult to sleep. And even when he did manage to drift off, there were the dreams.

The night in the cavern under Beaconsfield played over and over in his mind: Sir Mason Green using the stolen Noor Jehan diamond to unlock a legendary casket that had lain hidden in a burial chamber for seventeen hundred years; Green reaching into the casket and removing an ornate golden scepter and gazing upon it like he'd found some lost love. He'd grabbed Gerald by the hair and laid the rod across his forehead. That moment was now etched in high definition in Gerald's mind: the brain-collapsing vision that Gerald had experienced, the sensation of being shattered into an infinite number of particles and blown by a hot wind into every moment throughout the sands of time. He hadn't told anyone about this vision, not even the Valentine twins.

"Green's someplace overseas for sure," Sam said. "He's a billionaire—he could be anywhere."

"Don't let it hassle you, Gerald," Ruby said. "Inspector Parrott will take care of it. You don't need to worry about Sir Mason Green."

Gerald picked up another pile of envelopes. The top one had an elegant letter *R* embossed in red on the back. He tore through the stiff paper.

"Hey, look at this," he said. "A get-well card from Lord Herring at the Rattigan Club."

Sam laughed. "Didn't think you'd hear from him again."

"Unless he was threatening to sue you," Ruby said.

Gerald smiled to himself. The exclusive Rattigan Club—they'd got up to some mischief there trying to find the stolen diamond. All that old-world finery and stale cigar smoke. Those garishly decorated rooms. The Pink Room, the Blue Room, the—

"That's it!"

Ruby and Sam stared at Gerald with alarm.

"What's it?"

Gerald jumped to his feet. "I've got to call Inspector Parrott."

The next day, Gerald, Sam, and Ruby stood in a long corridor on the first floor of the Rattigan Club in London outside a door painted a lustrous bottle green. Mr. Fry had driven them up—three hours in the upholstered comfort of a customized Rolls-Royce limousine. Fry didn't utter a word the entire trip.

They were joined by Inspector Parrott and Constable Lethbridge of the Metropolitan Police, and the Rattigan Club chairman, Lord Herring.

"We've searched every inch of Sir Mason's office and his house and found nothing," the inspector said. "This investigation has reached a dead end. And a great deal of the interview evidence central to the case has gone missing." He cast a furious eye at Lethbridge. The constable glanced down at his shoes and absentmindedly slipped a hand around to scratch at his left buttock. "I hope this theory of yours leads to something, Gerald," the inspector said. "We need a breakthrough."

"It just struck me," Gerald explained. "I'd been in the Pink Room and the Blue Room and we'd run past a door to the Green Room."

Lord Herring pulled a key from his vest pocket. "Sir

Mason was a member of this club for a very long time. He had the Green Room for his exclusive use. He said it was a tidy space away from his office—handy for his private papers and such. The staff tell me no one except Mason has been in here for five years. He even employed his own cleaner."

Herring placed the key in the lock and turned. A heavy deadbolt slid aside. The door swung in and seven heads peered into the dark room.

"Hold on," Herring said. "There should be a switch." He fumbled a hand around the wall. A bulb flickered on. Seven sets of eyes adjusted to the light.

After a moment of shocked silence, it was Ruby who spoke.

"Oh my," was all she could say.

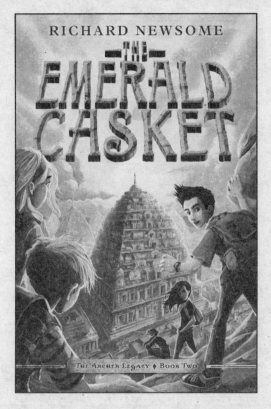

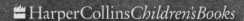